The Scent of Time

Alan T. McKean

Alan T. McKean

Black Rose Writing

www.blackrosewriting.com

ISBN: 978-1-61296-128-6

PUBLISHED BY BLACK ROSE WRITING

www.blackrosewriting.com

Printed in the United States of America

The Scent of Time is printed in Perpetua

To the Lord Jesus Who gave me the story and enabled me to write.
To my wife Stephanie, without whose love and care
this would not have been written,
and to my big brother Ian, who always believed in me
and was always there for me.

The Scent of Time

PART 1

Edinburgh, Scotland
21st Century

CHAPTER 1

He was too stupid to have seen me, the moron who was driving the red Ford while having his cell phone glued to his ear and primeval drum music pouring from his window. There was no doubt he was "sent" and so was I—nearly over the bonnet of his car. I could lip read what he said, but by the time I could think of a suitable reply, he had vanished into the throng of Edinburgh traffic. "Away ya' stupid statistic," I called after him, but somehow the words changed to a frustrating vapor instead of fulfilling their intent.

When you come to the end of a perfect day, boring with no future to look forward to, the only compensation may come through the mail in the form of an e-mail or otherwise. In this case the letter among the usual "offers of a lifetime" was from my Uncle Adrian Conroy at Bellefield, his lovely home outside of Huntly in Aberdeenshire. I had been to Bellefield a couple of times when I was about ten, but sadly had kind of lost touch until recently when we had renewed contact with each other.

Everyone has an "Uncle Adrian." My dad had thought he was a dreamer—the kind of dreamer who made things happen. He was a physicist, and when he spoke about his subject—so I was told—you nodded and said, "yes," and, "no," in the right places, with the occasional "Mmmmm" thrown in for good measure.

"Drew," the letter asked, "Can you come up and see me? Your mother says you have been working too hard and that you are having problems with young Meryl." (How could my mother possibly know that?) Meryl Scott, my girlfriend, had turned out to be a complainer.

Worse yet, she kept attempting to psychoanalyze me. She was gorgeous on the outside and as cold as ice on the inside. She made me feel like a slide under a microscope. Anyway, the idea of going up to Uncle Adrian's made good sense. I was due some time off work from my job as a book illustrator.

The journey up was good and once out of Edinburgh, I was free of traffic. When I go on a longish journey, I like to leave early and get a clear run. I drove one of the small Fiats, and despite the derogatory remarks about its size, at the petrol pump I was gassed up and away while some of the bigger cars still stood, their owners watching in distress as clicks portended the rising cost displayed on the face of the pump. There was a standard joke that someone should open a mortgage company for motorists.

As I got closer to Bellefield, the wonderful scent of fresh pine filled the car and the sun began sinking in the sky, turning it the color of fire. I turned into the drive way of Bellefield and memories swept back. Memories of picnics, trips, and hide and seek with my cousin Phyllis, who had shared the adventures of childhood with me even though I must have bored her stupid. The conversation of a boy of eleven and a girl of thirteen never addresses the same interests.

I parked my car and took the steps to the big front door two at a time, beginning to feel at home. Bellefield was the kind of place that wrapped itself around you and embraced you like a coaxing lover.

When you see Bellefield from the road, it looks as if it has had a succession of coaches and horses coming to the house and it is easy to imagine that house lit up for a grand gathering. How many adventures had started in this house? How many romances? What great projects? Little did I know that I was about to embark on a terrifying and deadly adventure of my own.

I rang the bell. There was a sound of footsteps, then the rattling of a bolt and muttering behind the door, "I must get some oil on this blasted lock." More rattling and suddenly the door shot open and I was face to face with Uncle Adrian. The light flooded from behind him and he peered out at me. "Drew? Well, you have grown."

"I do my best Uncle, but cornflakes help."

"Come in, man, and let me look at you. Lord, you are like your father—if that is a compliment. Still your mother must have thought something of him or else you wouldn't be here, eh?" He broke into a loud laugh.

My uncle Adrian was more than six feet tall, with a shock of black hair and green eyes. His open face displayed a broad smile. He wore a tweed jacket with a pipe sticking out of the top pocket, the contents of the bowl still glowing a somber red. He also wore cowboy boots—yes, real cowboy boots—yet as I got to know the man, none of it seemed out of place. He must have been about fifty-five. Despite his obvious intelligence, he gave the impression of attempting an escape from being seventeen. He refused to take life with the seriousness, which I at twenty-five, thought it should be taken. Apparently he kept a twinkle in his eye even when he had a cold.

"Come on. You'll be hungry and needing your tea," he said. "Got steak and kidney pie followed by clootie dumpling. Victoria makes lovely tucker—you look as though you could do with some packing. There is also a bottle of something unpronounceable from Spain with which to wash it down."

Flashes of the house forced themselves from my mental filing system. "It's starting to come back to me now," I remarked. "Isn't there a long gallery with a whole lot of pictures in it? There seemed to be a lot of tea sets—but I remember it as being darker than this."

"Aye," he replied. "Thought I had better get some decent lighting in before someone did something to themselves on a dark night." He stopped and turned to me, adding, "And all the better for folks to see the pictures at their best advantage."

It was only later that I understood the significance of that remark.

He continued in a philosophical tone. "You love history. Did you never look at the picture of a famous person and wonder what they were really like? What made them tick, what was going on behind the eyes? They were human and in their time there was so much to be discovered, so many dreams to come to pass."

"Uncle, you are getting romantic in your maturing years," I accused.

"No," he replied. "If you wanted to go to Australia or India, it took months. China was a long haul. You had to have a good reason for going." He walked on.

"How about money as a reason?" I suggested.

"Ach, Drew! You sound like one of these nine-day e-wonders. Where's your sense of romance, your sense of adventure, your sense of vision?"

"Under one of Meryl's microscope slides," I said half to myself.

He gave me a paternal look, "Aye, you can pick them. When are you going to learn to look deeper than what is on the surface? Remember the sirens of Greek mythology—singing with breath-taking loveliness, yet intent in luring sailors to their doom?"

I suddenly visualized Meryl sitting on a rock trying to sing. Singing was one thing she could not do. I focused on that image for a moment, then shuddered. Some things were best forgotten. Meryl, I was beginning to realize, was one of them.

By this time we had reached the entry of the oak-paneled gallery. Lighting had been installed first of all to make sure that nobody would trip over the uneven wooden floor, as Adrian had already postulated, and secondly to flatter the pictures, mainly portraits. On both accounts, the endeavor had succeeded. Halfway along the hall there seemed to be an alcove with a couple of windows in it. Looking at well known kings and queens was one thing, but looking at this lot who were painted "warts and all" was fascinating.

The flattering or critical result of portraiture, I realized, really depended on whether the painter had been "for" or "against" you. I remembered seeing two portraits of Richard III. One had obviously been done by a Riccardian fan. The other made him look like the worst villain in the board game *Cluedo*.

"This is John Binion," Adrian said. "Served as second officer on the Orion at Trafalgar, so we are told. He was killed the day after he made Post Captain in 1810."

"Careless," I replied for want of something better to say.

"You had better be grateful it was not 1809," my uncle admonished, "or else you would not be here." My wit somewhat subdued, we moved on. "John Malvern, here," Adrian informed me, "owned this house for yonks and never bothered with it. Left it to his factor who did only what he had to. Malvern, amongst his other business interests, had a house in St. Lucia in the West Indies. He died there of yellow fever. However, Mrs. Malvern, being made of tougher stuff, married a second time to a lad who came up with a process for improved Rum distillation—the rest was history."

"Don't we have anyone in the family who just did an ordinary job of work and died of old age peacefully in his bed?" I asked hopefully.

He shook his head. "You are getting old before your time …tut, tut. Well, just one more picture to go. I will leave you to see that on your own. It's in the alcove. Victoria will have tea ready and I will open the plonk."

Oh well, I thought. *One more picture and duty done.*

I turned into the alcove to come face-to-face with a painting of the most beautiful girl I had ever seen. I used to laugh when talkative people said, "words failed me." Now I understood. She was about my own age and I looked at the name inscribed below the portrait, *Lucy.* I stared at Lucy and her smile flowed back to me.

My spine tingled and I could hear my heart thumping in my ears. My mouth went dry. This was the kind of girl who only appeared in dreams. Her head tilted slightly in the painting and she wore a quizzical look on her face as if she were assessing you.

Cascading locks of the most gorgeous Titian-colored hair I had ever seen flowed like a banner of autumn about Lucy's shoulders, but it was the opal green eyes that transfixed me as if she could see into my heart. At the corner of her beautiful mouth there was just the hint of a smile.

I had never thought much about God. I was too locked into my humdrum existence of going to work, hanging out at the pub, then forcing my body that had eaten and drunk too much too many times to get down to the gym and exercise or hone my fencing skills, to have time to think about God even to the point of deciding whether or not I believed that He existed. But I suddenly believed in creation because there was no way that someone this lovely was a result of chance. *Imagine,* I thought, *of holding this in your arms.*

I was so gone—so out of it—that when Uncle Adrian looked round the corner of the alcove, he found me in front of the picture on one knee. I didn't understand it at the time, but a broad smile crossed his face. "I see you have met Lucy," he remarked.

I think my reply was, "Ohhhphewe," or something equally as honoring to the English language.

As I studied the picture, I realized two details were missing or had been covered up: her second name and the dates of her birth and death. She was wearing a gown that looked like something out of the American Civil War era, but she would have made sackcloth look stunning. Or more to the point, she would have looked just as stunning even in sackcloth.

Adrian pulled me away from the picture and into the dining room, sat me down at a table and commanded, "Food—eat!" The food reminded me that it had been a long time since my last meal.

I bombarded Adrian with questions about Lucy. "Where did she live? What did she do? Did she get married and when did she die?" Death had, after all, had been the common factor in all the pictures I had seen, so I assumed sadly that it had been the same for Lucy. The other thing I had noticed was that although the portrait was in an old frame, the picture itself did not look old.

"Time enough for questions—eat up," Adrian ordered. So the courses were brought in by the housekeeper, Victoria, who seemed to make a point of hiding her face from me. She put the food in front of me from over my shoulder. I didn't try to look at her, thinking that she might have had some kind of facial disfigurement that embarrassed her.

My uncle got on very well with Victoria and when he smiled at her, a kind of melting gentleness came into his eyes.

After dinner, Adrian ignited his pipe and a thick blue haze of smoke began to work its way round the room. Then he began to tell me about

Lucy. She had been born in 1846. At the age of sixteen, she and the rest of the family had moved to China. Her father, Maurice, had been in the tea trade. The tea trade had really only opened up after the advent of tea clippers, sailing ships like the famous *Cutty Sark* that could do the China-London run in ninety-something days, instead of the age it had taken before. I had been to Greenwich to see the *Cutty Sark* before the fire that nearly consumed her and even then she was magnificent. There had been some fantastic renovation work done and I hoped in my heart she would be around for many years to come.

Suddenly, Lucy began to make her lovely presence felt in my mind. "Did she marry?" I blurted into the silence.

Adrian answered, "Married...errr, no, not to my knowledge."

Amazed, I demanded, "Are you trying to tell me that a girl like that never married? Were all the guys in 18-whatever it was visually impaired?" Then a horrible thought descended upon me. She must have died of some illness or fever. "Is she buried somewhere? Is there a grave I could go and see?"

"No laddie, no grave, nor lost at sea, nor is she some kind of apparition."

Did she ever exist? I pondered. Or was she perhaps a composite painting of several girls that the painter knew? Before I turned in for the night, I photographed the portrait with a digital camera. That was unnecessary. I already carried her picture engraved on my mind. What had she been like? What had she done? The more I looked at the picture, the more I wished I had been alive some one-hundred-and-fifty years ago. Viewing her picture on the camera, I addressed those nagging questions to her gently smiling face and wished that she could answer.

Talking to a picture...Boy, Meryl would have a field day! "Focus on reality," she would tell me. "Lucy is a fantasy." Then she would return to her antiseptic world where anything she didn't need for social climbing would be consigned to the recycle bin of her mind. She cared about other people's feelings with the tact of a Storm Trooper, or so I thought, not realizing that I would eventually be proven wrong about her.

I dug about and enquired, but could gain no more information about the startlingly beautiful girl in the portrait.

Adrian had been busy for a couple of days and when the pressure eased off, I quizzed him again. "You show me a painting of the most beautiful girl I have ever seen—then give me only vague details. Come on, Uncle. Spill the beans. Who was she and what did she do?"

I had not noticed Victoria enter the room. This time when she put my coffee in front of me as we sat after supper, she made no effort to hide her face. "Drew," she said in a soft drawl, "Lucy is my daughter."

CHAPTER 2

"Your daughter!" I exclaimed. I think my mouth must have fallen open. "But she is in 18…it must be 1860-something and you are here…how did you get here? You don't look a hundred-and-fifty-something-years-old."

Victoria smiled and her smile almost duplicated the smile Lucy wore in the painting. There was no doubt the resemblance was striking. Victoria looked at me and remarked, "I think I may take that as a compliment that I do not look one-hundred-fifty years old. Thank you, kind sir!" She treated me to a mock curtsy.

"You really are Lucy's mother," I marveled. "But how?"

Victoria smiled mischievously and asked, "Do I really have to explain that to you? At your age?"

It took me about thirty seconds to realize what she meant. My cheeks blazed with embarrassment. "No, not that! I meant …"

My uncle, who had been trying to get back into the conversation again, came to life and said slowly, "Drew…how would you like to meet Lucy?" Seeing the incredulity on my face he added, "No. Straight up. No messing. Hands that you can shake, a figure you can see and lips that can talk …"

"And kiss," Victoria added seductively. "That is—at the right time, of course," she concluded with a maternal tone.

"Yes, but how do I meet her?" I gasped.

"Before we tell you that," Adrian replied, "you must sign the 'Official Secrets Act.' Otherwise, things can go no further."

Lucy had bedazzled me and insatiable curiosity about her had stolen my common sense. I would sign anything for even the remotest chance of meeting the subject of the portrait in person. I complied with my uncle's orders and Victoria removed the documents quickly, as if fearing that I might wake up and start thinking again and change my mind. She left the room, returning after a few minutes to sit beside Adrian.

Adrian treated her to an enigmatic smile, then addressed me. "The answer to your question is that you go back to 1867 ...or more succinctly, time travel."

I looked at them both. "Yeah. Right. That's a great storyline—but it can never happen—can it? I mean, it's impossible isn't it? People don't just jump from one time to another?" Even to my ears, my voice was becoming more and more unconvincing. If Victoria really was Lucy's mother...I looked at her and demanded, "Are you from 1800?"

"Certainly not!" she replied indignantly. "I'm not that old. I was born in 1823 and Lucy was born in 1846."

"Did you get here by time travel? How did you get here? How did you decide one morning that you were going to travel through time, like hopping on a bus or something? If you are from 1867, why didn't you just bring Lucy with you? And what does her father say and think about all this?"

Victoria held up her hand to stem the flood of questions. "Tarry, sir. My name is Victoria. My second name was Oxford until I met your uncle in China and married him. I had been widowed the year before. Adrian had come in search of a tea clipper. He can tell you that part. My late husband, Maurice, had left me not too badly off, but I had been unable to get a passage home. The prospect for a woman on her own sailing for three months on a tea clipper had all the attractions of getting a tooth knocked out. I had been left financially fit by Chinese standards, but what it would be like back in Scotland, I had no idea.

"Lucy was able to accomplish more in China than I could have. She and a friend had set up a school for orphans and children whose parents worked in the tea trade.

"I met your uncle and fell in love with him. He was caring and loving. Most of all, he respected me for being the person I am. He made me feel wanted and needed. I have since learned that he is a man with deep feelings."

"It was her steak and kidney pie that did it, you know," Adrian joked.

Victoria smiled at him, then continued, "I was treated with more respect by your uncle than any of the men in the 1860s had treated me with—or Lucy for that matter. Adrian explained to me that time travel was possible. I believed him. He tried to prepare me for the changes I would find in his time. All that he said and all that he showed me could not have prepared me for the pace of life today."

Victoria was silent for a while and Adrian said nothing. Then she continued. "All the advances in medicine—they're wonderful! No more diphtheria or croup or smallpox—not to mention what I now know was polio. The power to combat infections that killed hundreds, if not thousands. The amount and choice of food you have—round the clock strawberries and pineapples."

She shook her head and sighed. "All this, and yet millions are still hungry. Why? Millions have no clean water. Poverty is still rampant. I wonder frequently—has nothing been learned about sharing in the past one-hundred-fifty years? That terrible Adds disease…"

Adrian coughed. "Hem. I think you meant to say AIDS."

"Maybe I did," she replied. "Adds, AIDS. It still kills too many people. What about sharing some of the wealth to find a cure for that?

"In my time, the individual was still respected and valued. Well, that is to say—men were. Women have always had to fight for their rights. Only Jesus—as you know from the Bible, Drew (I didn't)—treated women with respect and as equals.

"Since getting to this time, I have learned that individuality in people nowadays is seen as something to be 'corrected' or even feared. Populations are controlled like they were in the old Roman Empire with 'bread and circuses.' There seems to be no vision, no dreams. Some may want to end poverty, but they can't agree how to do it.

"Drew, you have fresh water. Do you know how precious that is? You have never seen what cholera does." Then Victoria stopped and said slowly, "And the saddest thing I have seen since coming here is so many trying to do without God. They don't ask God for wisdom in dealing with all these issues. They have the arrogance and false pride to think they can solve everything on their own. Yet when they fail—they don't understand why."

I moved uncomfortably, feeling guilty for some reason. I had never felt that it was necessary to request wisdom from God, if He even existed. I was smart enough. I believed in figuring things out on my own. Of course…my life had pretty much consisted of wasted time and space. "Yeah," I muttered. "It must be real shock to you. I can't begin to imagine." I found myself thinking that her discourse would have made a fascinating dissertation for a Ph.D. paper.

There was silence in the room and I inquired, "Why not just bring Lucy back here?"

Victoria sighed. "When I came back here, I barely made it. The journey nearly killed me. Adrian had a medical friend of his examine me and do a battery of tests. I have, it seems, a heart defect exacerbated by the journey. The doctor couldn't understand what had caused it to flare up.

In 1867, it would never have been detected. Heaven alone knows what reason would have been given for my demise. The important point is that it may be hereditary. Fine without the rigours of time travel, but…" She looked thoughtful, as if she were trying to solve all the woes of the world in an instant.

Adrian took over. "The point is that if we tried to get Lucy here the journey might kill her, while if she lived out her life in 1867—even if she became pregnant and had a child—she would be in no more danger than any other woman of her time."

"So you want me to go there and stay? Why do I think that with the kind of people who must be behind this to finance it—to make it possible—concern over my love life is not the only reason, or perhaps not even the real reason. Or, am I being cynical in my young, old age? Suppose Lucy doesn't like me? Suppose I don't throw her switch and she looks at me and heads for the hills. What then?"

Adrian exclaimed impatiently, "Drew, for crying out loud! Your father had piles as well as pessimism. Try not to follow him in that sense."

"Lucy will fall head over heels for you," Victoria assured me, then giggled and added, "at least as far as an 1867 corset will allow her to fall! But, Drew, you must have confidence—faint heart never won fair maiden."

"No," I replied. "In the old days, all you had to do was to slay a dragon or something simple like that."

Victoria sounded exasperated. "Drew get some ice!"

Adrian put down his pipe. "Hmm. Life, dear, in this case. 'Get a life.' Or, you might mean, 'chill.' Don't worry so much."

Victoria was right, I realized. I was starting to sound like my dad who had fallen into the curse of our modern society, settling for the mediocre and calling it the best. To be honest, my life wasn't going anywhere. And I was right there with it, not going anywhere either.

"Okay," I relented. "But you will have to coach me on life in 1867. I mean, didn't they still hang people in public then and pursue other cheery pastimes?"

My uncle saw his chance to jump back into the conversation. "Good lad, Drew. Now let me explain the technical bit. You remember the comet that fell in Arizona about two years ago? Well, we took large core samples from it and found that the clocks in the lab went funny. Sometimes they would go fast—not just by hours or minutes—but by days. I remember my poor colleague was working at his desk while eating chicken sandwiches. Well, two days later, the sandwiches reappeared on his desk—the same ones he had eaten two days before. Said he thought the Cajun sauce he had made them with was strong, but not that strong. This only happened in the places where samples of the meteorite were stored. So we poked around ..." Poking around was my uncle's way of describing intricate scientific investigation. "We poked around and isolated a substance called Kairon."

"Wizard name," I said. "One of two Greek words for time."

He continued, "A few of us had been working on the 'Varley'

project—that being the ability to send very carefully chosen people back in time or even forward, though that has proven more difficult. Imagine stopping crashes before they happen. Stopping terrorist attacks. All that kind of thing."

"Forgive me for being dense, Uncle, but wouldn't they have had to have happened first before you could go stop them? What you try to stop from happening would already be history—not something that was going to happen. Wouldn't that be changing history?"

"You are getting moralistic," Adrian complained. "Must take it after your mother. Anyway, we found we could target Kairon on one object and the space round about it …well…" The technical details tumbled out and were totally lost on me. I was too busy trying to think of the implications. "So therefore, "Adrian concluded, "the number of journeys that can be made may not be limitless. We just don't know how many journeys can be made." He shrugged unscientifically. "The further back you go, the quicker the power source can deteriorate."

"What happens if the power source deteriorates in the middle of a trip?"

"We think you land at the nearest year to where you are at the time —if you pardon the pun."

"So I could be coming back from 76AD to now, the power could run out and I end up in 1776?"

"Well, technically, yes," he said slowly.

"Mmm. Better take a toothbrush or two then," I said trying to make light of the crazy mess I seemed to have somehow created for myself. I took the opportunity of the ensuing silence to go back out and look at Lucy's portrait again. She was so beautiful that "beautiful" was not a descriptive enough word for her. I went back in to enquire who had done the painting.

"You won't have heard of him," Adrian said, "but you will have heard of his teacher, Sir John Everett Millais, the Pre-Raphaelite. Besides you don't need to rely entirely on the painting. We can give you a DVD of Lucy."

"Uncle, have you thought of the consequences of this technology falling into the wrong hands?"

"You mean a different end to World War II or Waterloo, if Grouchy had got back on time? We must not be dramatic. There are safeguards."

"Uncle, think! If Robert E. Lee had won Gettysburg, there might have been two United States and world history would have been very different."

The volume of smoke from the pipe increased before being expelled in a large plume. "Look, Drew. There are things going on which do not really concern you or Lucy."

Why did I think I had touched a nerve with Robert E. Lee and Gettysburg?

My uncle continued, "However, I do need your help to get money to Scotland in 1867, so that this house stays in the family." He smiled apologetically. "In short, Drew, I need you to win Lucy and get the biggest shipment of tea you can get back here—or to London. All official and above board. Oh, yes. You will be given the money to buy a tea clipper."

A tea clipper! All sorts of pictures raced through my mind— mostly of the *Cutty Sark* and *Thermopylae*, the two classic clippers along with the host of excellent American ones. Sailing pirate-infested waters…that thought was off-putting. It would be like watching a film —except when the word "cut" was used—it didn't mean to stop filming.

Adrian continued, "You will need a bill of sale for the tea to present to the lawyer Isaac Porthero in Aberdeen. He is covering the purchase of the house. This will be added to the money he holds on Lucy's behalf. You have to go, Drew. I can't leave Victoria. Besides, there is another reason."

I suddenly got the impression that my uncle was trying to tell me something unpleasant. Things are rarely as simple as they seem in my life, probably similarly in the life of any who may chance to read this. My spine began to shiver, a bit like opening a carton of cream and finding a dead fly inside. "Let me guess, Uncle. Gorgeous girl. Commerce, and what seems to be a difficult task. There has to be a spanner or two in the works. My guess is he is male, and trouble, and is after Lucy, after the tea, after the ship—or all of the previous. Just to make life interesting. Right?"

My uncle looked at me with the look of a parent who, after thinking his child is dumb, suddenly realizes that his child is actually bright.

"Yup, you have hit the nail on the head. His name is Caleb Bryant."

If I had known then what that name portended, I would have left my uncle's house at a run and never looked back.

Adrian continued, "Bryant is a New Englander. He is now full owner of the clipper *Allegheny*, having won the other two-thirds of it from his former partners in a poker game. He knows and detests me on sight, but you he does not know. You have got to get there and take care of Lucy. Bryant is obsessed with her. (I could share that sentiment!) He would stop at nothing to get what he wants including kidnapping her."

"Please, Drew! You are the only one who can help!" Victoria cried.

Adrian added, "You have been psychologically profiled—sorry, laddie—without your knowledge, which is the way it had to be, and they reckon you could adapt and settle in that time."

I thought, then asked, "psychologically profiled? What? To see if I get withdrawal symptoms from *Starbucks?*" How had I been watched and tested without my knowledge? Suddenly the suspicion in my mind materialized. The door to the room opened behind me and Meryl's voice purred, "Hello, gorgeous!"

CHAPTER 3

At first, I couldn't believe it. There must have been something in the steak and kidney pie that caused hallucinations. Meryl came in and dropped her handbag beside the chair opposite me. She put her navy jacket over its back, sat down, crossed her legs, and sighed. I have to admit she looked lovely. Her blonde hair had just been cut and styled to frame her face. She was lovely, but not in the same league as Lucy, a sort of eight out of ten, perhaps, if one believed in using numbers as a rating system.

"Sorry, darling," she said perkily. "I was sent to profile you, and to provoke you, and frustrate you. We had to find out how you handled a crisis, how you handled your emotions, and how you coped with frustration."

I looked at her out of the corner of my eye. "You succeeded. So it was all a windup—and frustrated is hardly the word. Didn't you feel anything for me?"

She leaned forward, a motion that sent a wave of blonde hair falling across one of her blue eyes. The upturned nose wrinkled and the eyes lightened to baby blue. "If you must know the truth, Drew, I loved running my fingers through your lovely dark curls and staring into your lost puppy hazelnut eyes. I loved being the one to get to look at your beautiful face and hear the sound of your voice telling me how often you thought of me even when I wasn't there. Darling, I still have the poems you wrote me."

Adrian jumped in. "Look, when you two are quite finished, maybe we can get on with the job in hand. Meryl is here to help you and you need her help." He added, "Drew, think about that girl in the picture—Lucy Oxford. Meryl did what she was supposed to do. Now, we need to get you to China and 1867."

At the time, I thought that I must have imagined the tears I saw springing up in Meryl's eyes. Later, I was to learn that I owed Meryl not only a debt of gratitude, but my life as well. None of that was apparent that night at my Uncle's home, and there is nothing so foolish as flaming youth. With no apologies at the time, I was behaving like a flaming youth.

I told myself that I was going to drive back to Edinburgh and hope all this was a bad dream, but the truth—the stupid truth—was that I cared more for Meryl than I was ready to admit. Oh, why couldn't life just be simple?

Victoria came after me down the picture-lined corridor and took my hand. At the time I felt she was the least to blame of the whole gang. She got down on her knees in front of me in the hallway. "Drew, I beg you! Help my Lucy, please."

I pulled her to her feet in exasperation. "Victoria, for crying out loud, get up. You make me feel like the lowest form of insect life."

She responded by giving me a look of sheer desperation. "Drew, Lucy is in real danger from Caleb Bryant and she has no one to protect her. It was different for women in 1867, from what it is now. A girl needed a father or husband to protect her. Lucy doesn't even have a brother!"

Somehow, Victoria—or was it Lucy?—seemed to be winning my heart. I returned her look with mock sternness. "One question, how am I going to make mother-in-law jokes when my mother in law is around a hundred and fifty!"

Looking relieved, she burst out laughing. I added, "Do you realize what an awful job it will be to get Christmas cards to you?"

When I went back into the dining room, I reckon I had seen happier people at the dentist. "I am going to have a glass of wine," I declared. "I suggest that all of you do the same thing. Then you can show me what exactly is going to get me back to 1867 China, complete with

Lucy and tea clippers."

Adrian looked as relieved as Victoria had. Meryl smiled at me. "Knew you had it in you, gorgeous."

"Don't look so smug," I replied. "You still owe me about two hundred coffees for the length of time I had to wait for you coming out of your lectures—but in the interests of time and economy you can buy me tea at the *Ritz* or, failing that, *Starbucks*."

She pouted, and somehow, her reaction didn't seem totally mendacious.

"Sorry," I said contritely. And while she didn't speak, she mouthed, "it's okay," with her lips. "By the way," I added, "I like the outfit."

"When you two lovebirds have finished, we have a time machine to see," Adrian interjected.

We left the dining room and followed Adrian back along the picture-filled passage and I stole another glance at Lucy's portrait. Was I really crazy? Then again, how often did a life-changing opportunity like this proffer itself?

We trailed Adrian down a flight of stairs and along a dark passage below the house. Strangely, what I could smell was the scent of jasmine. We stopped at a sliding door and Adrian passed a card through a green light and the machine did an iris eye scan of Adrian and Meryl. Then at the press of a couple of buttons on the panel, it scanned my iris, too. I was given a card on the other side of the door that I assumed would get me in and out providing I didn't lose it. We then passed by a couple of 'heavies' armed with Uzis, who scanned me with care and obviously knew the others. "Doctor," one of them acknowledged Adrian.

The room was brightly lit. To the left of the door on the wall, there was what appeared to be a control panel. To the right of the room there was a steel car that turned out to be titanium, half-in and half-out of a tunnel in the wall. It looked like one of these contraptions you find at gaming centers. You go inside and the machine, with you at the wheel, takes you down harem-sacrum roads and over bridges, complete with the sound of screaming metal, screeching tires, and breaking glass. You get bounced up and down and from side to side and wish you had not eaten so much curry half an hour before as it now seemed to be on the move in your stomach. Additionally, you wished you had taken water instead of beer—for as you get thrown about—the beer starts to demonstrate its increased fizziness, to your increasing discomfort. At the same time, you are desperately attempting to prove how macho you are by not throwing up on your girl. as she clings to you, a course of action guaranteed to nip any romance in the bud.

"Here it is," said Adrian as a side door in the car opened. "Set the date and time on this dial…" Again, I smelled a scent like jasmine. "Pull the switch—and after a five-second delay—you are off. Don't pull the switch first and then shut the door. Shut the door first and do not open it again until the humming has stopped and the yellow light has come on."

Meryl, who had been watching us, said, "You want me to come along and hold your hand?"

"No. You might lose me halfway. My feet could be in 1914, and my head in 1850."

I noticed a door next to the car that seemed like a smaller version of the tunnel. "Is that for vertically challenged travelers?" I asked

"That is for the transportation of your kit and anything else you may need in a hurry," my uncle explained. "It costs less power to send it this way. Much of your gear will be transported and sent ahead to where you will be staying. One of our operatives has your picture and you will be given kit and clothes for 1867. You will be given money to buy anything extra you may need, but we will allow you to forego the endemic wooly long johns during your time in Foochow. One more thing: here is the DVD of Miss Oxford. She did not know it was being taken, but she has been told that someone might be coming out from Scotland to see her."

Adrian added, "You will be given survival training, the kind of thing that Special Forces get. You will get along fine with Angus McTurk. He will provide combat training and teach you how to shoot and hone your fencing skill. Fencing, particularly, may be useful. In 1867, some still used swords, but this time there will be no button on the point of the blade. The experience you've had in the army re-enactment group will be helpful. Listen to what Angus says and don't try to be smart with him. Meryl will be down in a couple of days with some files for you to read and remember. The important thing is getting down your life story for the 1867 Drew Faulkner."

Trying to lighten what was beginning to possess a severe chunk of seriousness, I asked, "It's not one of these things that you have five minutes to read and memorize before the contents self destruct?"

Ignoring my flippancy, my uncle continued, "You must sell your car and your flat and put in your notice at work."

No more nights at the Finlander Bar—would it be such a miss?

"Only one other person knows about this," Adrian added. "Connie."

I was taken aback. "Mum? But how?"

Adrian replied, "Not your concern. She is happy for you and is even prepared not to see you again after one more visit."

I sighed. "Okay, but I'm bushed. I'm off to bed—night folks."

I got to my room. There was a song going through my mind about what a difference a day makes. Yeah, this was really happening to me, but would I wake up tomorrow and find it was all a dream? I was deep in thought when there was a knock at my door. "Come in."

It was Victoria, and she had brought me tea with some rum in it. "Help you sleep," she explained.

"Tell me I'm not dreaming," I begged.

She looked at me with that kind of knowing smile that some women have. A smile that tells you that they know more than they let on —as if they know a secret that you, being a man, would never understand—even if they tried to share it in one-syllable words.

"You are not dreaming. You and Lucy will make it." She headed toward the door to leave.

"Good night, Mum," I couldn't resist saying. I smiled as she turned back to stare at me. "Just practicing in case I don't get to say it to you for real."

It was her turn to smile. "Just get to sleep, you. I don't want you meeting Lucy with big bags under your eyes. That's unromantic. Just a bit of motherly advice."

I fell asleep with the light on.

CHAPTER 4

I awoke to find dawn making its gentle presence felt in every corner of the room. I flicked off the bakelite switch on the light, had a quick breakfast, and jumped into my car, heading back to Edinburgh. I had a great deal to think about.

Here I was at twenty-five, fomenting a change in my life that would require selling my car and flat—ditching all their happy memories—as well as my job. Transcending common sense, I was starting to fall for a girl I had never met and with no guarantees that after I left my comfortable, reasonably undemanding life in my century and appeared in hers, she would love me in return.

In 1867, love would mean marriage—no turning back. What If I couldn't settle in 1867? What if she didn't love me in return? I loved history, but what would it be like to live it when you knew what was coming before it happened? I was reminded of Cassandra, the mythological daughter of Priam, king of Troy, who was condemned to always speak the truth. No one believed her.

The inimical factor would be Bryant. Once he discovered my intent, what would it be—sword, knife, or bullet in the back? A soft-nose slug from an 1867 Colt could take a sizeable chunk out of my 21st century carcass. A long life in early 21st century Scotland, or life with the most gorgeous girl I had ever seen? As the old program used to say, *Answer on a postcard...*

What was my life now? Existing from one TGIF until the next, endless curries and carry-outs. There had to be more to life than this, and what was "this" anyway?

The estate agent Caramel &*Co (Stick With Us &We'll Sell Your Home),* assured me that a flat only a short walk from the Scottish Assembly would soon sell. I tried to picture a member of the Scottish parliament in my flat, attempting to frame laws now for a country that had been totally different in 1867.

I sold my car to a medical student who needed it for his journeys to hospitals and his various girlfriends. I kind of wondered when he found time to study. My social life at Glasgow University had not been as varied as his—at least what I could remember of it. That reminded me of the various alcoholic concoctions that we passed round—beer and cider mixed in a sauce pan—with a little white wine for good measure. And the consequences. The following morning when the previous night's creations mimicked the impression of a jet Phantom flying at Mach 1.5 between your ears—oh, happy days (*Yeah right!*).

Meryl stopped by the flat a couple of days after I got back, arms full of files and magazines. The do's and don'ts of the 1860s man. Manners, dress and coping with servants, along with files of legal and maritime procedures. I had to purchase the tea clipper in 1867, for in 1869, the great rivalry would start between the *Cutty Sark* and *Thermopylae.* There was always the *Sir Lancelot,* with which to contend, as well as Bryant's *Allegheny.* Then there were the pirates and getting round the Cape of Good Hope. Suddenly morning traffic jams in Edinburgh did not seem so bad.

All these deep thoughts, I realized—as well as the surreal adventure itself—should be recorded. I decided to keep a journal so in the years to come I could read it and know it had not been just a dream. And if I survived—which was doubtful—my children could read it. They would know that their dad had made a difference and been a success at something.

The ship I was advised to attempt to purchase was the *Night Arrow.* She had been built in Stockholm, but operated from Scotland. There was no picture of her, but the specifications looked good. She should be able to match the *Allegheny,* if not outpace her. Yet a ship was only as good as the crew, and above all, the captain and sailing-master. A good captain could by sheer force of personality make an average crew do above average things. All these musings about ships and captains made the assumption that Lucy and I would get out of Foochow, China, in one piece. What if I had to kill someone in self defense? Fencing with a button-ended blade, face mask, and padded suit was one thing—but having a pointed blade come at you full speed and in low light was far less enchanting.

I suddenly came to the end of my dreaming when I heard Meryl's voice in my bedroom. I had forgotten she was still here and it was getting dark outside. I went through to the bedroom to find Meryl sitting up in bed like a sleepy kitten and wearing one of my shirts.

"I forgot my nightie," she said, but her eyes gave everything away. "We can't have you meeting some floozy and giving the game away, so I have been sent to 'make you comfortable' and keep you on the straight and narrow. Please use a condom."

She was suddenly and unexpectedly in the place where I had been trying to get her for weeks. I could almost feel the sheer physical relief that would come in coming. I sat at the side of the bed and she tried to kiss me, but when she got close, I realized that there were tears running down her cheeks. She wasn't doing this because she wanted to—or because she wanted me or loved me. She was doing this because she had been told to—ordered to make me "comfortable."

"Do you want me on my back?" she asked slowly, obviously not a happy bunny. "But if you want me to …"

I put my fingers across her lips and kissed her forehead. "I'm on the couch," I told her. "You stay here just in case your boss is eyeballing the place." She looked amazed.

"You and I have to work together. You are beautiful and you glow when you're not trying to be wonder woman. I promise you, no floozies. I have a lot to think about. It's not every day you get to be part of history. Nor is it everyone who gets an opportunity like this."

She looked at me and smiled. This time it was natural and made her lovely. "Thanks," she said. "I won't forget that I owe you."

The course of events later proved her statement to be more than mere words. We put the light out and I crept next door.

The following morning she ate all my Muesli and kissed me on the cheek. Her hair smelled deliciously of coconuts.

"Are you sure you wouldn't like to meet a nice guy in 1867?" I asked. "He couldn't treat you any worse than the creeps for whom you are working."

She smiled, shook her head, gave me a huge hug and left. Meryl deserved better than to be forced into doing something she didn't want to do. Every woman deserved the right of choice. Okay, call me old fashioned, but that's what I believe.

What does the well dressed young man of 1867 carry? Well, at least in China, the idea of a knife occurred. My friend Alec was an armorer. He made knives and swords and blades of all kinds for reenactment groups. I asked him to make me a Bowie knife.

"A Bowie knife!" Alec exclaimed. "You must tell me about the kind of parties you go to." Nevertheless, when I went to collect the Bowie knife at his workshop, he had made a good job. I tested the balance and swung the blade around a bit.

"Hey," said Alec. "Careful! You might cut off something that Meryl will need later."

"Man, you've done a great job!" He had even engaged a leather-working friend to make a sheath for me. Strangely enough, the pattern on the sheath was a sailing ship.

"Drew, in the name of the wee man, be careful! That thing is sharp. Would a pencil sharpener not be easier? If the police find you with that, they will take a dim view and eyebrows may be raised."

"Don't worry. Just taking a trip for old time's sake!"

Breaking the rules (since there were no sunglasses in 1867), I brought two pairs of wire-framed sunglasses. My final purchase was a sword stick, bought in the back streets of Portobello. I felt it might prove useful.

The shop owner took the money and said, "I have long ago given up trying to supply mental reasoning for the purchases of my fellow man. I just supply the goods."

Thoughts of Meryl reminded me that the past was going to be my future. I was going to have to cool down to win Lucy. I spent time looking at the DVD of her. I was mesmerized, both with her voice and her smile. I tried to imagine what it would be like to wake up lying next to her every day. She could sing like an angel and play the piano and flute. She sang ballads and hymns and read passages out of the Bible. When she read the Bible, she made the words in the Bible seem real. She spoke with passion about many things, including the type of man she hoped to marry. She looked at the girl who was doing the filming and her face broke out into a smile again. When her head turned just a bit to one side, the painting on Adrian's wall came to life.

It was shortly after that when I received instructions to report to *Kinimouth Brae,* a big house on the road between Peebles and Kelso. This was the training I had been promised. I drove the hired car provided and was met by Meryl, who suddenly appeared from nowhere as I got out of the car. "Come on," she said eagerly. "I will introduce you to Sergeant Major McTurk." Why did I think that this was going to be one of those experiences I was not going to enjoy? Computer games were much easier.

Angus McTurk was about forty years old, thin and wiry with not an ounce of fat on him. His eyes never left you and he was never taken off guard.

"Laddie, I am here to help you continue breathing. If someone sticks a knife in you in the right place, that breathing stops. If you stick a knife in him—or her—tell me, did you hear me, laddie—or her—they stop breathing. Get it wrong and it will be fatal. Remember that word when you use the knife—FATAL—fast and target aiming low."

We were in a gym and he produced a knife. "Sykes and Fairbairn Commando dagger—used only for one thing."

I mentally tried and discarded the quip about peeling potatoes that was forming in my mind. He shot the knife across the floor to me. "Right. Pick it up and attack me like you meant it."

I bent down to pick up the knife and felt a chop at the side of my neck that floored me. "Never, ever take your eyes off your opponent,"

Turk hissed. I picked up the knife and went for his chest …again I felt the edge of his hand across the muscles of my forearm and the knife dropped from my numb fingers. I ended up with the knife at my throat.

"Listen….aim low. You want to stop your enemy first. Killing is secondary. Right. Again…"

After forty-five minutes, I was sore. I had thought that I was physically fit. Now I knew better. Compared to my instructor, I was about as athletic as a broken-soled training shoe. I got a crash course on vulnerable points on the human body. The human body possessed so many vulnerable points it was a wonder anyone survived! This was going to be a long haul and a painful one, but then I remembered that someone coming at me in China would not be kidding—nor attempting to instruct me.

The other part of McTurk's talent was fire arms drill—shooting a revolver. "You ever fired a pistol before?" he asked.

"Not since I was a kid," I replied.

He looked at me with that, *Don't get smart with me,* boy, kind of expression.

"My dad had a 9-mm Lugar," I hastened to explain. "And by the time I was ten, I could strip it down and put it together again."

McTurk went to the wall, took a Lugar down and handed it to me. "Okay, let's see you."

I obliged. His eyebrow moved up about three millimeters, which was a sign that he was impressed. This time he turned to the desk and produced a revolver. "Okay, this is yours. The permit is also on the desk. This is not a toy. It is a working replica 1868 Webley No. 1 revolver, six shots. Fires a 14.6-millimeter bullet. It will stop anything—any pirate *and* the pirate behind him."

He taught me target shooting and "snap shooting," where a target appears and you have to decide in an instant if it's friend, foe or neutral. Get it wrong and your popularity with the locals can take a downward spiral. The Webley, even in a two-handed position, had a kick like a mule. My wrist ached. Additionally, I had to learn to strip it down and clean it. I shot from every angle, even a moving platform to simulate a moving ship. The gun was powerful, but not too long to be concealed in a coat pocket, as well as a holster. I also purchased a thousand rounds of smokeless ammunition, although that did not become available until about 1870.

The other aspect of 1867 life was dancing. This, too, was included in my repertoire. If you could not dance, you would be at a major loss. Dancing a la 1867, and particularly the waltz, required practice. So, too, it was important to learn your part in set dances. My teacher, Anna, was Swedish and beautiful and could move as gracefully as a feather on a breath of wind. She was the most graceful woman I had ever seen, real poetry in motion. With her blonde hair and white dress, she was like a gentle flurry of snow that had somehow managed to find its way onto the dance floor.

"Drew, you must concentrate. Stop looking at your feet. Look at your partner. What is the point of dancing with a beautiful woman if you cannot look her into her eyes?"

After four weeks of hard going I was able to "trip the light fantastic," or at least to trip. Perhaps my celibate life was getting to me, for Anna's close proximity was leaving me both shaken and stirred. We danced, and then she would separate from me to show me the move. There was not one unlovely thing about her—she was doing what she had been born to do, dance. After our time was over, I said to her, "I will miss you. You have not only been a delight to the eyes, but a treat to the spirit."

Her blue eyes flashed and her nose crinkled with pleasure. "I bet you say that to all the girls!" She reached out and kissed me and, unexpectedly, I did not want to leave her. I had an erection that I could not hide. She put the music on for a tango. "Dance," she commanded. Thankfully, by the time she was finished, the sweat had increased and the erection had gone, replaced by a sense of relief, but having left a somewhat embarrassing stain on my track suit front. It made, *"Come Dancing,"* take on a whole new meaning.

"Go," Anna said, picking up her towel, "or we will get into trouble." She left by a door at the other side of the gym.

Outside, I headed for my room I did not want to be seen like this, but Meryl came down a corridor towards me and her eyes took everything in, my sweat-covered clothes and heavy breathing.

"So you and Anna got on okay then?" she remarked on the way past.

You can go off some people.

After a shower, I landed at McTurks' den. "I could use a few more weeks with you," McTurk told me. "But remember: watch the eyes, get in first, and you'll be fine."

Heavens, I thought. Anna's advice for dancing was almost the same as McTurk's for unarmed combat! "You'll be fine," McTurk repeated, forcing his face into what passed for a smile. "After all, laddie, you've had me to teach you."

"Thanks for the bruises, Sergeant Major!"

McTurk looked at me steadily. "Bruises heal. Make sure your opponent doesn't. We may meet again."

I drove away with the thought that life would go on in Edinburgh without me. The same group would meet in the same pubs and go to the same restaurants. Work would continue from day to day. The traffic would get worse. The 1867 Edinburgh that I hoped to survive long enough to experience would be smellier and smokier. Nobody would recognize me, as if I had never been there. I thought of Anna and our last dance, but I had to focus on Lucy. If I even mentioned Anna, it might go bad for her. Like Meryl, she had only been doing the job expected of her.

You dream and plan for a change, then out of the blue the opportunity to make a change comes. The planning follows. And then you have to make the journey—take the first step. In my case, the first step involved going back some one-hundred-fifty years. Yes, I could back out if they let me, but I would end up an old man, wondering what would have happened if I had gone.

Then the day arrives when you finally get on the plane, or train, or time machine and start the journey. Suddenly, you reach your destination and are left wondering if it is real or a dream. The reality planted in my mind was that I would know for the rest of my life what was actually going to happen. Suppose something I did in 1867 changed history? How did I know that history, as I had already learned it, had not already been changed by perhaps even the very people who were behind this? Yet, I had to be prepared to take a risk or just be one of the sheep, waiting for someone else to make decisions so I could blindly follow.

My saying goodbye to Mum was traumatic and personal. How do you say goodbye to the person who has loved you all your life? "You always were going to be different, Drew," she observed. "I will miss you, but I want you to be happy, not just ordinary. Just be sure that this is what you really want." The conversation continued, but some things are personal.

"Love you, Mum. Thanks for everything and for being there. Keep eating and don't fade away."

She looked at me as only a mother can. "Love you, Son. And don't forget to wash behind your ears." This was followed by a hug, grin, and photograph. Yet when I arrived in China, Mum would not be born for another hundred-odd years.

"So you are going to work in China, then little brother?" Ian asked. My elder brother by ten years had a bald head, which had given him an appearance of worldly wisdom as well as kudos as a teacher. "I can come and see you, then?"

"No, Bro, I will be moved about. You may arrive somewhere you cannot pronounce to find that I had been shifted to somewhere else you can't pronounce." He cast an enigmatic look in my direction. "There is something you can't tell me. Okay, I get the picture."

When Ian looked at me again—still quizzically—I realized that he had always been there for me even in tough times. Dad had been an alcoholic, but had beaten it in the end. Ian and Mum had gone through some rough times. "I'll take care of Mum," he promised. "Just watch your back, Bro. Love you." And he gave me a big hug.

There were medical exams, treatments, dental checks, implants and teeth coating. My appendix had gone. I felt healthy except for sore arms from all the shots I got to advance kill every disease that it was possible to eliminate through inoculations. I felt like an immigrant going to America in the 1880s. I had made fun of some of the immigrant songs, but now I began to understand them. Now they spoke my language—me going to another time to meet a girl I had never met, hoping to make a good first impression on her and pick up on 1867 chat-up lines. Lucy and my relationship would have to be serious. Yet, if I had said that to anyone they would probably have replied, "Seriously? (In my time, people were often "partners," not spouses.) You can't mean it." I tried to imagine myself in 1910, surrounded by grandchildren. What a tale to tell!

I collected my hired car, a good bit bigger and zippier than I had been used to, a real thoroughbred. I headed for Bellefield, for my last time in this time. I was scared and not ashamed to admit it, but it was not enough fear to stop me. Would I remember everything I had been taught and read? The key was Lucy's love. If I could not win her, then everything else would change. This was not 21st century girl—in 1867 things were different…but how different? That is what I could not possibly know.

CHAPTER 5

I got to Bellefield in time for what I hoped was tea. Adrian opened the door, still blasting the lock. He sprayed me with conversation. "How did you get on with Angus? Good to see you are still standing. He's a great boy in a fight, even the SAS get nervous when he is around."

"Even my bruises have got bruises," I said. "Look…I'm aching all over."

Adrian looked at me with a wry smile. "That is him being nice. You should see him when he gets upset—or perhaps you shouldn't."

Victoria took me along to a different bedroom. I dumped my kit on the bed and she sat down on the edge of the bed and indicated the vacant space beside her. I sat down and got the feeling that I was going to be told something the magazines had not covered. "How you feeling?" she asked.

"Scared," I replied. "But not scared enough to send me back to being a nonentity."

"That sounds sensible. You will manage, Drew." There was a pause. "Drew, there is one thing they probably have not covered. You are used to girls, for want of a better word, smelling a certain way. Perfume, deodorant, scented soap."

"Yes, its part of the charm, especially the right kind of perfume. It can do wonders for the love life." I tried not to think about Meryl's coconut-scented hair.

Victoria adopted her motherly look. "Hmm. Drew, in 1867, girls smelled differently from now. So did men for that matter. When you get there, you will find that girls are still girls, but with earthier, more natural scents and odors, and heavier makeup. Clothes are much thicker and corsets are not the most comfortable things to wear. What I mean by that is that sweat builds up."

She produced a ladies' magazine from 1867, and handed it to me. "This has some articles which you should read, just to put you in the picture. This is where Lucy and some of the others are at." Then she took my hand and looked me straight in the eyes. "Drew, it is not what Lucy does or does not do, it is what others think she has done. Please do not compromise her. And you will have to get used to a chaperone, at least until you are engaged. Don't let Bryant compromise her, either. If you love her, marry her. Don't use her. My daughter is clever and intelligent and artistic, but very naive in some things. And I'm not there now to help her, guide her, or teach her."

I squeezed her hand. "I understand what you are saying and I want to marry Lucy and take care of her if she will have me."

Victoria took a couple of items out of her pocket. The first was a half-coin. "When you meet Lucy, give her this half-coin locket. She has the other half. Give her this letter—and this photograph if you think it is appropriate. It should be enough for her to trust you. The rest is up to you. Treat her as a friend, as well, and watch out for her."

I let some of my thoughts slip. "Am I crazy to do this?" Suddenly all the things I was used to seemed comfortable and safe. They started to wrap themselves round my thought processes like a mental duvet against chilly thoughts. Sometimes you begin imagining what could happen, instead of focusing on what actually is happening.

Victoria seemed to read the sudden confusion of mind that followed my question. "That is the difference, Drew, between those who get things done and those who just talk about it. No matter how you try to hide it, you will be different from the average 1867 man in your outlook. The way you talk to women as equals is not the norm for them. You will turn heads in that respect. Beware of a Russian woman, Julie Lacota. She is cunning, and dangerous, and has broken many hearts. Butter would not melt in her mouth, but do not let the little-girl-lost-look fool you. Come on." She got up and headed for the door. "There is stew and dumplings and peaches and brandy and cream for tea. Ready in about twenty minutes and don't forget to wash behind your ears."

On the way down I had time to look at Lucy's portrait again. There she was with that same air of peace. The thought struck me, *peace, perfect peace, and for such a time as this.*

After tea, Adrian handed me a letter. It was addressed to the Vicompte Louis Fumarle. My uncle explained, "He is the French Chargez d'affairs in Foochow, and you must get this letter to him and tell no one else about it and give it only to him, not some minion."

"Holy Moses, Uncle. James Bond has an easier time of it than me and he's trained. Are there any other requests—like stopping World War I from breaking out? If I remember my history, I am right in the middle of the expansion of Prussia—fighting Austria and in what will become Italy and in the Franco-Prussian War. I knew this wasn't just about my love life!"

I asked him if there was another time machine. He hesitated too long before answering in the negative. He also assured me that Lucy knew nothing of this and that I was free to back out even now if I wanted.

"Yes, I'm sure," I responded. "I know too much and I reckon if I took cold feet my life expectancy would be about two weeks before I became another statistic. No, you don't have to worry. I will carry out the plan, if Bryant doesn't get me or a dozen other things that could happen don't happen."

Adrian nodded approval. "You go tomorrow. You will get details of your rooms in Foochow and who to look out for. How do you feel?"

"Scared," I replied, my voice coming out higher than I intended.

"Why?" Adrian demanded.

"Because, Uncle, you are a whiz kid and a very clever one. The trouble is you are not the only clever whiz kid on the block. There is probably an 'Uncle Adrian 2,' to whom the possibility of time travel has occurred. Or am I just being pessimistic? Suddenly I feel like the guy who gets invited up to the bridge of the luxury liner and finds Daffy Duck in the captain's chair."

Tea was a subdued affair. I walked outside afterwards and sat on one of the steps of the front stairs. The stars shone and I ignored the slight chill in the air. I thought about the vast distances of space and tried to work out light years, but gave up. Maybe time travel was easier. I really thought about nothing because what I was about to do was way beyond my experience. I knew I was doing the right thing, in spite of the way my insides seemed to be quivering all the way out to my extremities.

"Penny for them," a voice said. I was suddenly aware of Meryl standing in front of me. She smelled deliciously of coconuts. She wore long cotton socks and black shoes. Her blue skirt swung gently as she bent down to pull me to my feet. Her yellow top showed her lovely figure to advantage. "Come, on. Let's walk. You will get piles if you sit on that step much longer." She slipped her slender arm through mine. "You go tomorrow?"

"Yeah." As we headed away from the house, I began to shake. "Some hero I am! Scared because he has got himself way in over his head. Scared because he is leaving everything he knows to go to the unknown. Scared because he might get a knife in the ribs."

"Shhh," she purred. "Just look and listen. Look at the stars and the vast expanse of the sky. We seem so small, just you and me. All we have is tonight and nobody can take that away from us. Tomorrow everything changes. Drew," she whispered, looking into my eyes.

We stopped walking and the moonlight reflected her tears and I wanted to hide in the beauty of her eyes.

"Tonight love, I am here because I want to be. Nobody has told me or ordered me or bribed me." She put her arms round my neck and looked up at me. "This is the real me. The Meryl who wants to shout for all the world to hear, 'I love you, Drew!' The head-over-heels, backward-flips type love."

She kissed me then, and had I been able, I would have willed the night and the kisses to never end. Gone were fear and doubts. We slipped into a grove of trees together.

"Love me, just love me," she demanded, passion rising in her voice and finding eager response in me. I pulled her to me hungrily—then the searchlight hit us both, revealing anything that we would have rather kept secret.

"Sorry to interrupt the party." Angus McTurk's voice came from behind the light. "But not on my shift you don't."

I looked into the light and said angrily through clenched teeth, "I wish I could speak Gaelic. Then I could freely express my opinion and you wouldn't have a clue as to what I was talking about."

Meryl squeezed my hand. "Come on, love." We headed back toward the house. I wanted desperately to hang onto Meryl—to feel her warmth and to study her face and commit it to memory. But she had withdrawn from me and sounded as cold and calculated as I had always thought her.

"Darling—go. Sleep. You have a long day forever tomorrow. Know that no matter where you are, I will always love you."

Once back at the house, we kissed again briefly, then parted under McTurk's paternal eye. I had never felt so bereft, so miserable, so empty. I guess that had been the story of my life. Wonderful things happened, but they happened at the wrong time or in the wrong place. There wasn't much sleep, just the memory of Meryl.

It must have been about 3:00 a.m. when I felt someone get into bed beside me. The lovely coconut scent and softness of form divulged the secret. We had to love in silence, yet it was a deeply beautiful oneness we shared, filling each other with a memory that would be in our hearts like the touch of the summer sun in the in the depths of winter. I knew I would carry the orchid of her love always.

We rested briefly and then came together again, hungry for each other's bodies, loving until our passion—but not our love—was spent.

I awoke and she was already gone. She had not asked if I loved her as if to leave me free. Yet there are some freedoms that by their presence become heartbreaks. I didn't want to get her into trouble. I must get on with things. I must get going. But now, what had been like a boy's own story had become duty—Lord, what a mess. I pulled out my journal and unburdened my heart and mind, pouring them into its copious pages.

I wished I could just switch my heart off, along with all my emotions. I wished that I could build a rock wall where the memory of Meryl's love had planted a blooming, scented rose garden in my heart. And how I hoped that no one would realize the depth of my suffering and guess at what it portended.

Victoria helped me with the studs of my shirt. When I landed in China, I would have to hit the road running. The clothes felt heavy and strange with no zips, just buttons. I had had my last shower and use of soft toilet roll. It's funny the things you know you will miss.

"Your things are in these two cases," Victoria instructed. "The rest has been sent on to where you will stay. You will like Mrs. Jamieson. She is a mine of local information and a good cook. Take care of my little girl and…Drew, what's wrong? There is something wrong, isn't there?" She looked hurt and bewildered.

"Victoria, it's nothing." I had to lie. "Just pre-flight nerves like in bungee-jumping."

"What's bungee-jumping?" she inquired, still bewildered, but not looking quite so hurt. I managed a smile. "You will have to ask Adrian to explain." I gave her a big hug, then added something that surprised me, "Mum, pray for me." That from me, a person who had no confidence in God or His existence, much less prayer.

She nodded. As I carted my case down to the basement, she waved at me from the doorway of the room I had just exited.

Adrian was waiting for me in the basement, just past the guards. "Have you got everything, even the letter for the Vicompte?"

"Yes, and yes."

He continued, "When you get there, it should be towards the middle of April. You have about six weeks."

Crikey! I thought. *How can I get Lucy to fall for me in six weeks?* Already, I felt like a heel. If Lucy were as innocent as Victoria and Adrian claimed and she did fall for me…what then? I didn't have the right to break her heart, and yet the memory of lovemaking with Meryl seemed to seep into every pore of my mind and body, gaining and regaining entrance no matter how hard I attempted to expel it.

Adrian continued his discourse and I tried to wrench my mind away from Meryl and concentrate. "When the tea is loaded," he warned, "you have to be ready to go. You will not be able to use the transportation door for equipment once you leave China and get to Bellefield in 1867 or '68. You have your files on Lucy, on Bryant, and the history books. We have done all we can. The rest is up to you. Victoria gave you details about where you are staying. Watch out for Julie Lacota. She is a man-eater and I don't want you ending up as one of her pot roasts, so to speak. Even McTurk couldn't help you there."

"Is Meryl okay?" I asked.

He looked at me thoughtfully. "It seemed best if she had something to do this morning. I think you two have said your goodbyes."

With Meryl, for the first time I had been myself, not the cool dude trying to impress others, but the real me. I had spent so much of my time trying to live up to other people's expectations and to be something I wasn't and probably wasn't even meant to be.

Then—dare I say almost magically—I had met someone who loved me for me. Someone who loved the real person I was, even though she had had to mine my depths to reach that entity.

Reluctantly—almost unwillingly—I got into the time car and Adrian put my bags beside me. "Good luck Drew. It's all set. You throw the red switch and when you get to your destination on the other side and the yellow light comes back on, count five before you open the door." He began to close the car door.

"One more thing, Uncle…"

He looked alarmed. "What?"

I managed a shaky grin. "Get some oil on the lock on the front door."

He laughed. "Will do, Drew, promise. Safe journey now." And he closed the door. I heard the hiss of the seal. I sat and took a deep breath and was about to throw the switch when I felt a lump in the padding at the back of the seat. I put my hand down the chair behind me and extracted a small package. It turned out to be a small bottle of perfume and a letter. When I opened it, Meryl's photo tumbled out into my lap.

"My darling," she had written. "I love you always. What we have will always be magical and time won't stop me from loving you. Who knows? Perhaps one day… Do what you have to do. All my love, Meryl xxx."

Could anyone even imagine how I felt? Amazingly, I found myself doing something that I had never done before. I wasn't even sure that I was doing it right. I stumbled over a few words that I hoped might qualify as a prayer. "God, if you exist—help me."

Then holding the photo to my heart, I threw the switch.

PART 2

Foochow, China
1867

CHAPTER 6

The shaking and the sense of being pushed through the back of my seat eventually stopped. I put Meryl's photograph in my pocket and wrapped her scent in my handkerchief. I stepped out to get my first sight and smell of life in China in 1867.

At least, I assumed that it was April 1867, a close April 1867. There was noise, the noise of hustle and bustle, but two things my ears missed almost at once were the sound of cars and the sound of music—at least canned music. It was amazing how accustomed I had become to them, but they had not yet been invented. The closest I was going to get was probably a brass band since China was under British rule and bands were popular in the Victorian era.

The next thing that hit me was the smell, at least where I was. It smelled like a stagnant pond where marsh gas had bubbled somewhere to the surface. I had come out from what looked like a warehouse, with another next to it. Dusk was approaching. My reverie was disturbed as a nonchalant rat looked up at me, as if I were an inconvenience, someone rudely blocking its way. Then it disappeared under one of the warehouses as a cat shot past me and tried to grab it. The cat looked disgusted with herself for having failed to catch her quarry. Suddenly realizing that I was there, she greeted me with a "Meowerrr." The first acknowledgment of my existence in 1867 came to me from a cat. Well, they do say that children and animals are good judges of character. I thought I had better find my rooms, so puss and I parted company. She disappeared into the darkness to hunt elsewhere.

I moved into the light of a lamp coming from a grubby window and was able to read my directions. I had to turn right at the end of the warehouse in front of me, and the road I needed to follow was the road that seemed to go past the harbor where the ship the *Carlisle* should have docked. If everything had gone according to plan, my cases would appear to have come from that ship. It should be April 21 and I would need to mingle with what I hoped were people still disembarking. In the event the timing proved just right and I was able to mix with the people —perhaps even waving to someone on the ship—I could grab my cases, then continue along the road.

As I consulted the mental map of my directions, I began to inventory my surroundings. There were food booths and smells of cooking—spices and noodles mixed with the scents of camphor and jasmine.

The name of *Tea Street* was painted in both English and Mandarin. The third door on the right, according to my instructions, should have a copper lion's head on it. It did. It was touched by patina but the occupant had done her best to keep it shining. I knocked on the door and surreptitiously polished the toes of my shoes on the backs of my trousers. The door opened smoothly. "Yes?" enquired a gentle-voiced Irish lady of perhaps forty-five summers.

"I am Andrew Faulkner. You have rooms for me. I am not long off the *Carlisle,* newly docked. It's fine to be on dry land again."

She smiled. "Meester Faulkner, it is right glad I am to see you. You have three rooms on the one floor, plus the best food in Foochow or County Kerry. A young gentleman like yourself will not find better rooms anywhere, except maybe in paradise itself. I am Mrs. Jamieson."

"I am gratified to hear that. *A good 1867-type phrase, if there ever was one*, I thought. "May I ascertain their exact location?" *Oh,* I thought, *that sounds educated!*

"I don't know about that, Meester Faulkner, but I can show you where your rooms are. Your other luggage was brought earlier and I did wonder where you were. But now, if you would bring your cases and follow me." She then had a second thought. "Oh, there is a letter on the hall stand for you."

"Me? Ah, yes, of course." I bluffed my way with a knowledgeable nod as if I had been expecting correspondence. In fact, I didn't have a clue. One person I realized it would not be from was Lucy.

The house, what I could see of it, was of Chinese design. Fortunately, as it turned out, it sported quite good plumbing facilities for 1867. Why should I be surprised? There had been major civilizations in China while we were still living in mud huts. The rest of the rooms looked comfortable, but also very Victorian as if Queen Victoria *not being amused* had even reached Foochow.

A couple of the lamps were huge. Mrs. Jamieson's voice interrupted my *so this is home reverie.*

"Tonight," she said with pride, "there be stew and dumplings, followed by fruit and custard. I will tell you when it is ready. You will find water in your room. It is boiled, just a habit I got into."

"Sounds wonderful," I said as she closed the door behind her. My luggage resided on the floor behind the door. At least I assumed it was mine, not having seen it before. I looked out of the window and found that the view overlooked the harbor, a fact for which I was thankful. I then began the business of unpacking.

Among other things, I took out Meryl's photograph and put it by the bedside. I loaded the Webley and put it in the bedside drawer, then put the Bowie knife under my pillow. I felt alone. Then I remembered the letter on the hallstand and ventured downstairs to retrieve it. It was an invite from the British Commission, if that was the right word.

"His Excellency Sir Charles Gray"—then the letter listed a whole host of decorations—"requests the presence of Lt. Andrew Faulkner at the Chinoiserie Ball at...etc."

I walked to the shadow of the window and in the video screen of my heart, all I could see was Meryl. "I will always love you," I said, feeling a warm unwelcome swelling of tears pricking my eyes. "And if I were to die unexpectedly and they were to do a postmortem, they would find your name engraved on my heart."

What good was it to feel like that when she was—not just miles— but years away, as well? A knock at the door brought me out of my reverie.

"Your meal is ready when you are, Meester Faulkner."

Right now food seemed a good idea. I went to the dining room and there was a place set for me and another place that turned out to be for Mrs. Jamieson—which was fine for me, feeling so alone, lonely and vulnerable.

The stew was a gastronomic delight, as were the dumplings. There was even a green vegetable of sorts. The taste was like a memory of childhood, wholesome food and then some. There were no additives, no e-numbers—just good food. It would take some adjusting to become used to the new bugs and changes in the work my digestive system had to do. I had anti-diarrhea pills, but these were a last resort, should the need arise. I was glad to see that boiled tea was plentiful. The custard had been well heated, but of it I only took a small amount. We enjoyed our meal and Mrs. Jamieson filled me in with all the local details of where and where not to go, of who sold the best tea and the process for buying it. She had heard it was going to be a good tea season.

"There is a clipper called the *Night Arrow* coming in," she informed me. And they say she is up for sale." My ears perked up. I must locate that ship.

"It's supposed to be stormy, so things might get delayed," she continued. "You must have noticed this yourself."

"Mmm, yes," I said. "But we had more weight and a deeper draught as well as being slower."

She poured the tea. It was delicious and my taste buds were flavourized to its quality.

"Oolong," she said, sensing my obvious approval.

"Well," I responded, "that salt air and dry food give a chap a capital thirst." I had thought "capital" was a good word for 1867. Four—or perhaps five—hours ago, it had been breakfast time a hundred and fifty years later. Now—suddenly, unexpectedly and almost alarmingly—it was teatime in 1867. There was a companionable silence as I demolished one of her scones, without the jam.

"Can I ask," she addressed me curiously, "is there a Mrs. Faulkner?"

The question was not unexpected. I smiled and put on a wistful expression. "Not yet. One day." It seemed an opportune time to follow that tidbit with a sigh.

Mrs. Jamieson put on that motherly look I would get to know so well. "Ah now, there is someone for everyone and plenty of young ladies who would suit a young man …" her voice drifted away as I heard Meryl's voice, "I will always love you…"

Then Mrs. Jamieson's voice intruded and I realized that I had missed something. "It was getting to the stage of bridal gown sure," she said.

Improvising, I said, "I can only hope when she comes along she will feel the same way about me." I put on the chin-up smile, but inside I wanted to scream, *"I don't want to be here with you! I want to be in Starbucks with Meryl—loving on her, looking into her eyes—telling her how beautiful she looks."* Knowing the trouble that both Meryl and I would get into if I returned to headquarters now, I bit back the words, almost choking on them.

We enjoyed some more tea. Then I ventured, "A while ago on the way here, I had a dream of marrying a girl named Lucy. She had a cascade of Titian-colored hair and eyes as green as cut emeralds and a voice as soft as the gentle wind that stirs the summer leaves."

Mrs. Jamieson put her head to one side and said, "Keep talking like that and you will have all the girls queuing up."

Then I said one of these things that you do when you are sleepy and relaxed and your thoughts take on voice. "I don't want them queuing up. I just want one and I hope she will want me."

Mrs. Jamieson, like a good mother, knew when to ask no further questions, but just nodded her head. The conversation had come to a natural stop. "Well," I said, "if you will excuse me, I think I will retire for the night. Maybe read for a bit. It will be nice to be on a bed that does not rock from side to side."

In my heart, I knew there would be no Meryl coming through the door to join me in bed this time. *Focus*, I ordered myself. *You have a job to do.*

"Will eight o'clock for breakfast be satisfactory?" Mrs. Jamieson wanted to know. I waved acknowledgement and was followed by a, "good night and God bless you, Meester Faulkner," as I headed upstairs.

I must have her call me Drew, I realized. This 'Mr. Faulkner' business made me feel like a Latin teacher in a down-at-heel public school.

Once upstairs in my room, I succeeded in lighting the lamp after burning my fingers a couple of times. Oh, for the modern simplicity of turning on a switch! It was not too bad for light—if you held what you wanted close to it. I did my teeth carefully and found my nightshirt, which was standard kit of the day. Meryl would have laughed if she could have seen me. Well, maybe not. We would have both been thinking about all the good things that could start happening once we got into bed together. I got into bed alone and touched the face on the picture. "Goodnight, my love. Think of me." I blew out the light and tried with all my heart not to wish for Meryl and Edinburgh.

I dreamed I was back in Edinburgh with my fencing buddies in the *Finlander Tavern,* near Brunton Street. That place had the most fantastic Finnish cuisine. *Sourmali*—stuffed cabbage leaves—was especially good, along with boiled carp and dill sauce. In the dream, I was feasting on this and drinking *Korsenkorva Vodka* to the haunting sound of the kantilla, a musical instrument of ethereal quality. In my dream, I was waiting to find out what activities my buddies had planned for the following weekend. I awoke with a start. After remembering where I was and why, I walked around the room, pausing to take a look out the window through a crack in the curtain.

When I next awoke, dawn slid through the windows. Despite the chatter of voices and the noise of the docks, it was quiet compared to the Edinburgh rush hour. Slowly, the memory of where I was—and most importantly—*when* I was, came back to me. Now I must learn what I could do without from my old life. Much of what I had considered "absolute necessities" were not even proto-prototypes yet. How could I really manage without a power shower? My thoughts on ablutions were interrupted by Mrs. Jamieson's voice and a bump outside my door. "That's a big jug of water for you to wash with, Mr. Faulkner. They say it is going to be close today."

Victoria had warned me about what scent Lucy might exude. I was beginning to wonder how I would smell myself within another day or two.

"Just so, Mrs. Jamieson," I replied. "Just so." I managed to shave with a cut-throat razor like Great-Granddad. I got all the studs done upon my collar and checked all my buttons on my trousers before venturing outside my room. When I got to the dining room, I found Mrs. Jamieson bustling about, doing three things at the one time.

"Lord save us if the bread did not rise and the porridge had gone lumpy," she muttered.

I sidestepped the offer of bacon, realizing the necessity of being careful until I had assessed the level of hygiene. There is an old Scots' saying, "Ye eat a ton of dirt afore ye dee." I didn't want to exceed my quota.

Mrs. Jamieson and I had another "get to know you" type chat, and I returned to my room. It was 10:30 in the morning—time to venture out. I had to find out where everything was—get the lay of the land, so to speak. I put the Bowie knife down the waist belt at the back of my trousers and was glad to see the longish handle was covered by the back of my jacket.

I thought I had better attempt to locate the bank where my money was. I located a big grey building which had obviously been there for some time. The front bore the logo, *Parsons and Sons—Bankhouse Established 1750.*

Venturing inside, I was greeted by a very nasal-voiced clerk who condescended to examine me through his pince-nez glasses. Then, though not entirely approving of what he saw, he at least decided to attempt civility. "May I be of assistance?" I noted the absence of the word "sir."

I gave him my details and identification and said that I wished to ascertain the state of my account. He looked up his ledger, (not saying "ba humbug," which surprised me), then looked back up at me. "If you would care to wait, sir…(Oh, ho! Money talks!) I will locate our Mr. Hall."

"Our" Mr. Hall duly appeared and I was ushered into his office. "My apologies for keeping you waiting, sir," he tendered. Being a cynical Scot, I assumed the contents of my account were above the average.

"What I need to know, Mr. Hall, is do I have enough to buy a clipper?"

He eyed me with the obvious joy of one about to convey good news and responded, "Enough, sir, for a clipper, captain, crew, and a considerable quantity of tea even down to the catty boxes. You know that if you are first home, your profit will be considerably more— perhaps even three pence a pound more."

"Thank you, Mr. Hall," I replied. "Apart from a small sum just now, I will 'hove too,' so to speak, when a suitable clipper comes into view. Oh by the way, perhaps you know the name of the large clipper in the harbor. It was too dark last night to see."

His face clouded. "Hmm…that is the *Allegheny,* captained and now owned by Mr. Caleb Bryant. He has a reputation, which to put not too fine a point on it, is not of the best and he does not bank with this house, so I tell no tales out of school."

I thanked him, and pocketing the 100 guineas I had retrieved, I walked out of the building into the sunshine and scents of the street and its interminably busy inhabitants living out their lives under the spring sun.

I headed for the harbor and checked the *Allegheny* over. She was a lovely lady, yet not as well cared for as she might have been. Still, the two hands at the top of the gangway looked chipper once you overcame the signs of growing boredom.

I walked on past the ships toward the quieter and further side of the harbor. That's where I saw the child fall into the water. He was small, and at first his mother had not noticed that he was missing. Then her fear turned to panic as the current began sweeping the child away from the jetty.

I had no choice. I was not going to let a child drown. I raced to the edge of the water, dropped my jacket on the jetty and dived in, with the possibly irrelevant thought going through my mind, *God, if you exist—now would be a good time to show up.*

The current tugged hard at me, but with an effort, I swam back to the jetty with the semi-conscious child. Onlookers had gathered. I clambered up onto the bank, put the child in the recovery position and started resuscitation. He coughed, opened his eyes, and began crying for his mother, who was working her way through the crowd. It was then that I noticed my jacket was missing. A Sikh policeman tried to keep the crowd back. The boy's mother picked him up smiled at me, bowed and said something.

I smiled at her and said, "I'm sorry. I don't speak Mandarin."

"She was saying thank you for saving her son's life."

I glanced toward the voice, but could not see the speaker's face, as I was looking directly into the sun. Two women were standing together. I shielded my eyes, and from under a straw hat, a pair of lovely green eyes looked at me. A mane of beautiful red hair tumbled around the face. She held out my jacket. "You may be glad of this, sir. We took the liberty of guarding it for you. Perhaps, sir, you should go home and seek a hot bath and toddy."

I tried not to stare at Lucy. I felt like a half-drowned rat and my shoes began to squelch. It was my first introduction to Lucy, quickly followed by a hearty sneeze.

"I pray you, sir. Please get out of those wet clothes as soon as possible."

There was a touching concern in her voice. I bowed and promised, "I will endeavor to follow your wise council with the utmost alacrity. Thank you for taking care of my jacket. Now, if you will excuse me…" I bowed again.

"Good day to you, sir."

"Good day," I replied.

What a first impression to make, I thought forlornly, as I put on the only dry thing I had left—the jacket. I slipped my hand into a pocket and felt a handkerchief. When I pulled it out of my pocket, it was a lady's handkerchief laced with the scent of lavender.

Mrs. Jamieson boiled up a bath for me. "Lord save us! How did you fall into the water?"

"I turned left instead of right," I replied. "Or perhaps it was right instead of left."

She produced a glass, filling it with boiling water, a spoon of brown sugar, and a large quantity of whisky. "Irish," she assured me, as if to alleviate any doubts I may have had about its medicinal value. "Now upstairs, then into the tub, then into bed—and stay out of the heat of the day."

I succumbed to the mixture of her motherly and medicinal advice. During the soak I used some 21st century shampoo. (Well, how often was I going to dive into the harbor?) I cleaned and dried the Bowie knife and went to bed and woke up to find it dark outside. I did the rest of my unpacking, finding in a false bottom in one of my trunks *Semtex*, and what I recognized after Angus McTurk's instructions as detonators.

Sitting on the end of the bed, I scratched my head and wondered why I would need Semtex. What would I need to blow up and why? Suddenly, I had the feeling that I had not quite been told everything.

At the bottom of my other trunk was an M79 grenade launcher with various kinds of shells. There were also canisters of *Oblivon*, a kind of knock out gas. That was marked as my "Contingency Kit No 2." All I wanted was green and brown "cammo" paint and I had it made.

CHAPTER 7

Here I was in 1867 China, a walking arsenal. Putting everything back, I covered it up and tried to reason things out. I had not been told everything, that was for sure, but what had I not been not told?

I thought it was going to be a simple: boy meets girl, falls in love, buys clipper ship and tea, carries said girl back to her home to Scotland and lives happily ever after. But even without the newly discovered weapons, it could not be that simple. For one thing, I already loved someone else—my "former" girlfriend, Meryl. Figuring out that romantic quandary took more energy than I possessed, so I returned to the easier, less-threatening puzzle of how and why my life seemed to be threatened.

What was I supposed to use Semtex to destroy? A bridge, a building, a ship? Was I supposed to preempt something, stop something from happening in the future—or was it just contingency? You might well fire a revolver in the street to protect yourself, but a grenade launcher and risk killing innocent people? I remember McTurk's words about people taking a dim view if you killed the wrong person. Wait, what was I doing even thinking about killing? For crying out loud, this was Drew Faulkner, ordinary bloke who liked a good time on the weekend, and now suddenly, had been propelled into the twilight world of God knows what. You can imagine what you want, but truth is stranger than fiction and this was no fiction.

I woke up the following morning feeling much better and a lot less tired. I had (thus far) not suffered any ill effects from my change in diet or my unintended dip in harbor water. Mrs. Jamieson had left my hot water, as usual, along with a bar of what turned out to be soap. I felt squeaky clean but did miss having a shower to use.

Breakfast was welcome and my landlady had just baked bread and made marmalade with some Chinese fruit (when did she sleep?). I declined butter, using the excuse of cholesterol—which she took to be some kind of an allergy. "Probably bring you out in a rash in this heat and you would not be wanting that!" She paused. "I heard what you did yesterday in rescuing the little boy. You will find that the Chinese have long memories for evil but also for good. Well, I must get busy. One or two things to do this morning."

I decided to find to find the French Chargez d'Affaires and deliver that letter which had been burning a hole in my pocket since I arrived. I was glad I had left it in my room yesterday. I suspected the Marquis might have found it distasteful to read a communication that had suffered the baptism of harbor water. I would probably have to make an appointment to see him, but one could live in hope. What I was trying to avoid was a large "to do" list.

Some dozen streets away past the center part of the docks, I came to a white

stone building above which the *Tricolor* hung with the air of one that had seen better days. Inside the building, fans were being operated by unseen hands and the clerk behind the front desk looked up at me with a weariness that not even two weeks in Deauville would have taken away. He looked at me over his pince-nez. "Oui monsieur?"

Okay, here goes the schoolboy French. "Je cherche Monsieur le Marquis de Plombal, j'ai une letter pour lui; c'est tres importante."

He sighed in that Gallic way and extended his hands, "Toutes les letters sont importante. Give it to me, monsieur, I will see it is given to 'im."

"Pas possible. I was instructed to give it into the hands of the Marquis himself, by Monsieur Adrian Faulkner."

The clerk sighed with the resignation of one who finds himself in a spy novel but never quite manages to get the girl. He took out his ledger, and running his finger down one of the pages, said, "Monsieur le

Marquis can see you for a few minutes (emphasis on few) on Monday at eleven in the morning. Do not be late. The Marquis does not suffer fools (followed by a head to toe look) gladly, nor those who do not keep appointments."

"Merci, monsieur," I replied with a bow. Then I returned to the dusty street.

There was not much to do until tonight. I had not realized that so many of the conveniences of modern life existed to take up time. For example, if we lost or broke our cell phones, then we ended up in a near state of hyperventilation. I was under the impression slavery had ended. But it hadn't: we had just exchanged masters.

Okay, I thought. *What about a stroll through the neighborhood?* Only perhaps being dressed as a "gentleman" in that area might not be a good idea. I searched the dock and found a ships' chandlers. They sold everything any Jack Tar would need to blend in. I would just be another salt looking for a ship home.

It seemed by the looks of it that no standard kit existed. The naval folk had a uniform. The average seaman wanted to be warm, dry and have a good grip on the deck and rigging. If you were sent up the mast to make sail in all types of weather, you didn't want to be slipping and sliding. It was no fun going round the Cape of Good Hope at the south tip of Africa cold, wet and in a constant state of danger, even with a captain who knew what he was doing.

I stopped short at getting a tattoo. I didn't care to risk infection from dirty needles. The necessity of sterilization had not caught on and while Dr. Pasteur's work would come to the fore in the next few years, I still knew of folk in modern days who thought hygiene was a way of greeting an acquaintance named "Jean."

I bought what I thought I needed to at least to look the part. The chandler who came from the west country could not understand what a well dressed gent was doing fitting himself out to look like a deck hand. He then gave me a lecture on the evils of drink and gambling. I thanked him for his advice and he added, "Well, I hopes that things goes better for ye when you get back to England. Find a nice young lady and settle down."

When I left the shop, believe it or not, he was singing "windy old weather, stormy old weather..."

Trading was going on everywhere. The sights and sounds; the food vendors; tea sellers with mah-jong going on in the back shop. Women with bound and unbound feet; silks whose translucent sheen reflected all the colors of the rainbow. I could take some back for Meryl. Then I realized there was no Meryl and no going back and that pervading sense of loneliness returned. I passed another house with a group of girls sitting outside, one attempting to attract my attention by showing a considerable amount of almond-colored leg. I continued walking and about two houses down, there were two middle aged men sitting with a group of children. As I passed, one of the men pulled a girl to her feet and smiled, pointing to her. She must have only been ten or eleven and I felt sick with disgust.

Then I began to feel the frustration of knowing that something needs to be changed—cleaned out—but not being sure what to do about it. I will never forget that little girl's pained, yet strangely impassive face, as I passed. Yet some one-hundred-and-fifty years later, the revolting practice of child prostitution continued. I noted the name of the place: "House of the Little Cygnets." I had to get the girl out of there—but when and how were two things I would need time to figure out.

Major contrasts existed between rich and poor. Remembering the comfortable lifestyle that I had left behind only seemed to polarize things more. One elderly aunty had relished regaling me with the fact that in her day, "we were poor but happy." In my experience, poorness never produced happiness. Too bad aunty couldn't come here to experience this steep learning curve. In the era I had left, it was good public relations to appear to care about other people's poverty and problems. It resulted in good publicity. Here, there was no publicity seeking. Folks just used whatever resources they had to ameliorate situations.

Many of the Chinese had learned to live with the "foreign devils" and be useful to them. This almost, at least in the port areas, made the Chinese foreigners in their own country. Yet, I knew that within five generations this country would be the most powerful country on the face of the planet with an economy on steroids—the very opposite of what I was seeing here.

* * *

Friday evening arrived and with it, the "Chinoiserie Ball" at the governor's residence. I got into my evening suit, but 1867 buttons were murder to fasten. I checked out of Mrs. Jamison's sight to make sure that my fly buttons were all done up. I did not want to suddenly feel an embarrassing breeze.

Mrs. Jamieson gave me the once over. "To be sure, Meester Faulkner," she said with the look of an artist who had just sculpted a masterpiece. "When all the young ladies get a look at you, you will be kept cool by the breeze coming off their fluttering eyelashes."

"Sure Mrs. Jamieson," I responded. "George Bernard Shaw didn't have a look in on you."

"George Bernard who?" she asked.

"George Bernard Shaw was an up and coming Irish writer," I explained, which brought a twinkle to her eyes.

"Now would there be being a Mrs. Shaw at this moment?"

I smiled and winked at her. "Ah, but to be sure now, that's a thing I would not be know'n.'"

She looked at me with a serious expression, then it was like someone taking the cork out of a champagne bottle. "You will be tellin' me you have Irish blood somewhere in the family!"

I stuck my thumbs in my waistcoat pocket and said, "My grandfather on my father's side came from County Antrim." The bit I neglected to tell her was that he would not be born for another eighty years.

In fact, I was starting to develop a sense of not knowing who had been born yet and who hadn't.

Mrs. Jamieson clapped her hands together in glee. "I knew it! I knew it as sure as barnacles cling to a ship's hull, I knew you had Irish blood in you."

If I could have got Mrs. Jamieson back to my time she could have done a wonderful one woman show—it would have been a sell out —"An evening with Mrs. Jamieson."

"Be off with you," she said. "Have a good time and don't eat the fish."

I went upstairs to collect the Webley and the sword stick. My jacket covered the shoulder holster very well. Then, putting on my hat, gloves, and cape, (I would have felt silly, except this was 1867 and everyone dressed this way), I headed for the ball.

CHAPTER 8

The Residency was a magnificent building with a light at every window. The closer I drew to the house, the more the windows glowed like misty diamonds. There were carriages coming and going.

Inside, the smell of cigar smoke hung in the air and the hum—first of chatter—and then of music, greeted me as I entered. I mentally tallied all Anna had taught me about dancing and hoped I could match the steps to the dance. Her words floated back to me as gracefully as the memory of her lovely image. "Remember, Drew. Look at the lady, not at her feet." In the films it was easy—but this was not a film, it was real life, as if a Margaret Mitchell novel had jumped off the printed page and started moving and breathing. I handed my cape, hat, gloves and stick over to the footman, who also took my invitation and handed to another footman, whom I took to be the guy next up the foot-pecking order. We were to be announced. As you were announced, you had to pose for the count of five at the top of the ballroom steps. This was to aid anyone who felt they had any business with you and to let them know that you had arrived. It beat e-mail with its cryptic, "Jst land Hong Kong thowt to touch base wth u."

I joined the queue waiting to be announced. "The honorable Gervaise St. John and Miss Belinda Huntingdon-Fortescue" were announced. Being just Andrew Faulkner made me feel inadequate, except that my rigged up past was going to catch up with me.

"Lt. Andrew James Faulkner." Mentally, I paused and counted, *one, two, three, four, five. Okay, let's go.* I had posed to the haughtiest of my ability and then joined the mob of guests.

It was starting to get warm. I noticed a mixture of lamps and candles. Where did one start in a posh "do" like this? Suddenly, as if by magic, a glass of champagne appeared in my hand. Okay, what now? A nod here or there—food would be a good idea.

In the films you meet all sorts of people around the food. I headed for the huge quantity of food laid out on tables. Austerity had not yet been invented. The only time I had seen food like this was at a conference I went to one time to discuss poverty in the third world. There was every kind of meat, cold cuts, things in sauces, and things in jelly. Further down there were desserts, frappe, flambeaus, and bombes, as well as fruit salad. Some of the cold desserts were looking a little distressed in the increasing heat. There were overhead fans, but they could not fan too energetically for fear of blowing out the candles. I stood wondering what to take when a voice beside me advised, "Leave the fish. You never know where it has been or where it has come from."

The voice had a Russian accent and the speaker's manner was friendly and helpful. I turned to be met by a man of about my own age. His black hair was cut short and he had a small moustache. His brown eyes possessed a strangely sage-like quality for one so young. Then the face broke out into a broad, good-humored smile.

"Thank you," I said, extending my hand. "My name is Drew Faulkner." We shook hands.

"Anton Devranov, and how do you English say it? How do you do?"

"How do you do," I repeated, "except that I am a Scot, which is different."

"Is there a difference?" he asked in surprise.

"Is there a difference between a Russian and a Pole?" I retorted. He looked thoughtful, then replied, "Only in the amount of vodka they consume," before breaking into a hearty laugh.

I followed his advice on food selections and we went and sat at a table together and began to eat.

"I am part of the Russian Delegation here and maybe I will get back to St. Petersburg one day," Anton said. "God knows, I miss it." I noticed he had kind of a dry cough that seemed to annoy him when he spoke too long. He added, "My sister Julie and I stay in the delegation. Julie is unfortunately divorced from her husband, but the name which she still uses is 'Lacota."

Victoria's warning about Julie Lacota rang loud and clear and I had a mental picture of this femme fatal. Anton was likeable and entertaining and I thought that if I ever needed help—at least in some things—I might be able to engage him. I had the feeling that a friend fighting in my corner might prove both useful and reassuring.

"Is there a woman in your life?" he asked.

At this point I spotted Lucy and a slightly older woman at the top of the stairs about to be announced. "Miss Lucy Oxford and Miss Caroline Harper," came the pronouncement.

"The answer to your question," I told Anton, "is not yet. Excuse me. I don't want her card to get full."

Anton looked at the top of the stair, "I admire your taste. A woman worth dueling for."

Lucy had her back to me talking to Caroline as I approached them.

"Miss Oxford? Drew Faulkner. We met at the harbor." She turned, and after the briefest of moments, recognition swept over her face. She made the beauty of the rose look like a weed. The saffron flowers in her hair intertwined with cascading titian ringlets. She wore a saffron ball gown with a cream lace top and lace sleeves. A ruby necklace resting against her slender throat finished the stunning picture she presented.

"It is Miss Oxford, isn't it?" I asked when she failed to speak. "We met at the dock when the little boy…"

She still hadn't spoken, but I read a welcome response in the lovely green depths of her eyes. *Calm, calm,* I militated to myself. *Don't rush it.*

"Miss Oxford, yes, but one day I hope that will change and I can be a serious grande dame."

"It would be a happy man who could bring about such a change," I replied almost reverently with a slight bow. The head tilted slightly, suddenly duplicating the pose in the portrait. "You flatter me sir," she replied.

"No, Miss Oxford. I just speak the truth. I love to walk—to view the sunrise. The joy of its beauty fills my heart." She wore her quizzical smile. "You compare me to a sunrise?"

"No, Miss Oxford," I replied. "For a sunrise has to learn to be beautiful." Even in the lamp light, I caught just a flushing of her cheeks before I added, "May I have this dance?"

She nodded. I offered her my arm to lead her onto the dance floor and forgot to stay focused on anything else for a second. Lucy was going to take my arm when my vision of her was blocked by someone coming between us—a bearded man a fraction taller than me and in his middle forties.

Shouldering me out of the way, he growled, "This dance and the next one are promised to me, so weigh anchor, boy." He reached out and grabbed Lucy's wrist.

My hand shot out and grabbed his. "Sir, I do not believe that Miss Oxford has indicated her wishes." It did not take rocket science to realize that I had been introduced to Mr. Charm and Personality, Caleb Bryant, a name I was not likely to forget. Call me peevish if you wish, but when you have the chance of dancing with the most beautiful girl you had ever seen and some folically challenged moron barges in, you tend to take exception. And if you had seen the look of desperation on Lucy's face, you would have stepped in too. She was clearly terrified of him.

"Get your hand off me boy!"

"Let go of Miss Oxford's wrist," I countered.

"Why, you young..." He reached into his coat pocket.

That's when I heard over the noise of revelry, a clear click of a hammer being pulled back on a revolver. Anton stood behind Bryant and said in a soft but steely voice, "The inadvisability of that move, Meeester Bryant, will become evident should you try to carry it out."

Bryant glowered at Anton, then at me. "We will finish this another time, boy. You can bet on that," he hissed. He walked away in a slightly unsteady gate, banging into a small table on which sat a tray of full champagne glasses. Liquid spilled down the front of his trousers. Lucy hid her smile behind her fan. Bryant turned and saw her and shot me a warning look to indicate this was a contest "a l'outrance"——to the death, as they used to say in knightly combat. I had this stupid mental picture of Bryant on the psychoanalyst's couch and her pen poised over notepad asking him, "Mr. Bryant, do you want to talk about your aggressive feelings?"

"Thank you, Anton," I said.

He smiled. "Think nothing of it. That's what friends are for." Bowing to Lucy, he disappeared back into the crowd.

Lucy looked stressed. "I am sorry you have been distressed," I said. Caroline joined us. Lucy inclined her head at me, treating me to a little, trembling smile. "Thank you, Mr. Faulkner."

"I would not have wished you upset," I added.

She blinked like a little kitten that had just been awakened from a nap. "You stood up for me," she whispered. "Thank you." I looked up for inspiration and suddenly my attention was taken up by the moving of one of the window shutters on the ceiling. It began to open and a barrel of a rifle inched its way through. I could hardly believe what I was seeing. I kept expecting the director to jump in and say, "cut! Let's take that again," but this was really happening and there was no director. I tried to gaze along the possible line of fire. The barrel seemed to be aimed, as far as I could tell, at Sir Charles Gray, the British Ambassador, who was circulating among the crowd. The muzzle followed his movements. Sir Charles turned his back and the muzzle steadied. No one but me had noticed. The phrase, "someone ought to do something about it," leapfrogged in my mind——but I seemed to be the only possible "someone" at the moment. The music playing was a *Chardash*, a Hungarian tune that involved some shouting on the dancers' part.

So I acted as the necessary "someone." I pulled out the Webley, aimed and fired twice through the ventilator just a fraction of a second before the rifle discharged. The rifle wobbled and then crashed onto the dessert table. A motionless arm hung half out of the vent. Everyone looked up, then looked at me still holding the Webley. The rifle bullet had grazed the arm of a man three people down from Sir Charles.

Suddenly the room fell silent. Sir Charles looked over to where the rifle lay on the dessert table. 'Sorry," he announced, "but that rather seems to have put paid to the fruit salad." There was laughter and the music started again. Lord, Sir Charles was a cool customer. The would-be assassin's arm was being pulled back up through the ceiling vent.

Sir Charles walked over to where Lucy, Caroline and I stood. Along the way, he thanked the people for their good wishes, brushing off any concerns. "No, it's nothing. Thank you. I am unhurt."

After firing the shots, I looked round the room. My idea was that where there had been one assassin, there might have been more. I scanned the room and noticed two men in dinner jackets, one holding in his hand something that made my blood run cold—a 9-mm Lugar pistol, which he was replacing in a leather shoulder holster and which the guy with him seemed to be remonstrating with him for exposing. The Lugar at the earliest did not appear till 1908, and this was 1867. How did the Lugar get here forty years before it had been invented?

Perhaps the more important question was how did the owner of the Lugar get here? I wondered if they were Prussian. Germany did not come into existence until 1870, after the defeat of the French at Sedan in 1870.

Sir Charles reached us. His secretary, Willoughby, whom I suspected was the man whispering to him, offered, "Miss Lucy Oxford and Lt. Andrew Faulkner."

One thing I noticed was that when our names were linked together, Lucy did not seem upset, even though we were virtually strangers. Sir Charles looked as if he were out for an evening stroll—as cool as the proverbial cucumber.

"Miss Oxford," Sir Charles acknowledged. "You grace our gathering. I do hope the fracas did not upset you. It is part at least of being a diplomat. My wife is indisposed and could not be here tonight, so at least she has been spared this."

Lucy curtsied. "Thank you for your gracious words, Sir Charles."

He then focused his attention on me. I still held the revolver down by my side. "I owe you my life, young man. Your quick response saved the day. Thank you. Excellent shooting." Someone brought the rifle over to Sir Charles after having cleared the pudding from it first. The concept of fingerprints had not yet come to the fore. Sir Charles took it and tested its weight and balance in his hands. "Quite a beast. It looks military."

I looked at it in his hands and recognized it. "If I may say, Sir Charles, I think it is an 1862 American Springfield rifle."

He looked at me and nodded. "I think, young man, there is more to you than meets the eye. Will you and Miss Oxford—and of course your companion, Miss Oxford—come and see me Tuesday?" He transferred his look to his secretary. "Shall we say 3:00 p.m., hopefully in time for tea? There is a little matter in which you may be able to assist."

"Of course," I readily agreed. "I shall be delighted to help in any way I can." Lucy nodded and said, "Likewise. And I can answer in the affirmative for Miss Harper."

Sir Charles thanked us. "Let us try and salvage something of the evening. The night is yet young and I have much tedious mingling to do." Then he looked at me and at Lucy and smiled. With a sigh, he said, "Oh to be young again."

A young man came and asked Caroline for a dance. She looked at Lucy and Lucy gave her an almost imperceptible affirmation. The two Prussians had been staring at me and when they saw me look back at them, they faded into the crowd.

When Sir Charles moved away, I began shaking. The import of what had happened finally hit me. Lucy touched my arm. "Are you alright"… then with the slightest hesitation. "Drew?"

"I have never shot anyone before, but I had to react."

She agreed with alacrity. "Of course you had to do it. Had you been able to prevent Sir Charles' death and failed to do so, it would have been cause for much sadness and remorse."

After a pause she asked, "What about Mr. Bryant?"

"What about Mr. Bryant? I wasn't going to miss the opportunity of dancing with you or give it up lightly. I've been looking forward to it all week." Then I realized what I had said and tried to gloss over it. "I don't mean that I had spent all week just thinking about you…well, what I meant was if you should be here. Not all week, just part of it." I was digging a deeper hole and the slight smile tripped back into Lucy's face.

"I presume you mean that you had a few minutes to spare in thoughts about me when you were not pulling children out of the harbor. Sir, are we not supposed to be dancing?"

The music and dancing stopped when Sir Charles raised a gloved hand. There was a long silence, then Anton rushed to my side. "It would appear that they are waiting for you and the beautiful young lady to lead off the dance. Do hurry. The champagne is getting warm."

Like a fantastic dream, the real Lucy was suddenly in my arms and the music played and we danced as if nobody else in the room existed.

Coming out of nowhere, it nearly ruined the dance for me. "I will always love you." Meryl's words spilled out from the open treasure chest of my heart and evoked a sigh where one had not been intended.

I knew that when I left the dance—and Lucy—I would write down the night's events before one train of thought in my mind gate crashed another. And inexplicably, Meryl would find her way from a 21st Century that didn't exist yet into the year 1867—not through a time machine—but through the open doors of my heart to spill down across the pages of the diary that I resolutely kept of my adventures.

CHAPTER 9

As Lucy and I danced, we talked. I learned that she and Caroline were teachers in a school for Chinese children. Lucy said, "They are very bright and keen—the girls as well as the boys. They learn English but stay close to their own roots as well."

"Can I help?" I asked. "Is there anything you need like books, maps, or whatever is necessary?"

"We need a lot, but it is getting them here," she replied thoughtfully.

"Give me a list," I offered. "I have some surprising friends."

She shook her head in disbelief. "You, sir, are an enigma."

My mouth must have fallen open. "You are addressing me as if I were a public meeting. I hoped I might be considered a friend. May I come to the school to see you and get that list? What about next Tuesday?"

She stopped dancing. "Are you really sure?"

"Yes, I am," I stated emphatically. At that point, the music stopped and an elderly gentleman stepped forward to Lucy and said, "I have come to claim my dance with the most beautiful lady in the room." His accent was Swedish. "Count Stockmann, from the Swedish Delegation." The two took to the floor—a case, I thought, of the oak tree dancing with the rose.

Caroline was standing nearby. I went to her and said, "May I have this dance, Miss Harper?"

She smiled. "Of course." The dance was a *mazurka*, which Anna had taught me, "just in case." Caroline was older and taller than Lucy—

approximately my height. She proved a good dancer and it gave us a chance to talk. The first important fact that Caroline disclosed was that Lucy still missed her mother, who had mysteriously disappeared. There was an air of pathos about Caroline, like an opera heroine who suddenly finds she is to be forced to marry someone she doesn't love. She wanted to help Lucy but didn't know where to start.

"It's the first time I have seen Lucy smile for a long time," Caroline confessed. "I mean when she was dancing with you. I would hate to think that she was fated for hurt again. Mr. Bryant would be an excrescence, not to put it too strongly. Thank you for your understanding and intervention."

I reminded her, "It was really Anton who saved the situation. I got a bit caught on the back foot."

Caroline stopped in the middle of the dance (I was beginning to notice that it seemed to be the thing in 1867 for girls to stop in the middle of the dance). "Do you think," she inquired with a spate of inspiration, "that it may have been because of what was going to happen afterwards that he did'nt make more of a fuss?"

I drew in a sharp breath. "What! That he had something to do with the attempt on Sir Charles' life?"

She shrugged her shoulders and pointed to Lucy, who had quit dancing and was heading toward us. Caroline smiled at me. "Take care, Drew."

As Lucy joined us, a silk flower fell from her hair. I stooped to pick it up and handed it back. She raised her arm to take it and then said, "Please, keep it if you wish."

In answer, I jerked a button off my suit and carefully replaced it with the flower. Lucy looked slightly puzzled. "Forgive me," I said. "But it is the closest place I can get to my heart. Good night and safe home." I bowed to them both and walked away.

After that, I mingled with some people, but it may have been my heart that told me to have one more look. Lucy and Caroline were at the top of the stairs. I said to myself, *if she turns and looks back, she is interested*...Lucy turned and looked back.

Things fell kind of flat after Lucy left. Anton found me. "Brother, you have a face like a grave digger who has forgotten to bring his spade to work. Come and meet my sister, Julie."

Anton had saved my life if that had been a pistol that Bryant had been going to pull on me. How could I refuse him? I followed him to a row of tables. Seated at the middle table was a woman surrounded by three men, one of whom was trying to get her slipper off so he could drink champagne from it. Two of the men were in military uniform and Julie was obviously loving every minute of it, every nuance of attention. Anton interrupted the party.

"Julie, meet my friend Drew. He is Scotch and likes vodka."

Julie Lacota dismissed the three men with a wave of her hand, then she looked at me and the room seemed, suddenly, to grow hot. I remembered being at the zoo one day and seeing a beautiful caged snow leopard. The leopard and I exchanged long looks, but I had absolutely no doubts about what would have happened if I had been in the cage or tried to stroke it. Now it looked as if my snow leopard had left the cage and taken human form.

Julie rose to her feet and she was just about as tall as me. Her raven black hair bounced and swung with every movement. Her eyes were violet and my thoughts went back to the snow leopard. Those eyes could have melted steel. Julie held out the back of her hand. Then as I was about to take it, she changed her mind in mid-lift and instead stroked the back of my cheek. Yes, the room was getting hot. Must have been the wool clothing. Julie possessed what my father once termed, "bedroom eyes."

"You may dance with me," she purred. "I am ready now." The music flowed into a waltz and we went out onto the floor (lamb to the slaughter came to mind). *Get a grip*, I told myself.

Anton had covered his mouth but not quickly enough to hide his wry smile.

This was something they had neglected to cover in my basic training survival course.

Julie never once took her eyes off me, dancing as closely as her gown would allow. We danced two dances before she demanded, "You must escort me to the balcony, I want air."

I naively inquired as to where her chaperone was.

The violet eyes crinkled and with a shake of the head she replied, "Darlink…old Russian saying, 'When the she wolf seeks her love, the old cow stays in doors.'"

I had to think quickly and act without upsetting Anton. "Excuse me," I improvised. "I must go and attend to a call of nature. Let me take you back to your brother."

Her eyes lit up. "So you, too, feel the call of nature. We are two of a kind. You must give into it, Darlink, not fight it."

"Mrs. Lacota," I said, "If I give into this call of nature there will be a mess to clear up on the floor. What is the Russian for toilet or lavatory?"

Suddenly the penny dropped. "Oh," she said, then followed that comment by something in Russian. She spun on her heels and stormed off, leaving me to find the toilets, such as they were, myself. When I proved successful in finding the facilities, I was very thankful for 21st century plumbing! Then I went to look for Anton.

I caught up with Anton, who was just saying goodbye to a girl who was giggling and somewhat flushed. I tried to explain about the episode with Julie.

"Oh, do not worry about Julie," he said, waving his sister aside expansively. "She will recover even though it is true…" He looked pensive before finishing the sentence, "that she generally manages to get what she wants, one way or another. She has had three duels fought over her. Matters of honor, you understand."

"We have a saying in English," I replied. "He who fights and runs away lives to fight another day."

Anton looked at me in near disbelief. With a shrug of the shoulders he asked, "Where is the honor in that?"

"Probably not a lot of honor, but I think we live longer. I am going home. It has been quite a night and I think the effects of it are starting to catch up on me now."

"Come and call on us Wednesday afternoon at perhaps around three." (Which he pronounced "tree.") He gave me the address, which I duly noted.

"I have some real Finnish vodka especially for you," he added. "*Dosvedanya.*"

I went off toward the door. I was stopped on the way out by an American voice and extended hand. "Captain Luke Carter," the speaker of the outstretched hand said. "Attached to the United States Delegation."

The smile was open and friendly, as was the handshake. Luke was all of six-foot, two-inches, with blonde hair and blue eyes. I was kind of hoping there was someone waiting for him back home. I thought that if Lucy met this guy, I wouldn't have a hope. Still, faint heart never won fair maiden. The conversation continued. "Yeah. I am here for four more months, then I'm fixin'to head home. Then it's marriage for me, to Mary Ellen Darrow. Hey! Here! I have a photograph of her."

I looked at the sepia of Mary Ellen Darrow and felt that she was every bit his match—but not quite as nice as Lucy.

"Where'd you learn to handle a gun like that?" He asked.

"British Army Regimental Sergeant Major called McTurk," I said. "Crack shot and good with a knife."

He studied me briefly. "You must be in the military, then? Haven't we met somewhere? You look so familiar."

How was I going to answer that? I wondered. But before I could, a polite voice answered for me. "Lt. Faulkner is on special detachment to my delegation. He is one of the good guys, as you saw."

"Yes, Ambassador. I was just congratulating him on his shooting."

Captain Carter looked surprised, but Sir Charles had spoken for me and that was good enough for him—at least I hoped it was. I had to remember that Luke had almost certainly been engaged in the War Between the States from 1861-1865, and the fact he had survived that carnage and was here at the ball spoke positively on his behalf.

When Luke left us, Sir Charles turned to me. "You have been promoted from 2nd Lieutenant to 1st Lieutenant and your regiment, The

92 Gordon Highlanders, are excellent fighting men. You did not learn to handle a revolver like that at a funfair. Please, remember to come and see me on Tuesday, along with Miss Oxford and her companion."

"Yes. Tuesday." He nodded. I turned to leave—then turned back and asked, "There were two members of the Prussian delegation here." I described them.

"Ah," Sir Charles acknowledged. "Herr Regensbruck and Herr Kremmenfeld—strange characters. They seem to be paying attention to the French delegation, so my informants tell me. Herr Bismarck is turning into quite a political force. He and Napoleon III are like two stallions in a stable where there is only one mare."

Sir Charles looked at me as if he was seeing me for the first time. "Pardon my staring…it is just you remind of someone. The resemblance is truly uncanny. Nevertheless, I will not detain you. Thank you, again, for your prompt action. Your identification of the rifle, by the way, was quite accurate. The man you shot was tattooed, but carried no papers. Not surprisingly, he was either American or European. Good night to you. You will need to be careful from now on. My thanks again."

Sir Charles was joined by his secretary, a man with the amazing ability to appear out of nowhere just at the right time and the two went off in deep conversation.

Time for bed I thought, and I also considered what Lucy might be doing at this time. She had been fairly composed about the events of the evening, and people in 1867 were much more accustomed to guns than my generation. Certainly to Luke Carter, guns were a way of life and a way of staying alive. What about the Germans though? I was convinced they were Germans or Nazis and were not from this time. Why were they here? And how did they get here?

I had to get a note as quickly as possible to Adrian. He might have some intelligence that could help. If there were another time tunnel, where did it come out? How could I find it? I wondered if there were any Chinese who could help me. The Germans would stick out like a sore thumb to them. I was still pondering these imponderables when I got back to my room. Mrs. Jamieson was waiting up for me. When I arrived, she opened the door, beaming like some fairy godmother.

"Come away in. I have a cup of tea ready for you." The alcohol had dehydrated me, so I was glad of the tea. "Sure, an' you've got the stars in your eyes. How many young beauties did you delight?"

It was nice to have someone who believed in you.

"Someone tried to kill Sir Charles Gray," I told her.

She drew in a sharp breath. "Saints preserve us! What happened?"

"The would-be assassin got shot."

"Shot! Was Sir Charles hurt?" I indicated in the negative.

"But who saved Sir Charles' life?" she probed.

"One of the guests," I replied truthfully.

"And?" she asked in that way that only women can.

I smiled at her and replied, "And the dance resumed."

Mrs. Jamieson's look of alarm deactivated. "Did you make any friends?" she asked, "just in case someone comes to visit you."

A Russian and a snow leopard I replied, "Anton Devronin and his sister, Julie Lacota." At the mention of Julie's name, a worried motherly frown crept into her eyes.

"Meester Faulkner, she has a terrible reputation. The stories about her are more than fleas on the back of a Kilkenny hound."

"I think I will have to consider your advice, but it's too late for my brain to function. Goodnight to you. I am afraid I am half asleep."

She wished me goodnight. There was a lot to Mrs. Jamieson, as well as uncomplicated kindness. I think my head hit the pillow when I got to my room. I had started mentally composing my letter to Adrian, but gave up. It would keep, unlike my eye lids, which had suddenly decided they were going to go on a separate holiday from me.

CHAPTER 10

The morning light streamed through the window brightly, which was because I had been too exhausted to remember to close the curtains. Bright light, an empty stomach, and a raging thirst were not a good combination to invoke holistic happiness.

It was 10:00 a.m. and Mrs. Jamieson had waited until she heard me moving about before bringing up my water for shaving. I breakfasted on my own because she was preparing a bath for me, for which I was glad. The food was good and enough. "I must be cracking round the block a bit," I thought to myself, remembering the day when I could have finished a *Vindaloo* curry and all the fixings and still be hungry. But the tea with breakfast worked wonders. *Lapsong Souchong's* smoky richness chased away yesterday's taste in my mouth. When I checked, Lucy's saffron flower was still in my button hole.

The events of last night paraded themselves like some kind of cerebral *'Trooping of the Colour,"* the highlight of which had been dancing with Lucy. But the replay of watching the Springfield crash down onto the dessert table repeated itself seemingly endlessly. Anton's remark about Julie also came back to haunt me. "She generally gets what she wants."

After breakfast I returned to my room and wrote a letter to Adrian outlining the events of last night, including my suspicions about the Germans. Short of sending someone else through the tunnel, help in whatever form it took might have to come from this side. What could I do? Chum up with someone, buy them a few drinks and say, "Hey, what about helping me blow up a time tunnel?"

I decided it was necessary to visit my time portal at the warehouse, taking as long and as a circuitous route as I could engineer. This was turning into an 1867 rat race, and in that rat race I had actually shot someone. Suppose the boy who was killed had chums who did not take kindly to what had happened to their friend and thought that I had acted improperly or had made an error of judgment? In this rat race, the rats had guns and knives, which I did not want to experience.

Thus, I headed to the warehouse, as casually and unhurriedly as I could manage, stopping and watching at intervals to make sure I was not being followed. The only living thing that I spotted was a bluebottle fly that expressed its disappointment at my being alive by flying in the opposite direction. I felt like jumping into the time car myself and heading back to the Finlander Bar to see who was there, but in my mind I envisioned that action leaving me suffering from a lifetime of guilt because I would be left holding a whole handful of threads that—through my selfishness—could never be woven into the intended pattern. I could not run out on Lucy, nor the letter to the French, nor whatever it is that Sir Charles Gray wanted. What stuck in my mind like an ever-sharp, ever hurtful barb was the little Chinese girl in the child brothel and how to get her out of there. The image of the nefarious, leering owner burned itself hotly into my memory. I had not reloaded the Webley and wondered if another empty chamber would make all that much difference. Lucy and Caroline could help with the girl, I told myself. But while violence might be the fast, easy answer, it would be the wrong answer and might prove only a temporary surcease destined to callously hurtle the child back into misery and danger. Instead, I must attempt to buy her back from the fate that was stealing her life and had tragically already stolen her innocence and childhood.

Suddenly, I remembered my grandmother having said to me, "Drew, Jesus came to redeem you ..." Was that what I was hoping to do for the little girl? And then I remembered the other half of Granny's story—the cost that the Redeemer Jesus had paid. According to Granny, Jesus had paid for it with His life. Would that ultimately be the price I had to pay?

Lucy, at least, was set to get a shock fit to knock down an elephant. The last time she saw her mother was two years ago—1865—and now she would see her mum as someone from the 21st century. I placed the letter that I had written in the small tunnel and only just managed to close the door on time.

The proximity of the tunnel suddenly brought Meryl close again. "I will always love you." Her words and the memories of our first and only night together captivated me. I hadn't thought about her recently, which made me feel that I was betraying her. Yet she had demanded nothing from me. I guess real love doesn't militate. I realized, too, that love was not a gooey feeling. It was a commitment, regardless of what happened. I remembered two of my friends who had married and turned one of their wedding pictures into a refrigerator magnet. They had a sign shop print on it for them, "I do and I will for the rest of my life," along with the date. So far, they were making their marriage work.

When I emerged from the warehouse, two Chinese men were taking a shortcut and looked surprised to see me. I pretended that I was looking for something. I had palmed a guinea, and suddenly produced it off the ground, and with many sighs of relief, hopefully convinced them of my sincerity.

How long did I wait for an answer to my letter? I thought I would try evening. They would be aware of the time here as I had put it on the note.

Right; now home, or at least a diversion. What about Anton, even though it was not yet Wednesday. Would he be up yet and could I avoid Julie? I traced the Russian Delegation building by finding a picture of whom I took to be the Czar Alexander II, "The Liberator," outside.

The servant who opened the door went to get Anton after I had presented my card. There was a smell of tobacco and scent streaming out of the house. Russian tobacco has a unique smell about it that made me think of exotic places and I was slap dab in the middle of one of the most exotic. Anton exploded onto the doorway and looked pleased to see me.

"Drew, come in my friend, and we will show you how we live in this humid dump. I miss the snow and ice." I looked surprised. He patted me on the back. "It's true. You are looking at me as if I was yesterday's rye bread! The Russian winters are cold, but it is a cold that quickens the spirit and sharpens the mind, and sends the blood rushing round the body as you feel the wind blowing off the frozen Neva River."

"Hmm," I said. "I sense an old Russian saying coming up."

He paused, and summoning his most sage look said, "In winter, a woman and vodka will both keep you warm, only the vodka doesn't argue back."

"Very profound," I approved. He looked pleased.

"You like Russian philosophy? You have to be philosophical living under czar."

I thought to myself, *You poor guy. If you think the czar is bad, wait till you see the red storm that is coming in fifty years.*

"Maybe I write book one day," Anton mused. "Perhaps in your country there is not big market for book on haggling in the markets on the Don Basin."

I thought of the blur of publishers who would go for that! We had reached an inner room. "Stick to being a tourist guide for those lost in China," I advised him with a smile.

"Tourist, what is tourist?"

I hummed and said, "People who go and visit other countries for fun."

Anton looked astonished. "People would come here for fun when there are vodka and women instead?" The astonishment in his voice was genuine, as was the lingering dry cough that I had noticed at the ball.

A voice purred from behind us, "I like what my brother has brought in for fun. I knew you would not be able to stay away, Drew, darlink."

I suddenly realized how language misunderstandings could cause problems. I smiled at her and bowed formally. "I came to see Anton and to thank him for his help with Caleb Bryant. Your brother pulled me out of a difficult situation and enabled me to dance with Miss Oxford."

Julie's eyes widened and the look of the snow leopard was back. She nodded her head. "Of course, darlink. I believe you."

We sat down and tea and vodka were brought. I declined the vodka, explaining that it was a little early in the day. After the tea, Julie gave me a long, languid, look and declared she was going for a bath. "I love the caresses of warm scented water, the way it…"

Anton interrupted her reverie, "Julie please…"

In response, Julie slowly loosened her long black hair. She treated me to a smile that caressed like a silk scarf and shimmered from the room.

I noticed a chessboard. "Give you a game of chess if you want. I am not very good though."

Anton replied that the last time he played chess with someone who was "not very good," he had lost three hundred imperials.

"He must have been good!" I responded.

"He?" Anton snorted. "It was my eighty-six-year-old grandmother after she filled me with some of her home-distilled vodka. Never mix vodka and babushka. What really worried me was when I found out that what she did not drink, she used to fill her lamps with."

Anton went on to speak of Russia and his home in the area of Borodino. The "we" he mentioned was his Finnish wife, Irja, and their daughter, Sonja. "I do not think there was a happier man on God's earth," he declared, "the day that I married Irja. Suddenly, I realized that I had been living in autumn and it had become spring again. My health and my life improved. I can still hear her laughter and the very sight of her filled my heart with joy. Even in the deep winter it was like spring in every room of the house." He looked wistfully out of the window and was transported back to the place that his heart had never left.

He sighed deeply. "When Sonja was born and I held her in my arms, Drew, my friend, she was so beautiful and perfect—a masterpiece from God. This was my daughter. Our child. I was going to watch her grow up and love her and scold her and buy presents for her…Irja was a born mother." He took another mouthful of tea from his cup and I noticed that he had poured vodka, but not yet touched it.

There was silence. His tone changed, warning me that some admission was coming, borne on the wings of pain. "I had to go to St.

Petersburg to see my lawyer on business. That's what you call it. When you go away and you leave everything well, you expect it to be well when you return. Irja and Sonja were the two beats of my heart. I had been away four days. When I returned, the cabin door was open. I pushed on it and shouted that I was home, only to be met by a deafening silence. Then the smell hit me—that sweet, sick, smell of death. Irja lay in front of the stone fireplace, her head covered in dried blood." Tears swept into his eyes. "I took her in my arms and tried to breathe, to will life in her. She was as cold as the frost outside. I went to look for Sonja, dear God no, no... I moved round the house like a man in a nightmare who wanted to wake up. I found her in her room. She lay across the bed...she had been ..." He started to cry and I put my hand on his shoulder.

"Anton, shhhh. I see the picture. There is no shame in tears."

Tears! Dear Lord! They would have had to scrape me off the wall if that had been me.

Anton continued. "The neighbors came, as did the doctor and he gave me something to make me sleep. Sleep! I wanted to die! I woke up in a neighbor's house the following morning."

He reached for the vodka, then put it down again. He breathed in and suddenly became very calm. There was a silence of words in the room and the sun filtered through the spaces in the shutters and Anton's mind left the cold, bloody snow and returned to the close humidity of China. I had never met the victim of such crime face to face, what do you say? "Anton, I am so sorry." A bird began to sing outside the window.

"They found the two who did it, a father and son. I found them, too, and shot them both. The boy begged for mercy but I gave him none. He was sixteen." I marveled at his sudden calmness.

"The boy I shot was the wrong son. They were twins. He had been on his way back from university, coming home to find what his father and brother had done. He had not been near the house. I can still see the look of terror in his eyes. He said he had not been near the house, but all I could see was Sonja. 'For the love of God, have mercy!' He cried. 'I have committed no crime! Have mercy!' It was only afterwards that I found out he had been innocent. They arrested me and I was exiled to here. I wish to God they had shot me."

There was silence in the room and the bird outside continued singing. "Is there no way of getting back?" I asked.

"Yes, but only with a pardon from the czar. Julie could go back, but she will not leave me." My opinion of Julie changed. Her loyalty to her brother proved a depth of character that I had not expected.

I persisted. "Can you go anywhere else without prejudicing your chances of pardon?"

"Prejaundicing, what does that mean?"

I smiled. "Prejudicing, err…messing up…stopping something from happening." I could not think of a better way of explaining it.

Anton looked tired and spent, a man who had opened his soul to a stranger. I felt very privileged to have earned his trust.

Julie returned from her bath. She recognized Anton's torn, melancholy expression and rushed to his side. "We will go to the hills today," she promised him. Then she directed me, "We will pack some food to take along and my brother will recover."

I shook my head ruefully. "Sorry, but I have to go. I have an appointment in half an hour. Regretfully, I must dash."

Julie drew close to me, bringing with her the fragrance of jasmine. Suddenly, the snow leopard turned into a tame kitty. "Thank you for what you did for my brother. He needs a good friend. Someone who will just listen to him and let him talk." She touched my arm and went back over to join Anton.

Anton drifted back to the present. Suddenly remembering that I was in the room he said, "I'm sorry. But can we leave the chess to another day—next time, I swear."

We walked to the door together. "Anton, we all make mistakes. Sometimes terrible mistakes. But your mind was unhinged by such grief." I put my hand on his arm to try to reassure him, both realizing and regretting how inadequate words are sometimes.

CHAPTER 11

I arrived at the French Delegation and was ushered into the presence of the Marquis de Plombal. "You have a letter for me, Lieutenant?"

I passed it over to him. He indicated that I should sit down. He broke the seal and began to read. His face creased into a frown, then I heard a sharp intake of breath. "Do you know the contents of this letter?"

I shook my head. "I am only the messenger—I trust that you noticed the seal had not been broken?"

He said, "I must pass the contents of this to my government. Do you think you were followed here? You're already known after what you did for Sir Charles Gray. You must be careful."

Yes, I must be careful! I warned myself, yet I had to risk what was on my mind. "Thank you for your concern and for mentioning Sir Charles, but that event brought me to the attention of two members of the Prussian delegation."

Marquis de Plombal's eyes widened.

"I fear they are up to no good." I told him.

He inquired as to where I was staying and asked if it were possible to contact me there should the situation require it.

"Of course. I will not mention that I have been here or have seen you."

He thanked me and I left.

When you are scared, there can come a time when you don't get anymore scared. Fear just moves in to live with you like an unwelcome in-law.

I headed home for lunch and Mrs. Jamieson eyed me carefully. "Can I ask if there is something upsetting you? A good meal often helps." She had the table ready, filled with cold food and warm, freshly baked bread. Again, the tea was most welcome.

After we had eaten, I asked her, "How do you help someone who has made a terrible mistake? Someone who regrets with all their heart what they have done, but cannot forgive themselves?"

Mrs. Jamieson sat for a while before answering, "You try to love them. If they have an aching heart, they need a higher forgiveness."

I pondered her words. "Higher forgiveness? You mean God?"

She stirred her tea and nodded. "Only God, who made us, can help us forgive ourselves. Forgiving yourself is sometimes terrible difficult."

"I'm not sure about God," I admitted.

"Meester Faulkner, it's not about you that we were talking. It's about your friend and it sounds as though he needs peace more than anything. Sometimes, Meester Faulkner, we do not have to understand how help will come, we just have to believe it will. One thing that I have learned about God is that He has terrible big shoulders. Would you be going to church tomorrow?"

That course of action had not occurred to me. Yet, if I did, I could meet a lot of people. Then I remembered that it was 1867, and thought how patronizing I was being—no—how shallow. I suddenly felt ashamed and alone. These people staked their lives on what they believed. I had never taken the time to think about God, and here I was in a situation where God was not just important (if He were in fact real), but could be strength.

"I will go to early mass," Mrs. Jamieson informed me. "Then I can get back and have your lunch ready. You are a distracted young man. It must have been something or someone at the ball. It was a terrible experience for anyone."

We continued in conversation. I asked her where the United States Delegation was. She told me and remarked, "Sure, they are a friendly bunch even if wid'some of them I can't be understanding a word they are saying. Three days ago one of the soldiers carried home my purchases from the market. He was a fine young fellah to be sure. Oh, yes, a fine young fellah." That remembrance was followed by a wistful sigh that made me realize that my landlady had hormones. Judging by the slightly glazed look that came into her eye when she spoke about the soldier—her hormones were working full tilt.

"I think I will go for a walk and try to find their delegation," I told Mrs. Jamieson. "I might get a firsthand account of the War Between the States."

Back out in the street, I headed for the U.S. Delegation, which was a little way past the British Embassy, where clearing up from last night's ball continued. Somehow the place did not look quite so romantic in the daylight. I could not see a way up onto the roof and wondered how the would-be-assassin had managed his feat. Well, as the lawyer had said, "Where there is a will, there are relatives." I was pondering the lawyer's words when I was stopped by two Sikh policeman.

"Lt. Faulkner, sahib Sir Charles wishes you to see him immediately. Please follow us."

Following was not so easy, as they were very quick walkers. When we got through the embassy door I was passed onto a footman, who passed me on to the secretary, who passed me on to Sir Charles. He was behind a large desk in an even larger office. He got up as I entered. "Ah, Lieutenant, good of you to come."

I sat down in the seat indicated and asked, "How may I help?"

"I take it, that like most of us, you have seen a dead body before?"

I nodded, thinking that Sir Charles' question was an interesting conversation opener.

"Good. You are not long from the old country and may just be able to explain any new military developments."

I shrugged my shoulders.

Sir Charles frowned. "I am still not convinced that you do not know more than you let on."

I attempted a look of innocence, but people like Sir Charles did not survive in diplomatic circles by being easily fooled.

Sir Charles indicated that I should follow him and we headed down stairs to a cool basement. "Please give me your opinion about how poor Mr. Prenderleith met his demise." He lit two paraffin lamps and they exposed a body lying face down. The stench was starting to become horrific. On closer inspection, I found the bullet holes—arranged in a straight line down the poor man's back and administered with clinical precision. There were about twelve of them standing out like interloping potholes. It didn't take genius to see they had been made by a submachine gun. The only other alternative was that the man had been shot once and killed—then the other holes coldly and deliberately drilled into the dead man's body.

Yet what could I tell Sir Charles? After one more sympathetic look at the body, I asked if we could return to the land of the living.

Once back in his office, Sir Charles asked, "Tea? I find tea always helps. A calming reassurance of home."

After the tea had arrived he asked me what I thought. I felt that I was being interviewed by the headmaster about my choice of college just before going up to Oxford.

"Sir Charles, have you heard of the Gatling gun? It was used with effect towards the end of the American Civil War."

Sir Charles thought and remarked, "Yes. That was also a close run thing. We nearly came in on the Confederate side. I sometimes wonder what would have happened if we had.

"Yes, I have heard of the gun you mentioned. It is voracious in its consumption of ammunition. It could stop a charge of any mass of infantry. Are you suggesting it was Gatling gun that was used to kill poor Mr. Prenderleith? The poor chap went out to do some drawing—he was quite a good artist to all accounts. Doesn't a Gatling gun require two men and need to be on the level, not like the rocky place where his body was found?"

He was right. "Sir Charles, let's suppose that there was a newer development springing from the Gatling gun. One that could be fired by one man and was easily portable."

"That is a thought," Sir Charles acknowledged. "A few men armed with what you describe could stop a regiment of single-shot rifles."

I was, like Dorothy in the Wizard of Oz, wishing I was back in Kansas. "Is it a possibility that the Prussians (I nearly said Germans) could be developing a weapon like that? If so, they are probably developing it in some remote area. Even a quick-firing gun that one man could operate could jam."

He lit his pipe. "Mmm. The word of Herr Bismarck's remarkable victories have reached even here. Where next? He would not tackle Britain." There was a hesitation and he added the word, "yet." Suddenly, his eyes opened wide. "France! He is going to attack France, not to conquer it, but to prove it can be done. The implication being that you exist not by the will of Napoleon III, but by Prussia. Perhaps Napoleon III has plans to inflict defeat on Prussia in revenge for the part they played in his uncle's eventual overthrow. Then I should—were I he—be in a position to challenge Britain." Then he negated his own idea with a robust shake of his head. "No, it's a flight of fancy. Sheer imagination."

The idea had been planted, though, and nothing including Sir Charles' dismissal of it would make it vanish.

I attempted to appear very patriotic and very matter of fact. Inside, I was scared. I knew I had to find where the Germans were operating (if they did turn out to be Germans). I must also allow Lucy and Caroline get on with their teaching for now, at least until Caleb showed up again. I had to build my relationship with Lucy—but how far I could let it go, I was unsure. Of one thing I was certain; I could not hurt her and still live with myself. If only I could eradicate the sound and pull of Meryl's voice from my memory…lose it back—or would that be forward?—in time where it belonged so that it did not return to jeopardize my new relationship with Lucy.

"Sir," I addressed the older man. "We must try and find out if there is a focus of operation for whoever did this and then try and stop them. Any pressure in the wrong area could precipitate the development of this weapon. I know you don't want the Prussian delegation up in arms, especially with scant evidence."

The trouble was—and I could not tell Sir Charles this—that it was not a case of developing a weapon, but rather of loading a case of them into their time tunnel. Once a piece of equipment was invented, it was nearly impossible to un-invent it.

Sir Charles considered. "They must be operating somewhere outside Foochow. There are many valleys, hills and mines in remote areas. We have in the Chinese one advantage, that of many eyes. Eyes that would be quick to spot unusual European activity, even though some of the Chinese may be involved, albeit even under duress."

"Could some of them have been used as hostages? Would a Chinese man keep silent if his wife or child were in danger?"

Sir Charles stood up. "Lieutenant, I have found the Chinese to be courageous and loyal and trustworthy—a view not shared by some of the government in London. Their desire seems to be to funnel as much opium into China as possible. It is shameful and unforgivable. I have tried to do all I can to hinder the opium trade. It may be that the attempted assassination was a backlash from that."

More tea arrived, and our conversation resumed. Sir Charles assured me, "The Chinese themselves have taken very draconian steps to try and stop this trade. Sadly, the prime minister in London, the Earl of Derby, feels that the Chinese may have to be 'persuaded.'

"Economically speaking, opium is paid for in Chinese silver," he explained. "That silver can buy tea for an increasingly thirsty British nation. Opium rots the fabric of society and is responsible for killing women and children because it encourages their fathers to kill themselves. They talk of choice, but with opium, all too soon the element of choice is lost and necessity and addiction replaces it. Moral stances may make enemies, but I will not be responsible for ruining the lives of families while I can still make a difference."

Sir Charles stood up and stared out the window. I suddenly felt the shallowness of the existence I had been living. Both Sir Charles and Lucy —and even Caroline—held in common what many of the patronizing books of the 21st century sneered at as "Victorian morality." Such sneering attempted to ignore achievements and replace them with wind. These people I had met here in 1867 did not have to be cajoled or forced or asked a dozen times to do something. They used the resources they had to make a difference where they could. Sir Charles had used his influence to try to stop—or at least hinder—a nasty and evil trade that was a blot on Britain.

"Sir Charles, give me seventy-two hours to try to find something, if I may call on the help of others?"

"Of course," he agreed. "Do your best and keep me informed. And, please, do be careful. I don't want your body lying in the basement."

"Did Mr. Prenderleith have items on him when he was found?" I asked. "And if so, may I see them?"

A servant was summoned and returned with a small box containing a few drawing pencils which were broken, an eraser, and a drawing book. The last page had been ripped out of the book. I took one of the drawing pencils with a soft lead and ran it gently over the page. Slowly a drawing came to life, a landscape of rocks and caves.

"Sir Charles, do you have anyone else who can draw? Who can take this drawing and flesh it out?"

"But Lieutenant, why are we concerned about drawing? Surely we need to be seeking this weapon you mention?"

"Sir," I explained, "this page may contain the very last thing that Mr. Prenderleith drew—the last place that he saw. And it may be why he was killed. If anyone can recognize this place, then it may save a lot of wasted time in searching."

He smiled and nodded his head. "Well done, indeed. We have such a lady who can do that. I will inform you when it is ready, Captain." He saw the surprise on my face and chuckled. "I like to keep good surprises to the end. Your promotion came through by telegraph today. Congratulations."

We shook hands and I left, wandering into the street in somewhat of a daze. I kind of wondered if there had been anyone else who had been shot at, wounded, or even killed with the same weapon as the one that had killed Mr. Prenderleith. I had set about to be Sherlock Holms without the least clue of how to go about it. Who would have most contact with the Chinese? I was due to go and see Lucy's school; perhaps she or Caroline may have picked up some scuttlebutt. What about Luke? He was another possible source of information.

Lucy seemed the best bet if I could fill her in on what had happened. I found the school with the two classrooms and very attentive children. Lucy got up when I arrived at the classroom. She seemed to have the older children. It was at once evident that they were fond of her. I guessed that if she gave me her approval, the children would feel I was fine, too.

Lucy gave me a list of things needed for the school. I tried to explain to her quietly about what had happened to Mr. Prenderleith and the unusual way he had been killed. If the children knew of any activity that was out of the ordinary and mentioned it, I would be obliged for any help.

Lucy called one of the oldest boys over. He approached me and bowed. I returned the bow.

Lucy introduced us. "This is Ah-tee, the older brother of the child you saved from drowning." Ah-tee looked a little bit anxious. "A thousand thank yous, sir, for you saved my brother's life. May the wind of heaven blow upon you with favor."

I told him that I was glad his brother had recovered from the ordeal and added, "Please convey my good wishes to your mother and father."

He bowed again and said, "My father is dead. So my mother gladly receives his blessing from you as well."

He returned to desk and his writing. I took Lucy's list and headed straight for the time tunnel, pushing it inside the small door and trying to force myself not to think about Meryl. There was no reply yet to the letter I had already sent, so at the bottom of Lucy's list, I asked for help in case I had to stop the Germans.

I couldn't help thinking that if I needed some military brain Luke was the guy. I found the American Delegation and was stopped by one of the sentries. "Can I help you, sir?"

I informed him that I was hoping to communicate with Captain Carter. "Please tell him that this is Captain Faulkner."

The sentry came to attention. "At ease," I said. "I'm in the British Army, not yours." He called over one of his colleagues to talk to me while he went in search of Luke. It did not take him long. Luke looked worried. "Drew, this is a kind of bad time, but congratulations on your promotion. One of my men in a two-man patrol has been shot, but there are some things that are puzzling."

I gave him a quick sketch of what happened to Mr. Prenderleith and asked, "Just by any chance, were the two guys attacked by what could be called a fast-firing gun?"

Luke studied me briefly. "You better come and talk to them. They are still shocked and I tell you—it takes a lot to shock these guys."

We found Hank, who had pulled his buddy out of the line of fire. Billy, the guy who had been shot, was still with the doctor. Hank scrambled to his feet when Luke approached. "As you were," Luke ordered him. "Private, this is Captain Faulkner of the British Army. Can you tell him what you told me?"

Still shaken, Hank repeated his story, "The durn thing just kept firing and firing. Bullets and rock splinters went everywhere."

"Well done for getting your buddy out. You did the right thing." It sounded as if they had been victims of another two-man patrol. The two Germans must have continued firing. Hank and Billy had not tried to be heroes, and it said as much for their skill as the Germans bad shooting that they were both still alive.

"Did you see anything of the men who shot at you?" I asked.

Hank considered the question. "Only that they had green uniforms and metal headgear."

Luke asked me, "Can you have a talk with my superior, Major Piper? He's trying to make some sense of all this." He dismissed Hank. "Okay, soldier. Get some chow and you have the rest of the day free. Oh, and take care of Billy's mount for him." Still looking somewhat shocked, Hank saluted.

"Is Billy going to be okay?" I asked Luke.

Luke nodded. "Reckon so. I'm just fixin' to go see how he is now, if the doc has finished with him. Want to come along and see for yourself?"

We headed over to the medical facility. Luke was angry. "I don't like it when someone uses my men for target practice."

The doctor met us. "He's been shot three times, but by some miracle—no bones broken and no arteries injured. He's suffering from blood loss and shock."

Luke asked the doctor, "Can we talk to him? Just for a few minutes."

The doctor took a deep breath, "Well, okay. But not too long. He needs rest."

The room where Billy lay was cool. When he spotted Luke he struggled to get up. "As you were, son, just relax." Luke assured him.

Billy looked at me and Luke explained, "This is Captain Falkner of the British Army. He is interested in what happened because it appears you may not be the only one who's been shot."

Billy considered me gravely, wincing at a sudden pain. Then he explained, "This guy in a green uniform shouted something when he saw us and the next thing his gun started firing and forgot to stop." He rewound the picture in his mind. "One other thing, sir. I am pretty sure the language he was shouting in was German. My grandfather spoke German. That's how I know."

I could not keep from smiling. "Thank you, Billy. You have just given me the last clue we needed. Well done."

After talking to Billy for a few more minutes, we headed outside. Luke asked, "Do you know who did this?"

I looked at him. "Perhaps an idea. But let's find out from Hank where they were or what they were near."

Another quick word with Hank disclosed that it was near the Hanshee Caves.

I told Luke that I was ready to see Major Piper now.

Major Piper was an experienced soldier and he asked me about my regiment. I had been prepared for this, knowing that it could be verified by wire, but also knowing that those who were behind this and had given me the cover I needed had foreseen such probabilities. I attempted to remember all the details of my reenactment time of Victorian soldiery as I replied, "92 Regiment, formed in Aberdeen."

He nodded. "You are a long way from home, Captain." Going to his desk, he took out his pipe and filled it. Then he sat down in one chair and pointed me toward another. "Fill me in what you know about this business."

I told him and tried to emphasize the danger of the fast-firing gun the Germans had. "It probably would not be a good idea to go in with all guns blazing. Perhaps three or four could accomplish more than a whole battalion. The idea being that in the end these guys don't show up again."

"Maybe we could take one of their guns, let the folks in Washington see it."

I couldn't let that happen. Time enough in World War 1 for the submachine gun to make its scything presence felt.

Luke came back in and Major Piper asked him about a four-man raiding party to scout out the best way of dealing with this. I advised them about Mr. Prenderleith's drawing. "If we find a match, we'll have the right place," I explained. "If it doesn't match, we have two teams operating. I'll be in touch."

After I left, I went immediately back to Sir Charles and asked him about the drawing. Miss Dorothy, the artist, was summoned. "She has an idea where it may be," Sir Charles explained.

Dorothy entered the room and Sir Charles asked her to repeat what she had told him. "Well, I was filling in the drawing when one of my house boys passed and started to look very concerned. 'Don't go there, missy lady, he said. 'A very bad place, Hanshee Caves. Evil spirits there. No go.'"

"The poor boy got very upset and suddenly possessive." Her big brown eyes opened wide as she recounted the story. She produced the drawing and I asked if I could borrow it briefly. "I want to take a photocopy." When they both looked at me blankly, I explained, "Put a copy of it in my mind like a photograph."

Dorothy looked at me with eyes of 1867 understanding. After she left, I told Sir Charles what the Americans were planning and that they were somewhat miffed with the Prussians for shooting at their men. Sir Charles listened and I could almost hear his mind mulling things. "Captain, you seem to have made friends with Captain Carter. Perhaps you could go along as an observer. But please try not to get caught. On occasions, the Prussians can be singularly lacking in a sense of humor and I fear this may be one of those occasions. Do your best. Be careful. Try and be a shadow and forget about being a soldier."

When I got outside I thought to myself, *I need a holiday*—because it suddenly dawned on me what problem the Semtex might have been intended to solve. How long ago was it when I was in Edinburgh traffic with figuring out how to spend weekends the biggest challenge? And now I was almost going to start a war. Next time you don't like where you are, maybe think again. That fresh-looking greener pasture may boast a cliff just over the horizon.

I was tired. I could sleep for Scotland and I could murder a plate of fish and chips. *Come on,* I ordered myself. *Get a grip.* We used to have an expression that was a bit of a joke when someone told you something with too much detail. You cried out, "Too much information."

I had to chance the time tunnel again and send back a note about what was happening. It would be good if someone could help. But the one whose help I really needed was Angus McTurk and he was some one-hundred-and-fifty years away.

CHAPTER 12

I must have looked like death warmed up when I got back to Mrs. Jamieson's. I passed on my meal and went to bed, finally catching up with Luke some four hours later. We discussed plans. What worried me was how we were going to light our way.

Luke had already thought about this. "Two days from now is a full moon," he assured me. "It will be bright enough to allow us to move out."

After a moment of thought, I inquired, "What about snakes that may come out at night while we are going about in the dark?"

Luke grinned. "Well, I'm from the Texas—the part with a lot of what we call hills, because everything in Texas is big—and we won't own up to calling anything mountains unless they're huger than other folks' mountains. We have rattlesnakes and water moccasins, both of which are poisonous. But they like heat, not cold. I suspect the snakes here might have better things to do on a cold night than looking for people walking about in the dark to bite. Still, since you mentioned it, canvas leggings should help. We can only take the ponies so far. Then we will have to walk. We can loan you a Sharps if you haven't got one. They go a good five-hundred yards. But don't you already have a revolver and a knife?"

I took a deep breath and remembered McTurk's knife class—cutting edge technology, to be sure—but the thought of having to stick a knife in someone did not appeal to me. Okay, I could probably handle it if it were needed as self-defense. I nodded and agreed to meet Luke and the others in the American Delegation at 7:00 p.m., two days from now.

Meanwhile, I had to go back twice to Sir Charles before I found him in and could inform him of our plans. I asked casually if he knew of anything valuable in the area of the Hanshee Caves.

He was quick to answer. "There are large silver deposits there. Chinese silver is of a high quality. A lot of it goes to purchase opium."

Again he emphasized about being careful and then added that it might be a good idea if Miss Oxford was "kept unaware of these proceedings."

During the intervening time I did some ferreting round in an attempt to get the name of the girl I had seen at The House of the Little Cygnets. Her name was Mi-Ling. She was barely eleven. I expected that I could engineer a way of removing her from the brothel, but I would need help in taking care of her. The obvious person for that job, I thought, was Lucy. Instant parenthood had not been on the agenda when I left my going-nowhere and arriving quickly life in the 21st century, but I could not leave a child to Mi-Ling's present fate. Once I had rescued her, morally, I would assume the responsibility for her. She had good reason to distrust adults, but I had to do something. There was nothing cultural about the life she was living. She was being used and abused by a greedy, nefarious, bat-fowled bandit. I learned that she had not been there long. As with so many other child victims, she was an orphan. How could people do that to a child? I wondered. It was sick, sick, sick, disgusting, disgusting—so horrific that I lacked descriptive enough words.

Sadly, I could not rescue all the children who were being sold into child sex slavery. But I knew I could and must help one. This one. Mi-Ling. Something had happened to me when I looked into her dead, black eyes and now she sat on my soul, weighting it in judgment.

Nor would I allow her to go to an orphanage in Scotland in 1867. I had read enough about them. What Mi-Ling needed was love, a home, a family and parents who loved her for herself and not as a commodity.

I went to the school and spoke to Caroline, asking permission to call on them that evening for something that was vitally important and concerned a third party. She quickly agreed.

At tea that night, Mrs. Jamieson asked how I was getting on. "And," she questioned, "have you seen your young lady?" When I told her I was going to see Lucy and Caroline that night, Mrs. Jamieson pulled out her beaming smile. It spread like butter across her kind face. "Ah, when the calls come to evening it is a good sign. It's a full moon tonight, a lovers' moon." That followed by a deep sigh of reminiscence.

"Mrs. Jamieson," I asked. "Do you know anything about The House of the Little Cygnets?"

I had no reason to suppose that she would answer in the affirmative, but she did. "Oh, dear God! You're not going there—but they are only children! Children!" Her breast heaved with righteous indignation and she rightly remonstrated with me until I explained about wanting to rescue Mi-Ling and needing Lucy's help.

Understanding erased the ire that had captured the expression on her face and she apologized. "Forgive me! Of course, I will do all I can to help the wee lamb. You will really need to get her out of here and I suspect that will mean you and Miss Oxford leaving, too. You came by sea and it will be sad to lose you."

I needed the rest of the time between then and our planned nighttime raid of the caves to plan all potentialities and get myself mentally and physically ready for action. I was pretty sure whatever happened would be far from pleasant.

Luke was a military guy and I didn't know all the things that had taken place in the Civil War. There had been raids, I knew. Places got blown up and railway tracks were destroyed. I suspected Luke and his team knew a lot about guerilla warfare. The War Between the States wasn't all set piece battles like Shiloh. It was a wonder that a lot more were not killed. I had to think that I had been given the Semtex for such a purpose, but if I was caught with it, it would be a dead giveaway that I was not from 1867. I could imagine myself asserting, *no, really. It's for modeling—modeling clay, honest*.

I had to set the Semtex to destroy their time car. I could really do with help. But what could I say to Luke after this almighty explosion went off? Plus, I had to be far enough away so that none of his men got hurt or else the Prussians would not be the only ones for me to worry about!

I went to Lucy's house and Caroline opened the door and took me into their sitting room. Lucy gave me a big smile. "It's good to see you again…" and after a moment's hesitation, "Drew."

I bowed. "Lucy. Miss Harper." Some social chit chat followed before I broached the subject of Mi-Ling. Could she stay with them, or did they know a safe house for her? "I have to get her out of that life. She is just a child—barely eleven. Please help me."

Caroline asked severely, "What would you do with her, Drew? Would you put her in an orphanage if you got her back to Scotland safely?"

"Dear God, no," I said in horror. "Have you seen these places?"

At my reassurance, she looked almost joyous. "You would help a child who was not yours; take a child of a different nationality and adopt her yourself?"

Her question hit me like a public transport bus on an Edinburgh street. She was right. I could barely spell the word commitment and now I was suddenly committing myself. "You will help me, please? I will pay for anything she needs. I will go by your judgment."

Lucy got up and came toward me. "Of course, we will help, Drew. But give us time to formulate a course of action."

With that assurance, I felt happier—even lighter in body weight. I found myself almost praying, "Lord, don't let me get caught by the Germans now. I must rescue Mi-Ling."

After leaving Lucy and Caroline, I put another note in the time tunnel demanding help. Additionally, I asked for the loan of a submachine gun and a Heckler &Koch MP5K. I had seen one in the training sessions. It was only a little over twelve inches long, easily concealed, and fired fifteen rounds. That was what I needed if I were going to be faced with a couple of guys with World War II German MP 40s. Besides—their aim might have improved. They were killers. They had already killed. I put a polite RSVP at the end of the request.

As a last gasp of hope, I went by the time tunnel an hour before I was due to meet Luke and his men and there it was—with a paper for me to sign saying I had received it and the ammunition, and that I would be returning it as soon as practicable. I loaded Heckler & Koch and put it into my warm coat pocket along with two magazines. I would still take the Sharps that Luke offered. It would look odd to refuse it.

Luke and his gang scared the daylights out of me. They were tougher than any desperadoes. Luke was concerned that everybody had water, a knife, revolver and a Sharps. The Sharps had a longer range than the MP 40, but you only got one shot.

It was a moonlit night and we jogged along on our ponies in companionable silence, our mounts being remarkably quiet. We dismounted about a half mile away from the Hanshee Valley and saw no snakes, thankfully. We left one of the men with the ponies. The mounts were our transportation out again. That left two teams of two men, and yours truly by himself. There were a lot of caves and there was no way to explore them all. Mr. Plenderleith had been exceedingly unlucky. He had hit the right cave at the wrong time. How do you keep nosey people away if you are trying to conduct covert operations? The Chinese had more eyes than any, yet none of them would come near the "haunted" caves. We had failed in our attempt to secure a guide when they learned of the location. They warned us to stay away, explaining, "evil place—many bad things stay there. Screaming devils."

Luke had requested volunteers. I would have liked some back up, but "honor of the regiment and all that…we must press on." To the British Special Air Forces, this would have been a piece of cake. But I wasn't SAS—just a pretend soldier. It looked easy on the television, but reality was a different kettle of fish.

We had made it halfway down into the valley when suddenly all hell broke loose. The air was filled with evil laughter and screaming and colored lights flashed off and on in two of the caves. The combination of things scared me. What it did to the natives I could only guess. The two caves that were lit up were a distance apart. Luke used hand signals to indicate they would take the big cave to the right and I should go to the closer smaller one to the left. How long this racket would last was impossible to guess. It was not only hard to hear, but hard to concentrate. Anyone here would know that someone was trespassing in the vicinity. The fact that no gunfire had split the night air yet might indicate that we had not been seen. I felt the reassuring weight of the submachine gun in my pocket and resisted the temptation to pull it out in front of the others. I knew enough about caves to know that the entrance to a cave was not always a guide to what is inside, nor how high or low the ceiling is. I worked my way along the side wall of the entrance, really hoping there were no snakes who wanted a night's lodgings waiting to be trodden upon.

I unhitched the Sharps and went in quickly. There was an eerie green light inside. I fought down my fear. It's great when you can stop the DVD on the computer and go for a coffee or go to the toilet. Take my advice: if ever you are insane enough to do something like this, go before you go. As I moved inside, the racket suddenly stopped and the relief was wonderful. I pulled the hammer back on the Sharps and at the same time the lights stopped flashing. There were several dark corners in the cave. I decided to try to run from one to another. The trouble was that I didn't know what I was looking for. Maybe it was a time tunnel like the one through which I had come. Or perhaps the 1940s version was different. Or maybe it was more modern. Regardless, I had to neutralize it because one thing was for certain: if the Germans learned how deeply I had—and perhaps Luke and his men, too—penetrated, the guards would be at least doubled. I moved further inside and reached a section of curtain below which a wooden crate peeked out. I gingerly drew back the curtain to find a pile of long crates, one of which had not been fully nailed down. The silver inside could not have been ingoted that long, for it was not tarnished.

Then I got careless—that unguarded moment that had cost many a soldier his life. My boot lace had come untied and I forgot that I was dealing with professional soldiers. Yeah. I failed to look around carefully before bending down to tie my lace. Suddenly there was a whack on the back of my head and the lights went out.

I awoke tied to a chair and with the embarrassing realization that I had wet myself. This was not Hollywood. This was real life.

I regained consciousness to find what I expected was a German officer behind a desk. In front of him was all my kit, including the Heckler and Koch for which I had signed a chitty. It occurred to me that it was difficult to frame coherent thoughts after a cosh on the head.

CHAPTER 13

"So you have decided to join us after your little sleep?" the German chuckled. "Just be thankful you caught Feldwebel Ottmann on a good day, or else you would not have come round. You can choose to answer my questions easily or with difficulty. My name is Major van Haas of the Abwher. Who were those with you?"

I guess when you think that you are going to get chopped anyway, you become a little bolder. I decided to change my accent; put on the stiff upper lip, polite English accent. "These chappies were friends, old boy, who came along to see if there were any more baddies in the caves. You Prussian chappies have a flare for the dramatic—what?"

He hit me round the face with the back of his hand so hard that I felt my neck snap backwards frighteningly, although it must not have been broken because it continued—somehow—to hold up my head. To satisfy those with a morbid curiosity, it is nothing like the films. It's just blooming sore. I felt the warm, sticky feeling of blood inside my mouth and I did a quick check of my teeth, relieved to find they were all intact.

He picked up the Heckler and Koch. "Very good. Just the kind of weapon someone in 1867 would have. "You know more, Captain, than you let on—and we know more than you thought we did. I have some friends who are very good at extracting information. It is not a matter of if you tell—but when."

I could hear my heart beating in my ears. "Look," I said, trying to sound alarmed—and discovering that it did not take much trying—"you chappies are not at war with Great Britain and the Geneva Convention..." *Oh, big mouth! You stupid burke!*

He smiled. "I do not think the Geneva Convention was signed until 1923. How do you know about it in 1867? Clearly, you are a spy. You are not in uniform and I can shoot you and save the paperwork, but what we must find out is what you know or how much you know. My friends in Berlin will make sure you cooperate."

I replied trying to sound calm, "The other thing you do not know is how many know what I know. You are shipping silver back to the Reich to pay for the war effort, so why not go for gold? Silver tarnishes."

He smiled that superior Arian smile, "How do you know we have not? Besides, in a few weeks the Americans will not care and we will walk on through to victory. Heil, Hitler!"

Then he looked at me derisively. "You are too stupid to know anything." He picked up the Lugar and flicked off the safety catch. He pointed it at me. I closed my eyes. I guess I just gave up.

Then heard the sound of the door flying open. There was a startled grunt and silence. When I opened my eyes, McTurk was standing over the now-dead German cleaning his knife on the dead man's uniform. "Didn't I teach you anything?" he demanded. "You should have looked behind you, laddie."

"How did you get here and how…" He cut me off and severed the ropes binding me to the chair.

"You were microchiped, laddie. Once I was here, you were easy to find. He raked through a cupboard in the dead German's office and found a pair of black trousers, which he threw at me. "Go ahead. Put these on and save your embarrassment." He then gave me back the Heckler and Koch and my other equipment. "This time, try not to lose them."

We searched through the office found drawings and letters. McTurk spoke fluent German. "They are not trying to pay for their war effort," he informed me. "They are trying to buy opium to undermine our war effort. They are capturing troops and addicting them to opium. Then they release them and use the carrot on the stick. 'If you want more opium, do as we tell you.' Hundreds and hundreds of armed fifth columnists, right in the forces addicted to opium that only they can supply. They mine the silver here and get the opium from here and make it into God knows what. The soldiers, once they step out of line, become traitors. So they have to continue in the slavery they sold themselves into unwittingly."

We looked at each other in horror and disbelief. "You know," McTurk said, "this is stupid enough to work. We must find that time tunnel..." I was just relieved to be still breathing, so I followed him to find another figure lying in the tunnel. He was a Feldwebel and his MP40 lay under him. McTurk had found him before he found McTurk. He was dead.

We discovered cases of silver bars and about a dozen MP 40's. McTurk had something like a miniature radio in his hand. "This detects the presence of active, but also inactive, Kairon," he explained. "There is a source just ahead behind that jutting rock wall."

There were, as we quietly crawled along, two German guards at what looked like one of these doors of mini trains they have in airports to take you from one terminus to another. We crawled back round the corner. McTurk's voice was solemn, if ever a whisper can be solemn.

"Laddie, we have to deal with these two. It's best to try and split them up from each other. Remember, these guys will try to kill you. You have to get in first." He looked at me and put his hand on my shoulder. Laddie, if they succeed, the whole of World War II could be extended and thousands more people get killed. They knew what they were risking when they signed up.

"I will distract one and get him here and when his buddy comes round, you have to take him. If a shot is fired it could alert others and we would have another ten to deal with. We can't risk a fire fight against so many. The throat if you can. Wait behind the rock on this side until he comes round. You will get only one chance." He patted my back and went to the other side of the cave.

I crouched down. I had no choice. I tried not to picture the wife and kids who would never see their loved one again. McTurk began to ping stones off the wall. It sounded like the kind of noise an animal would make. I waited and then happened to glance at my feet and saw the snake. Where do you run to when there is no place to go? I am terrified of snakes. The pointed snout identified it as a hog-nosed viper, jokingly known as the "one-hundred pacer," because that was how far you got if you were bitten before the venom took effect, generally fatally. When you read such information or such statistics, you kind of wondered how they actually collated them. I really did wish I was at home in bed in Edinburgh.

McTurk must have seen me go rigid. It's amazing how little you breathe when you don't need to. He screwed a silencer to the end of a pistol and began to ping more stones, this time at the snake who had curled up in front of me about three feet away. The snake's head came up. Oh, dear God, what a situation. It birthed words that had never lived before in my mind. *Dear God, if You exist, I could really use some help. Please.*

The stones began to have an effect. The critter realized that the threat was not coming from me. It got down off its high horse, so to speak, and moved to the left of me before starting to coil up again—still about three feet away—but out of line with me. I had never seen a human move so fast. McTurk rushed round the corner and discharged the pistol twice, the 'phuts' coming in quick succession. Then he hit the dirt about four feet away from me and fired, hitting the snake in the head.

I remembered Adrian saying that McTurk even made the SAS nervous. Now he had saved my life twice in one day. To say McTurk shot up in my estimation was an understatement. I checked my trousers and this time I was dry.

There was no standing on ceremony. We opened the door of their time car, hauled, pushed and shoved the two dead Germans inside— then repeated the effort with the other two bodies (along with the MP40's). McTurk used some of my Semtex to set charges. Making a guess as to the journey time and concluding 1940s Berlin was about right, McTurk set the time car to "return."

"Laddie," he ordered, "when I shut the door and send it off, run like blazes for the exit and don't stop. It will be dawn. Get back to your room and don't worry about me."

We shook hands and he stopped me from thanking him for saving my life—twice. But I knew he could read the gratitude from my eyes. "Now," he said. "Move!"

I ran faster than I even knew was possible. Behind me there was a noise like screeching. I made it outside with about a five-minute gap before the entire hill blew up.

I kept running. What happened to Luke and his men, I didn't know. But a new day was walking up into the sky and I followed McTurk's instructions to get out of there. I hoped we had got everything and hoped that the explosion would be seen as an accident—underground gas or any one of a dozen things that could have happened. I guessed if there were any Germans hiding out in the cave that we hadn't found, they would have been killed in the explosion.

But in spite of McTurk's insistence not to think about him, I thought about him anyway. I hoped like I had never hoped before for anything in my life that McTurk got safely away. He was a remarkable guy and there was only one of him.

CHAPTER 14

Predictably, Mrs. Jamieson was up when I got back. She opened the door and said, "Glory be! If this is you, I would hate to see the other fellow." I didn't divulge to her what had happened to the other fellow. I guessed the German must have hit me several times. "I have got to go out..." I tried to explain.

She shook her head. "An hour and half in bed would do you no ill and a whole lot of good." She left me briefly and returned with things for first aid. "It's a pity, that," she remarked. "I've run out of iodine. Maybe Miss Oxford will have some. Why not go round and see?" I wondered if Mrs. Jamieson had really run out, or if it was her intention to help make the course of true love run smoothly.

I closed my eyes for a few moments and all I could see was the snake that had been facing me and its head exploding as McTurks' bullet hit. I decided that I had found a good name for an aftershave, "Close Call," for that's what it had been. I guess in my heart I wanted Meryl to tend me, not Lucy or the kind-hearted Mrs. Jamieson. I wanted to feel Meryl's touch and hear her voice tell me everything was going to be okay. Or was that really the whisper of my heart? Inexplicably, I was not sure. Perhaps it was Lucy I really wanted at my side. Post-traumatic shock. Hollywood was not big on that condition, but this was real life— not Hollywood—and I knew that I was suffering from post-traumatic shock—hang Hollywood or any other doubters.

I headed for the French Delegation and this time I was shown right into the Marquis' office. What I had not realized until later was that Napoleon III had designs on Prussia, only history says he did not act on them. Bismarck was to prove quicker on the draw and that would bring Napoleon III's downfall—the nephew was not the uncle.

I was beginning to get used to 1867 China, at least what I had seen of it, but I wondered how my 21st century attitudes were fitting in. In this busy port, the broken earthenware of humanity passed by on their way to anonymity.

"Monsieur Faulkner," Marquis de Plombal said, "the letter is quite fantastique, yet interesting. A warning from friends in England of an attack on France in three year's time. I believe the Prussian protestations of being peace-loving are not true. L'Empereur cannot act upon a letter alone, no matter or how sincerely meant. The letter will be on the next ship out to Paris, and France thanks you for bringing this to her attention."

He paused. "If the king knows an assassin is coming, is he not wise to shut the city gate?"

I walked to his window. "Monsieur Le Marquis, I try to stay out of politics and leave it to those with wiser heads. Sometimes it is good when we do not know what's coming."

When I looked out of the window and across the street, I saw the German who had pulled out the Lugar at the ball. He may have been looking for me, or for one of the French Delegation. Perhaps he had received word of what happened at the mine and realized he was stuck in 1867 China, unless there was another tunnel.

"Pardon Monsieur," I murmured, "but I think I am being followed by one of the Prussians."

The Marquis joined me at the window. "Gray suit, straw hat," I described. Staying back from the window, he followed my gaze.

"Hmm. Herr Doktor Kremmel. He has not been here that long. Still, it may be better if you left by the lovers' exit."

He smiled at my quizzical expression. "The side door. When the mouse comes into the cat's lair, it must have a good reason, n'est ce pas? You English, pardon—Scots—have a saying, 'One itchy back needs another to scratch it.' Non?"

I thought for a moment. "Well, yes. I think the exact phrase is 'if you scratch my back, I will scratch yours."

He laughed. "Why not, if she is beautiful!" He returned to his desk. "Now, I think it is my turn to help you. The Prussians have been buying opium from us and paying in Chinese silver. But why would they do this? It gets taken away, shipped out. Yet we are unable to trace it on any ship's manifest. It just seems that it vanishes. It is almost as if it is being spirited away."

We discussed the situation for a few minutes before the Marquis suddenly looked at his watch and exclaimed, "You must excuse me, Monsieur Faulkner, but I have an engagement soon. I will see you are taken to the lovers' exit. If you have any further information for me, I should be glad to hear it."

We shook hands, "Bonne chance!" the Marquis exclaimed heartily as I left.

I was as careful as I could be to determine that I was not followed, yet how could I tell in such a mass of humanity?

My next stop was Lucy. I knocked at the door of their house, after finding the school building empty. Caroline opened the door and looked alarmed. In the glow of conversation with the Marquis, I had forgotten the state of my face and he had been too polite to mention it.

"Goodness gracious, Mr. Faulkner, what happened?" Caroline asked. Were you attacked?"

I attempted to shrug it off with an, "you should see the other fellow"—until it suddenly hit me all over again that the other fellow was dead.

"Caroline?" Lucy's voice drifted from the other room, "Is it Mr. Faulkner?"

"Yes," she called over her shoulder. "He has been set upon."

I heard a couple of quick steps. "Mr. Faulkner—Drew what happened?" Then to Caroline, "Quick! Get some iodine and hot water—please."

Lucy seated me in the parlor and Caroline brought the water and iodine. An older lady had carried it in and was heading toward me to do the nursing when Caroline's hand grabbed her sleeve and restrained her.

I hummed and hawed, and then saw Caroline raise her fingers to her lips. "Please, give it to me," Lucy said. Then to me, "this will nip a bit." It did, but I looked into those lovely green eyes—not in a picture now— but alive and real and wide open with concern and intensity as she nursed me...the sting vanished. Her mouth was slightly open as if tender administrations to me required deeper breaths as she rinsed the cloth and reapplied it. I flinched. When she put on the iodine it did nip. Then I saw a tear struggle out from the corner of her eye and cut a silver furrow down her flushed cheek and it was as if that tear and her kindness and compassion toward me thrust Meryl back through the time tunnel into the 21st century where she belonged. Here, it was just Lucy. My Lucy, one day, I hoped.

As she nursed me, I told Lucy that I had been attacked in the hills and had been rescued. Halfway through the story I glanced at Caroline, who had not moved at all. To my surprise, she wore a definite smile as if whatever relationship Lucy and I were fated to have, she approved.

"We have to see Sir Charles soon," I said to Lucy as softly as I could.

"Yes, yes, of course, if you are alright."

The three of us made our way to the Residency, but a bit slower than I would have liked. I really didn't want Bryant or his cronies, or the Germans to see us. I was concerned about Lucy, but so far, Bryant had done nothing to echo his threat. The picture of that dead German officer played over again and again in my mind like the start of a movie on a DVD when someone forgot to hit the "play" selection. Had the time machine we had blown up been the only one?

We walked up the long driveway. "A penny for them," Lucy offered, and I was brought back to reality. Caroline had dropped back to what might be called a longish respectable distance. "Thinking thoughts of home?" Lucy asked.

"No," I replied, somewhat mendaciously. "There is nobody at home...not even Grandpa. He hasn't been born yet."

"Pardon?" Lucy looked at me wide-eyed.

"Sorry, it was a manner of speaking."

She shook her head, sending a wave like burning sunlight through her hair. "You are a strange man, Drew. You do not seem quite to belong here. You think further ahead, as if you are here for a purpose probably too deep for me to see or understand."

She was perspicacious, my Lucy-to-be.

We had reached Sir Charles' house, and I thought this was not the time or the place to start an earth-shattering conversation with Lucy about time travel.

We were invited into Sir Charles' office and tea was bought. I had to figure out how familiar Sir Charles was with ships' manifests. Would he be familiar with opium just being "spirited away?" He immediately noted the condition of my face.

I attempted an explanation. "The Prussians were shipping opium and maybe silver. Perhaps, to help pay for their war effort. Or, to build up a war chest. They wanted people kept away from the area. My guess is that the explosives they used for mining went off and maybe sparked the others. It may have been that and leaking gas. Anyway, there is not much left of their mine.

"They had developed a fast-firing gun. I saw one but whatever weapons they had stored there must have been lost in the blast." *(Oh, help! When you start messing with history, it creates a mess!)*

Sir Charles looked at me thoughtfully over the top of his glasses. "One would hope that—shall we say—the explosion was not encouraged in any way?"

I looked as serious as I could. "Only history will tell, Sir Charles."

Thankfully, the conversation switched to less perspiration-inducing topics. Sir Charles looked at a piece of paper on his desk. "There is a clipper coming up for sale, *The Night Arrow,* owned by the McCormack brothers who need to sell her to make one end meet the other. My informants tell me that that is your desire to venture into the tea business."

I nodded.

"You need a ship, a crew, and a cargo. I cannot help but think, Captain, that with you on the high seas, life will be very much quieter in our little corner of Her Majesty's domains. I will help you in any way I can."

Lucy looked astonished. Now I must tell her everything—but not here.

However, Sir Charles helped—unaware that he was helping. "Miss Oxford, did you ever think of going home? Going back to Scotland? Mr. Bryant may have been instrumental in the attempt on my life. I fear he is a man not easily put off getting what he wants—and that makes me fear for your safety."

Lucy and Caroline exchanged glances. "Please think about what I have said," Sir Charles added. "I cannot tell you what to do, but even though your work here is invaluable, your safety and person is of more importance."

Once we were back outside, Lucy was quiet. "Lucy, I need to talk to you," I said.

She took fast steps, outdistancing me so that we were no longer walking together, and shook her head. She turned back and spoke in anger. "You nearly steal my heart, sir, knowing you were going to leave! What kind of a man are you? I expected better." She ran on ahead and Caroline sprinted past me to catch up with her companion. Lucy's plaintive words drifted back. "I want to be alone!"

Caroline returned. By the look on her face, I was not flavor of the month. "How could you lead her on?" she asked. "Shame on you, sir!"

Before she could spit in my face or do something else equally drastic, I pulled out the half-coin and asked Caroline, "Do you recognize this?"

She looked with all the reluctance of a child looking at a teaspoon of castor oil. Then recognition flared across her face and she gasped. "Where did you get that?"

"As hard as it is to believe, from Lucy's mother, Victoria. She is alive and well and married. Let me come back to the house and explain."

Caroline stopped and looked at me. "Give me the coin!" I handed it to her and she jogtrotted up to Lucy and showed her the coin.

It was Lucy's turn to gasp. She turned around and looked at me, then ran back. "Where is my mother?" she demanded.

I handed her the letter and the photograph. Lucy took them and started to read. How many times she read the letter, I didn't know.

When she spoke to me again, it was with desperation. "Please, sir! You must tell me what you know!" I looked at her green eyes, brimmed with tears like a lovely rose spattered with the first snow of winter.

"I will tell you, Lucy. But let's get back to your house first. I must be mindful of unnoticed ears."

When we got back to their house, I asked the girls to sit while I related my story. Caroline had a right to know, too, for she would be directly affected by what happened to Lucy. "Lucy," I explained. "I'm not who I appear to be. Your mother is alive and well in the year 2012. She has time traveled. I don't know what she wrote to you, but she is, I think, quite happy except for missing you."

Lucy looked at me. The rose did not seem quite so shaken now. "Time traveled? But what does that mean? How is it even possible?"

"By time coach. There is a substance in the coach that causes time to move—rifts in time through which one can travel. I know it's hard to believe, but that's how I got here."

"But why would you? Why did you come?"

Her question caught me off guard. All I could tell her was the truth. "There is a lovely house in Aberdeenshire called Bellefield. You own it. Or you will do. It's my job to get you there."

"Then you will no doubt leave me and go back to your year."

"No, Lucy. I can't go back."

She looked at me wide-eyed. "But if things have improved so much as my mother says here in her letter, why give up all you have known? Why come to what must be a step back?"

I took a deep breath. "The people who enabled me to come here told me that it was a one-way trip. There's no going back."

Lucy shook her head, "But why did you come in the first place? Were you paid?"

It was my turn to join the head-shaking brigade. "I have more money than I will ever need—at least by 1867 standards."

Her eyes opened wide. "I am trying to understand what in the world would cause a man to give up everything. To leave all behind and go into the unknown. To risk his life. To risk everything. There is nothing that would make a man do that except…" her voice trailed off and she looked at me, "except love."

A voice and scent from another time came back to me at Lucy's words. "I will always love you…" and Meryl's face formed itself on the screen behind my closed eyes, her coconut-scented hair brushing softly across my face.

Then I sort of came to again. Mere seconds had passed. "In Bellefield, Lucy, your picture is on the wall. It entranced—captivated me. I could not believe such beauty existed. Thought that perhaps the artist had exaggerated. He hadn't. But what is on inside is more important than anything on the outside. True, I have discovered that your outward beauty is real—but even though I've known you but a short time, I've also discovered the depth and purity of your inner beauty.

"I wanted you to get to know me. If we left our discovery of each other to the time of the journey back, I thought, then we could talk and learn and see. And if fate, or God, or whatever you want to call it, wills, experience that unity of heart, head and purpose that are vital when two people commit themselves to each other for life. It's a dangerous journey, Lucy."

Her green gaze was open and accepting. "You have given me much to think about. I must try to take in all you have said. I must try…to understand."

"Lucy, please think about what I have said. If you have any questions, I'll try to answer them."

We parted. I realized that I must give her space. The last thing a woman wants is to think she's being forced into a situation. Love doesn't bloom in a hothouse.

When I got back to Mrs. Jamieson's house, there was a note waiting for me from the bank informing me that there was a clipper coming up for sale. The bank gave it a good report. The *Night Arrow* might do it for us, but *Aerial* would also be in the race. *Aerial* had won the tea race the year before.

The auction was set for ten day's time and if I knew about it, Bryant would know, as well. His ship, the *Allegheny,* would also be a serious contender in the tea race. And as captain, Bryant would not hesitate to use dirty tactics.

If Lucy got on board the *Night Arrow*, assuming we were successful in purchasing the ship, Bryant would not destroy the ship for fear of losing Lucy and because some of his chums would gladly take possession of another clipper, no questions asked. But before anything, I had to go and see Luke Carter, even it was only to let him unload his anger. He must have thought that I deserted him. I hated confrontation, but I might need his help.

I went over to the American compound. I told the sentry who I was and he engaged a stand-in while he went to find Luke. Luke quickly appeared. He dismissed the sentry and ordered him to be back in half-an-hour. The man saluted and marched off.

"Where in thunder did you get to?" Luke demanded tersely. "I ought to knock your block off! The only thing that stops me is that it looks as though someone else has already done it."

"The Germans may have invented kindergarten, but they did not invent Sunday school," I told him. "I got caught, knocked out and interrogated by a Prussian major who did not like my face. They're mining silver to pay for opium. So when I found that out, I decided to hinder their operations."

"Hinder their operations! You English are a master of understatement. You darn near got us killed!"

"You had help, Captain," I reminded him. "I got sent into that cave on my own with nobody to watch my back. I didn't know the place was going to blow up."

He looked at me. "We had to leave. We didn't have enough power to engage in a firefight with those guys."

I realized I must attempt to defuse the situation. "I'm sorry, but the guys with the fast-firing guns were lost in the explosion. I couldn't stick around when the powder started to blow. And why are you so mad at me, anyway?" I asked. "I have just as much right to be mad at you. It was supposed to be a joint exercise."

Luke breathed deeply. "That's the last time I trust a blasted English dandy."

It was my turn to vent. "I am not English. I'm Scottish. How would you like to be called Canadian?"

His hat snapped off. "Just try it for yourself and see."

I was too angry to avoid open conflict with this trained military dude, even though common sense warned me that he could pound me into the ground. Fortunately for both of us, Major Piper intervened. "Tenshun!" His voice lashed at us like a whip. "You two—my office, now!"

We picked up our hastily removed and discarded hats and headed to Piper's office. Luke came to attention. It wasn't my regiment, but so did I.

The Major ordered us into chairs. "What are you playing at?" Piper bellowed. "Two officers brawling—or at least a kick in the britches off from it. I don't care if you are or aren't in my army, your behavior affects the morale of my men." He looked hard at Luke. "Captain, this isn't like you. I ought to bust you to lieutenant, and then what could you say to that sweetheart of yours?"

Luke drew a ragged breath. "Permission to speak, sir, and answer the Major's question."

Piper nodded.

"I would say nothing to her, sir, because I can't. She was kidnapped, sir, by Commanche Indians in a raid." He produced a letter and handed it to the major, who asked, "May I?"

Luke nodded.

Major Piper read the letter, folded it up, and returned it to Luke. "Son, you should have said something."

"Captain Carter," I added, "if we had gotten into a fight, I know I would have lost. I'm so sorry about your news." I patted him on the back, then said, "Major Piper, please accept my apologies for my attitude. I'm sure you both have a lot to discuss."

Luke stood up and held out his hand. We shook and I left.

"Nothing is so bad that it can't get worse," or so some optimistic soul had said. I guessed I had better keep headquarters up to date, so I slipped around to the time tunnel and sent Adrian a message containing details of what had happened and what could be expected to happen in the near future. I was exhausted. Adding to the fatigue, the atmosphere was growing close and muggy.

I had to find out about tea; how to obtain some and what made up a good cargo. Being a coffee drinker, I sure missed *Starbucks*. But I had to admit that the tea in China was different. It had life to it. Which reminded me that I had embarked on a dangerous mission. It would be good if I could keep life in my life, too!

CHAPTER 15

It seemed that going along to see Anton and cheer him up would be a winning idea. I got to the house and the footman opened the door. I announced my identity and asked if Anton was in. Anton came to the door looking much happier than I had seen him.

"Come in have some tea…" His voice faded. "What have you been doing? You look as if you have been in fight with very big Cossack."

I wondered about Julie, but decided not to enquire in case it was misconstrued for more than a passing interest. "An argument with some Prussians. One, at least, as well as the one who knocked me out."

Anton's eyes lit up. "You need vodka. Good for the brain. Help it to recover. My grand-uncle Pyotyr once fell from a sled going at full speed down the Nevski Prospect. After the doctor had tied him back together, he had several large glasses of vodka and was as right as snow."

I smiled, something I had not done in a long time. "I think it's rain, my friend, 'as right as rain."

Anton laughed. "Rain, snow. Who cares? It's the getting right that's the important thing." Then he was thoughtful. "Poor Uncle Pyotyr. He was killed three days later by having a pot of flowers dropped on his head. Poor Uncle Pyotyr. If he had lived, he would have died of shame to have died in such a way."

The vodka was strong. It had a presence about it. I was beginning to wish I had eaten first. Anton vanished and came back with a chunk of black bread. "You need something in your stomach or you may not have a stomach to put anything in."

Then he produced a letter. "Here. Read it."

121

I looked at it and tried not to laugh. "Anton, it's in Russian and I can't speak Russian. Is that the royal cipher on it?"

He beamed broadly. "Yes! My case is before the czar and he is looking at it. Oh, to go home and get out of here! Back to crisp cold and good food and the improving society of beautiful women."

"The improving society of beautiful women…" Lev Tolstoy would put that in *War and Peace* in 1869. Anton began to sing. Began to sing in Russian. He had a good tenor voice. "Anton," I asked, "just out of curiosity, do you know a writer called Lev Tolstoy?"

He thought, then nodded. "Yes, he is an getting known writer. He is working on a very long book."

"Would it translate to *War and Peace?*" I asked.

He stared and had another sip—that is if a Russian ever sips vodka. "How did you know?"

I thought I should tell him. The vodka might help him believe. "I have a book I want you to look at."

He beamed—a smile that could only have been the vodka. "A book of beautiful English women, that sounds good."

I shook my head. "You are incorrigible."

He picked up the bottle again, then put it down. "How do you spell that word incorr, incorrig—whatever it is?"

"Incorrigible. Well, I'm not sure."

"Ah, old Russian saying—'you cannot be what you cannot spell.'"

I laughed, and then heard Julie's voice. "It is good to hear laughter here again," she said, making her snow-leopard entry into the room. When she saw my face, she cried, "Darlink, what has happened to you? I hope you killed him." She grabbed a cloth, poured vodka on it and headed for me—a Russian version of Florence Nightingale. She pushed me down onto a chair and began nursing my face. I guessed I was heading toward having the most nursed face in the whole of China.

To get to my face, Julie sat on my lap. I jumped up and said, "Thank you, Mrs. Lacota. But if you put alcohol on the wounds, they will start to bleed again. But thank you for your kindness. I must get Anton a book I promised him."

"Yes," Anton agreed cheerfully, "a book of naked English women."

The vodka added to the list of their attributes.

Julie tossed me a scornful look. "Darlink, you do not need the cold covers of a book. You can come under my covers anytime." Her eyes gazed at me with unrequited longing.

"Julie," I explained. "It's a history book. I mean, Anton knows so little of what goes on in Britain. I must go now. I think Anton may have fallen asleep."

She purred close to me. "Darlink, that means that nobody will miss us. I am sure there are many entertaining things we can do to pass the time."

Saved in a nick of time! For there was a Sikh policemen at the door seeking me. "Sir Charles," he informed me when he was admitted into our presence, "would like to see you. Immediately. I am to escort you without delay."

I looked at Julie and at Anton, who was lost in his vodka-induced slumber. "Please excuse me, I must go."

Sir Charles was waiting for me. "The *Night Arrow* is to be sold tomorrow," he informed me. "The McCormack brothers need the money and are willing to part with her for eleven thousand pounds. They have already had one offer. I have insisted that the sale be handled as an auction. Mr. Bryant seems to be the only one interested, however. If you get the ship, I can arrange that she be packed with tea first. That means you will be towed out first and on your way. That is the last way I can help you. After that, you will be in the hands of the Almighty. But first you have to get the ship."

After leaving Sir Charles, I went to my bank and arranged a draught for £16,000 to be ready the following day.

What was really bothering me was that I still had to buy the tea, then get it loaded and find a crew. Above all—a captain who could contact a sailing master.

I returned to Mrs. Jamieson's feeling hungry. She had somehow made ale and beef pie and bean shoots, which I was getting used to and even beginning to like, along with some stewed fruit.

"I am buying a ship tomorrow," I told her. The *Night Arrow*. Then I must purchase some tea."

"Do you have a captain? A crew?"

I sighed deeply, responding, "no," to both questions and adding, "Nor even as much as a packing case of tea."

She thought for a moment. "Captain Simon Searcher would be worth trying to find. He is a good captain and a man of his word."

I considered this and then asked, "Well, if he is so good, how come he doesn't already have a ship?"

Mrs. Jamieson poured me out another cup of tea. "Meester Faulkner, it is not for the want of capability he has no ship. The matter concerns a broken heart."

I was amazed and asked, "How come you ladies know so much about us men?"

She smiled at me with that look of a teacher trying to talk to a dim child. "Oh, Drew—if I may call you that?" I nodded hastily. "You have so much to learn. Just believe me and don't try to figure it out."

I scratched my head. "Foochow is a big place. How do I find him?"

She shook her head. "Now don't you be worrying your pretty head about it. Leave that to me. You just remember to watch your back."

I resolved to go back and see if Anton was awake and lively again and if he would agree to accompany me to the auction tomorrow. Then, I thought, an early night was indicated. As events turned out, I could not have been more wrong. I decided to take the sword stick with me. So, in my room, I took a few minutes to practice some of my fencing exercises. Maybe, I thought, the Bowie knife would help as well.

Anton had fully recovered. The guy must have had the constitution of a Clydesdale horse. "Of course I will come with you to buy your ship. So far, it's the closest I will get to getting out of here."

He did not offer me any vodka, which was probably an indication that he had a hangover or something else was coming up. I passed the something else on the way out, a beautiful brunette who spoke to me in flawless English.

As I was leaving, Anton called after me. "Julie will be our

chaperone, of course. That is, if she is up on time. My sister is not an early riser."

We arranged to be at the auction half an hour before it started. I set out for home, realizing that I was tired. When you get tired, you can get careless. I decided to take a short cut in the dark—*dumb, dumb, dumb.*

I had shot down an ally that opened out into a courtyard. Suddenly there was a figure in one of the ally ways—actually, five figures. I tried to turn and go back the way I came, only to find another figure blocking my exit.

"Well, boy," Caleb Bryant's voice mocked. "The Spanish have a saying that revenge is a dish best eaten cold. It's amazing what money can do. You are the only one who would bid against me tomorrow. Well, I want that ship. So I will remove the opposition. Then I can let Miss Oxford have the pleasure of a real man's company."

He proceeded to tell me what he intended to do to her, being a "real man."

Don't listen, I directed myself. *Get your back to a wall in the lightest part of the courtyard.* I drew the sword and the Bowie knife.

"Hey, boy," Bryant taunted. "Watch you don't cut yourself. Mommy wouldn't like that. After we've finished with you—even your mommy won't recognize you."

To say that I was scared was an understatement. And, yes, your bowels do feel loose in such a situation. Two of the thugs started to come forward. Suddenly, the thug who was blocking the ally screamed. A sword blade emerged from his chest and a figure shot past and joined me at the wall. "Hello, gorgeous." Meryl materialized beside me.

"Remember, honey," she said, correctly reading my amazement even in the dark, "you are tagged, not just in my heart. Bet you didn't know I was ladies' Olympic saber champ at the last Olympics."

I smiled—nerves make you do funny things.

Bryant commanded his execrable crew. "Rush them! What am I paying you for? It's only a woman."

If there was one thing I learned from this, it was never use the word "only" in reference to a woman. Two brutes ran at Meryl and two, including Bryant, ran at me. Meryl sidestepped one and ran him through. Her sword flashed and drew a weld down the arm of the other. He dropped his blade. I parried the one with Bryant, battering the handle of his sword stick down his nose. I spun around to face Bryant just as he turned to Meryl and ran her through with his blade. "That's for you, bitch!"

When you see something like that happen and realize the bad guy is getting away, something snaps. I slipped on blood and found myself behind Bryant. I drew the knife across the back of his legs. The blade bit deeper into one leg than the other and he swore at me. I hoped his ham string was cut. He wanted away badly. I badly wanted to finish him off, feeling a murderous rage that I would never have expected could exist within myself. But Meryl groaned. My first priority was to try to save her life.

Bryant limped off, snarling over his shoulder, "Better see to your girlfriend, boy."

I shouted after him in frustration, using profanity—which I almost never did. "Damn you to hell, Bryant! This isn't over!"

He vanished into the darkness at the end of one of the alley ways.

Meryl eyes flickered open. "You sound sexy when you're angry, darling." Her raspy voice testified to the struggle it was for her lungs to inhale every new breath. Her voice dropped to a whisper, "What is it they say in the films? They got me."

I cradled her head in my arms, feeling the warmness of her blood seeping into my clothes. "Don't you dare die on me, Meryl! You can't! You can't! You can't!" I barely realized that tears were raining down on her from my eyes. How could I realize that when I never cried?

A blood-stained hand reached up to caress my cheek. "I love you, gorgeous."

The time tunnel was not far away. It was her only chance. If she stayed here, she would die from infection and lack of advanced medical care. She had one chance to live. "I am taking you to the time tunnel," I explained, gathering her in my arms and gritting my teeth when she groaned in pain. "Darling, it's your only chance."

She grew limp and unresponsive in my arms, "Please, God," I begged as if I had some right to pray to a God I didn't even know existed. "Please don't let her die! Please, God!"

With Bryant and his men shunted, the streets were quiet and fortunately no one saw us. I eased Meryl's blood-soaked body into the seat of the time car. Then I admitted something that I had withheld even from myself. "I love you, Meryl! Live for me, darling. You must live for me!"

Briefly, her pain-shrouded eyes looked into my face. I kissed her gently. Her skin was smeared with red blood where it should have been white and her blonde hair was tangled and plastered to her cold, sweating face. "You are so beautiful," I whispered in wonderment as if seeing her for the first time. Perhaps, I was.

She managed a smile. "Bet you say that to all the girls!" Then she grew serious. She fought back the pain that rendered her nearly voiceless. "Drew, forget me. Do what you came here to do. Promise me, darling." Almost imperceptivity, I nodded "You must," Meryl insisted and new tears rained down my face and fell on hers, dislodging blood as I realized what an effort she was making to exact that promise from me. "But even so, Drew, I love you."

My pain and grief were so overwhelming that I wanted to crawl into the time car with Meryl and hold her into eternity, or wherever we wound up. But I had made a promise to my dying love. Instead, I set the switch, closed the door, and went out into the street to retch up my guts.

* * *

When I awoke the following morning, Mrs. Jamieson knocked at my door and informed me, "Someone found a walking stick they thought was yours, for some reason, along with a sword. A saber, I think. They said you had dropped them last night and told me to tell you that..." she paused to remember the exact phrase, 'the carrion had been removed.'"

I thanked her and left to collect Anton. The two of us headed for

127

the docks. Julie, as he had prophesied, was still asleep. Anton picked up on my quiet mood. "The wolf is strangely silent."

"Anton, if I told you, you would never believe me."

He chuckled. "Now, my brother, why should I not believe you?"

I faced him. "Bryant tried to kill me last night." I gulped a deep breath as the picture of Meryl's lovely face came back to me.

"Let me guess. He was not alone. He has the bravery of the wind. But—no. It is something else. Something has deeply hurt you. Maybe Lucy is not the only one who has a key to your heart. Let us watch our backs."

The auctioneer from the bank began. The bidding started at £11,000, and I finally silenced Bryant at £16,000. I had done it. The *Night Arrow* was officially mine.

"They say that fires can start mysteriously, boy," Bryant spat at me, hatred narrowing his mean eyes. "I hope she died."

I looked at him. Suddenly he did not scare me any more. Anger had replaced fear. So I shouted loudly, "Hey, Bryant—what happened to your leg? Cut yourself shaving?" Then I added in a lower voice, "I hope the wound turns putrid and poisons you."

Anton, who had been feeling neglected during this exchange, said to Bryant in a soft, icy voice. "There are many things that would burn nicely in your barque should anything happen to the *Night Arrow.*"

Bryant's companion, who had been standing just out of earshot, faced me. It was a face I was to regret having ever seen, although I did not know that at the time. James Lancaster, Bryant's sailing master, was later to prove the most evil man whom I had ever met.

"Come on Captain," he said to Bryant. "There's more than one way to skin a cat." His eyes were like the small, dead eyes of a snake, as if what motivated him was to see what evil he could conjure up. Before I had seen the last of him, I had learned that his capacity for evil was stomach-retching.

The tea auctions were due to start soon. I had the ship. Now I needed a captain. These men were legends—"White Hat" Willis, Captain Tobias Limeburner, James Moodie, and Joshua Slocum—

standing below the sails and masts of their *Moonraker* or *Cloudcleaner*, almost sniffing every change in force and direction of the wind. I must discover if Mrs. Jamieson had found Captain Simon Searcher. Time was beginning to be pervaded by the scent of apprehension instead of jasmine.

When I got home, Mrs. Jamieson had a bottle of champagne and was wearing her best beaming smile. "And am I addressing the new owner of the *Night Arrow*? A fine ship!" And without waiting for my answer, she pulled out the cork and filled my glass.

"Will you not have one, Mrs. Jamieson?"

She nodded. "I'll get my drinking thimble ..." After raking round a drawer she withdrew a thimble the size of a half pint glass. "Well," she philosophized when I looked surprised, "it's a special occasion. May the wind always dry out your peats and may there always be buttermilk in your bowl." After three thimbles, she hiccupped. "I have to get cookering," she said, Irish jigging around the room.

I managed to stop her with my question. "Mrs. Jamieson, did you manage to locate Captain Searcher?"

She looked at me, puzzled, before comprehension dawned on her slightly flushed face. She began searching the top of a desk. "He's gone to the moon, weeee..." And back to the Irish jig.

Okay, try again. "To what part of the moon has he gone?"

She looked at a piece of paper. "The Golden Moon. Doesn't moon sound like what a cow does—mooo. No moo, no milk. That's what they say. I have seen a silver moon but not a golden moon. I know that's why they called it that. So people will come to see what a golden moon looks like. It's in Divine Wind Street." She stopped jigging and added, "Cows get wind. Why, I remember..." then looking into her glass, "how do they get bubbles into this?"

Somewhat relieved that we were not going to get the cow story, I told Mrs. Jamieson that I would get something outside to eat.

She didn't seem offended. "Sure, do you not know it's no good outside? It's got to be inside before it does you good. Sure, you are a growing boy." She sat down. Her head hit the back of her chair and she fell asleep. I covered her with a coverlet and she broke into a gentle snore.

I left and went looking for Captain Searcher. Let's hope he was willing to take on the ship and a very novice tea buyer. I decided to take the Webley with me. I didn't want another horrible surprise.

CHAPTER 16

I found Captain Searcher at his meal, complete with a glass of rum with which to wash it down. He was in a vacillating mood.

"Captain Searcher, my name is Drew Faulkner and…"

He studied me. "You just bought the *Night Arrow* and now you need a captain and crew." He sighed deeply. "I am not the man. Sailing and a broken heart don't mix."

What do you say to that? I knew it wasn't a question of pay, which shot it right out of my depth. I attempted to persuade him. "I need a good captain—not just any captain. I can't afford to spend that much money on a ship and a cargo of tea, only to pass it along to someone who doesn't know what he he's doing." There was a long, awkward silence. "There is danger," I admitted.

He snorted. "There is always danger. You go to your bunk with it, you wake with it. It wraps itself round the helm and in every creaking timber." He pushed away from the table and went to stare out the window.

"It's not that type of danger," I said. "But two-legged. A captain called Caleb Bryant. He has threatened…"

Searcher spun around, looking interested for the first time. "Did you say Caleb Bryant?"

I nodded. "Yes. He has promised to stop me from getting home."

Searcher rocked on his heels. Then he returned to his table and slammed his fist down on the top. "Bryant and I are from the same town in Massachusetts—Nantucket." His voice sounded like it was being forced up through gravel. "Martha Slocum was my sweetheart. We were

131

engaged to be married until Bryant came along. He promised her everything until he got what he wanted from her. Then, when she told him she was pregnant, he laughed and said to her, 'What's done can't be undone. Besides, how do I know the baby's mine?' He shipped out. Martha killed herself. She was too ashamed to live. I didn't hear about it until later—when it was too late to save her. I would have married her and raised the child as my own."

He took a long, slow drink, then set the tumbler on the table with a thump. "You just got yourself a Captain, boy—and your crew, and the fastest run home, as God is my witness."

He was not drunk, for he had eaten a good meal, but there was a look of fire in his eye—a look of relief that at last he could do something about the pain that gnawed away inside him. I had my captain. Unexpectedly, I was beginning to think that God was real and that I would need His help to tie everything together.

* * *

There was a note from Sir Charles Gray. Could I call on him at my earliest convenience? I decided a good sleep was 'de rigeur' for functioning, so after breakfast provided by a somewhat subdued and embarrassed Mrs. Jamieson, I thought I had better see Sir Charles. And I guessed that I should also visit Lucy and ascertain her response to any approach I could make.

Additionally, I realized while I was going about chasing butterflies, my conscience over Mi-Ling was bothering me. The longer she was left in that awful place, the more danger she was in—not just from abuse—but also from sexually transmitted diseases. My mind did not have to spell out the details for me to realize how vital it was to get her out quickly. But first, I needed to find out if Lucy and Caroline were still willing to help me.

I sighed and shook myself. First things first—Sir Charles. When I arrived at his office, he was standing by a window. He pointed to a hole in the pane of glass. "Rifle shot. From across there by the looks of it." He indicated another building about four hundred yards from his window. They had telescoped rifle sights, had used them to serious effect in the recent War Between the States. Someone was trying to kill Sir Charles. I suspected it was because someone wanted to sell drugs and Sir Charles was rightly opposed to "that filth," as he called it.

"Thankfully, Captain, they missed—this time. Telescopic sights. What will they think of next?"

I looked at him, "I fear, Sir Charles, that it may get worse before it gets better." I looked around and asked where he thought the bullet hit.

He pointed to his book case and the second row. "Right in the middle of *Pride and Prejudice*. The book had absorbed enough of the force that the bullet had not harmed the bookcase. When I looked inside *Pride and Prejudice*, there was a minie ball. Evidently, Sir Charles must have put a lot of care into getting quality covers for his books.

"This could have been fired by a similar type of Springfield rifle as the one at the ball, only with a telescopic sight," I told him.

Sir Charles looked slightly lost. "Maybe the next time I will not be so felicitous." He had the look of someone who needed to go home to Wiltshire and write his memoirs. Slippers, sherry, pipe and grandchildren round him. Yet there was still that smoldering need for purpose in his life. He still had to be of use to his country. He walked over to his desk. "I heard you purchased the *Night Arrow* and that Mr. Bryant was not very content. In fact, you seem to have upset him."

I nodded.

"Then you will need tea," Sir Charles said. "If you accept my suggestion, you will hand the buying of tea over to my friend, Sen-shi Ivanovitch. Tea merchants may pull the wool over your eyes, but they will not do so with him. Taste is important, but taste that will still be there after a long sea journey. To find such tea requires the senses to be focused to the minutest degree. If Mr. Ivanovitch says it is good, then rest assured it is good. He will arrange it to be packed onto your ship, right down to the last catty box. He will obviously need to be paid for the tea, plus any gratuity you may see fit to give him." He paused, then added, "If anything unfortunate should happen to me, Willoughby will take over until my successor arrives from England. One last thing. Please get Miss Oxford home safely in so far as it lies within your power."

When I was nineteen, I had fallen in love with a girl from Finland named Soila. She had been tall. Like Lucy, she had owned cascading red hair that lacked the depth of color that Lucy's had, but her hair had been red enough for the sun to cause it to shine like antique copper. We were walking to the ferry for Sweden that left from Helsinki harbor when it suddenly struck me, "I'm not going to see you again." I just knew. Sometimes you just know because you know because you know.

Now I had that same feeling about Sir Charles, while at the same time hoping in my heart that I was wrong. "Please be careful, sir," I begged him. "Don't stand too near windows."

He smiled at me. "Thank you. But whether I live or die is in God's hands."

I left the building and started down the drive with a heavy heart. It was then I heard the shot. "Oh, dear God, no!"

I sprinted back up the drive and caught a glimpse of a figure on the neighboring roof carrying a rifle that looked like it had a telescopic sight. I pulled out the Webley and ran to the fire escape. The figure raised the gun and fired, missing me. I knew that if it came to close combat, I had the upper hand. I had to make up distance. Another shot rang out. This time I fired back. How could he get down from the roof? I had to block the most obvious route of escape.

There was a tree at the back of the house within jumping distance. I was relieved that with the Springfield he could only load one shot at a time. He was working back in the direction of the tree. Was there another way off the roof at the back?

Then I realized that there was only one place he could be. There was an ornate kind of roof garden with a sheltered pagoda. I could not keep firing in case I hit some innocent person. Just then, I heard girls screaming. Out from behind the pagoda James Lancaster came with his rifle slung over his shoulder and a knife held at the throat of a young girl. He smiled nastily. "Now, boy. Little missy and me are going for a walk down off here real slow and you can drop that gun of yours or else your posh friend, Sir Charles, is minus one granddaughter."

I held the gun directly at him and he continued to move backwards. He had to pass a corner where birds liked to congregate. There were a lot of bird's droppings, which when tread upon become slippery. He had not seen this yet. He was still taunting me.

When he slipped, he let go of the girl. She was her grandfather's granddaughter, spunky and quick-thinking. She rolled away from him right across the bird dung.

Lancaster regained his feet and a shot between him and the girl stopped him from grabbing her again. Instead, he headed for the tree and poised to jump. My bullet must have grazed his side, but he leapt and caught a branch and was down and away.

The girl, who had bird mess clinging to her long dress, looked at me with tears in her eyes. "I'm going to get in fwightful trouble for getting my dress dirty," she wailed.

I smiled at her and negated gently, "No, little lioness. I promise no trouble. You were a very, very brave girl."

She took off the white smock covering her dress. Her nanny came out, obviously greatly relieved to see her. I explained how brave she had been and Lady Gray also appeared. She was a handsome woman. She hugged her granddaughter tightly and smiled tremblingly at me. "Thank you, Captain Faulkner, for your courage and for saving Melissa."

I shook my head. "Lady Gray, if Melissa hadn't taken action and moved quickly when her chance for freedom came, I couldn't have helped her. She has her grandfather's courage."

Tears spilled down her face from fully watery eyes. "Charles is dying," she informed me.

I took her arm. "Please Lady Gray, I must I speak to Mr. Willoughby immediately. I know who is responsible."

She was a woman of steel and took me straight to Willoughby. I related the incident to him.

"Are you sure?"

I nodded. "Totally. The rifle will still be on the roof. It was James

Lancaster, Caleb Bryant's sailing master."

Willoughby thought for a moment. "We must inform the American Delegation. Mr. Bryant's ship is American territory, and remember, you are the only witness."

What about the attempted kidnapping of Melissa? There are two witnesses for that."

Leaving legal matters in Willoughby's capable hands, I went to see Sir Charles.

He lay in a room with his wife holding his hand. "Dearest," he requested, "please open the curtains. I do not want to go home in the dark to meet my King."

She hastened to open the curtains, then told her husband, "Mr. Faulkner is here, Charles."

He turned his head toward me and held out his hand. I looked at Lady Gray and she nodded, so I moved forward and took his hand.

"Several years ago we lost a son in an accident," he told me, gazing at me with eyes that struggled to remain open. "Richard was a beautiful boy and so full of promise. When we first saw you...you are so much his double, in character as well as appearance."

"Sir," I whispered, gulping back tears. "I am not worthy even to be related to someone like you. I wish I were. I wish I had your courage and character."

"Please stop calling me sir," he said, almost sternly. "You make me feel like a public meeting." I shuffled uneasily.

"What may I call you?"

Lady Gray looked up at me and mouthed one word, "Father."

"Father," I repeated somewhat hesitantly.

"Thank you." He closed his eyes and a smile stole across his face. "I never thought I would hear that again in this life from my son." He turned to Lady Gray. "Constance, the Russian medal."

She went briskly to his desk and came back with a box and handed it to me.

Sir Charles' words were labored. "Czar Alexander owes me a favor. If you produce this, he will fulfill his obligations. You or anyone who may have need of it.

"Remember me, Richard, but above all remember the Lord Jesus Christ. He made me what I am despite all my shortcomings. He can do the same for you. Trust Him. Talk to Him. He won't let you down. Promise me you will."

"I promise, Father."

His nod was barely perceptible. "Then I can go home."

"Home to the land of the dead?" I asked in horror.

"Oh, no," he said with peace like a tranquil river washing across his countenance. "I am leaving the land of the dying and going to the land of the living."

His eyes sought his wife. "Constance, I love you."

Her smile as she nodded at him held all the redolence and beauty of a bouquet of spring roses. "And I love you, dear heart, with all my heart."

Then the breath left his body. That quickly, it was over. Sir Charles was gone. Lady Gray said, "Thank you. I can never repay you for your kindness to my husband."

I shook my head. "For a man like that, I would die."

She smiled through her tears. "It's alright, Drew. Someone already has died for a man like my husband—and for all of us. Jesus Christ, Our Lord."

I left her bent over her husband's body, deep in mourning. Willoughby took my arm and led me to a small ante room. "You may need a little time to compose yourself before venturing out." He closed to door behind him. I fell to my knees and cried my eyes out.

CHAPTER 17

Willoughby had already contacted the Americans. I went to see Luke and was told, "Mr. Willoughby is with Major Piper now."

I was still upset. "Can we go in and pull that animal off the boat?" I asked. "I have a Bowie knife that will save the agony of a trial!"

Luke put his hand on my shoulder. "Calm down. We'll get him."

"Don't bank on it," I said through gritted teeth. "If I see him first—I don't care if he is one of your countrymen. I saw the look of terror in that little girl's eyes as he held the knife to her throat."

Major Piper came out of his office along with Willoughby. "Captain Carter, have the men saddle up. Twenty rounds apiece rifle ammunition, twelve rounds pistol. We will impound the ship."

Then Piper addressed me. "Captain you come along. You can be an observer. We do things right in the U.S. Army."

With alacrity, we followed his orders. Except when we got there, the *Allegheny* had gone and was just clearing the main harbor. It was a bitter, frustrating moment. Would they go somewhere else, or would it be like a great white shark—just out of sight, but waiting?

I had to tell Lucy. I found her at the school, teaching one of the classes. She looked surprised to see me, but far from unhappy. She called a break and we sat down to tea. "It's good to see you again," I told her. "But I regret that my news is of the utmost sadness."

She looked puzzled. "What is amiss, Drew? You look distressed."

I took a deep breath and was embarrassed to find myself yet again on the verge of tears. "Sir Charles was assassinated a short time ago."

She gasped in horror and disbelief, and unlike me, made no effort to stem her tears as I completed the story. "Lucy, he called me his son. He was perfectly sane. I'm not worthy of that. All I could do was take his hand. And he wanted me to love Jesus. I don't know how.

"The worst part, Lucy, is that I had been there visiting with him. I had only just left him. If I had waited another five minutes, I might have been able to prevent it. I know who shot him, but he got away, although I did prevent him kidnapping Melissa Gray."

She came out of her chair and knelt down to my level. Her clear green eyes looked into mine. "Not worthy? Drew, listen to me. You saved Melissa's life. You pulled the young boy out of the harbor. You saved Sir Charles' life the first time an attempt was made. You want to rescue the young Chinese girl..."

I couldn't help it. The memory of the last gallant memories of Sir Charles' life replayed in my mind and I started to cry again. Lucy knelt in front of me and put my head on her shoulder. "Hush, hush. It's alright, my poor brave boy."

I raised my head, "I'm so sorry."

She smiled, "Sorry for what? Tears that outwardly paint the colors of your heart? And now, you must get me back to Scotland. You know that's what Sir Charles wanted and if you will escort us, it is what I want too. And, yes, before you can ask me again, let me assure you, that Caroline and I will help you with Mi-Ling." She turned her head to one side in that quizzical look that I had memorized from the portrait. "Mmm...Papa? Yes, I think you will make a very good one."

I felt my face turning red. Caroline had joined us and had sat quietly through my account of Sir Charles' murder, reactions of pain, outrage and sadness taking turns playing across her face. But now, watching Lucy and me, a broad smile pasted itself to her lips.

"Lucy," I said after a moment, "Perhaps I have been thinking on too many things and have forgotten what matters. There was a song from my time which asked a question, 'Will you still feed me, will you still need me when I'm sixty-four?'"

Lucy considered me seriously. "If you commit yourself to love someone in marriage, it would not matter how old you became. For

139

me...should. Well, when... I mean, if he were here and he were to wonder about that, the answer would be 'yes.' That is if anyone did wonder—if that were the case. Uh...wouldn't you agree, Caroline?"

Caroline, who had not expected to be brought into the conversation, replied thorough a mouthful of cake. "Yes, Lucy. Of course."

It was time for classes to resume. As I walked past Caroline, she whispered, "Nicely done."

With a ship purchased and tea on the way, things must of necessity move quickly. Next, I needed help to get Mi-Ling out of hell. Luke was under orders and I could not see Major Piper agreeing to his intervention no matter how good the cause.

Anton might be more agreeable, but I needed someone who spoke Mandarin. I wanted to be sure that when I "purchased" Mi-Ling, the old fox—and that was being uncomplimentary to foxes—who owned the House of the Little Cygnets would not renege on the deal.

Anton was bored. I guess the place was getting to him. "I am rutting away here," he complained. "I will I never get out of here. In St. Petersburg, there is real life going on. Women. Balls. Hunting. And here I am in the land of noodles." He paused, then added sadly. "Without my wife and daughter—that is all I can look forward to now. The good time."

I had accepted the Russian medal Sir Charles gave me with the idea that it might help Anton return to his native land. But first, I needed his help here. "How can I get the young girl, Mi-Ling, from the House of the Little Cygnets?" I asked him.

His face bore a sudden resemblance to a vicious thunderstorm. "For God's sake, no!" Disgust underscored his horrified words.

"Anton, no! Dear God, not that! I want to adopt her. To give her a home and a chance."

He peered into my eyes suspiciously, then nodded his head, satisfied. "Good. You are serious." That I had no evil intentions toward a child apparently called for vodka, which duly arrived. "Just a small one," I protested. "That stuff is lethal."

Anton looked puzzled. "Lethal? What is this lethal?"

"It means it can kill you."

He laughed. "If you drink enough you may die, but your body will not rot."

Julie flowed gracefully into the room, looking as though she were in love. I did not flatter myself in thinking that I was the recipient. She had heard our scheme.

"How much are you willing to pay for her?" she asked.

I replied, "Three thousand pounds."

She thought. "Make it five. And he may not sell," she warned.

I stood up, all gusto and no brains. "Then I will take her by force."

She shook her head, the raven locks shining in the sun. "That is no good. The Chinese like to gamble. Get the money in nice, shiny gold, darlink, and offer to cut cards for her. He will know your cards by experience. If you lose, you give him the gold. If you win, you get the little one."

Anton looked at his sister with open admiration. "Of course! Perfect! You are a genius."

It was a terrible gamble. Suppose he wanted the best of three? Yet, it was the only legitimate way to get Mi-Ling out of there without the slum bucket snatching her back. If I had tried to force the issue, the Chinese dockers would not go near my ship. If I won... *Dear Lord, I must win!*

Anton agreed to come with me, along with the major-domo of the Russian delegation, Sir Charles' trusted Chinese friend, Sen-shi Ivanovitch. I wondered why I hadn't thought of him myself. Sir Charles had engaged him to help me purchase and pack my tea.

That evening at tea I told Mrs. Jamieson what I planned to do. "The good Lord is surely in that," she agreed. "Because it is a gambling debt, he will hold to it. I think you will find that he will want the best of three. Your nerve will be up to it. Just keep the picture of the wee lass before you.

"And Meester Falkner...Drew...since you have afforded me that liberty. She will need a whole lot of love and patience. She will need to learn to be a child again and to build up trust. You must be patient with her. You must prove to her that you are different and that you love her like a daughter."

I think she must have seen my brow wrinkle.

"Drew, if you can't really love her, love her like your own, you'd be as well leaving her there. If you were to break her heart again, she might not recover."

Mrs. Jamieson held no degree in psychology, but she was both wise and totally right. Was I ready to be a parent to a child—a child who was not even mine and who had been sprung on me half-grown already rather than as a baby that I could nurture and watch grow? Whether or not I felt that I was ready, it was something that I had to do. Mi-Ling had the right to childhood games, a good education, then eventually— marriage. She had the right to be married to someone she chose and to someone who loved her—not used and abused her.

Mrs. Jamieson put her hand on mine. "Drew, I'll not be knowing now what you believe, but with God, all things are possible. He knows your heart and He loves you. And He loves the wee lass."

Anton, Sen-shi Ivanovitch and I had arranged to go to the House of the Little Cygnets at ten the following morning. That night when I went to bed, sleep kept stubbornly out of my reach. Then I remembered Sir Charles' injunction to trust Jesus. I needed all the help I could get, even if it was help that I didn't understand. Slipping out of bed, I walked over to the window and said, "Jesus I don't know what to call You. I remember some of the Bible stories I heard when I was little and how You helped people. I am not asking for myself—but Mi-Ling is only a child. Please help me get her out of that place. And, please Jesus, give me a father's heart for her. I know so little about love—real love. But I have heard You called the Father of Love. So, please teach me, Jesus. Please help me to help her. Please, Lord. And I hope this is okay as a prayer, because I really don't know how to do it."

I went back to bed and fell asleep almost immediately. Before I knew it, dawn was pushing its way through the curtains imperiously.

Sen-shi and Anton came for me exactly at ten. Anton was very somber. Sen-shi predicted, "He will want three chances. I will explain, but he will not believe. He will think you want her for yourself."

"I don't care what he thinks. I just want Mi-Ling out of there."

Sen-shi directed, "You must have patience of the fox."

We got to the place and Sen-shi contacted the owner. He bowed to us and rubbed his hands together. "I get you young girls to have nice time with. They do what you want." A leer spread over his face. I had to control my impulse to wipe the leer off his face with my fists.

Sen-shi conveyed the fact that we wanted only Mi-ling.

"Three of you," the owner said, pointing toward a room. "I go get her. Other one wait here for turn. Two can go in at a time."

Oh, God, I whispered, attempting to control my rage. *I'm going to be sick.* I wanted nothing more than to take that leering rat and shove my knife through his heart. *Patience. Please, Lord! Help!* If I snapped and lost control, I would ruin Mi-Ling's chance for freedom.

Sen-shi explained that we wanted to buy Mi-Ling and we had an offer. The owner gave us his attention. Sen-shi went on, "Show him the gold. Open the bag." I spilled it out onto the table, 5,000 sovereigns.

"Cut cards for the child. If I lose, you keep the child and the gold. If I win, I get the child. Come. We are men of the world." I moved my hands in and out of the gold.

His eyes opened wide. He said something and Sen-shi explained, "He agrees to let the cards speak."

We handed him the sealed pack of cards. He opened them and looked at them, then nodded. One of the women of the house shuffled them. Anton decked them and the deck was put down in front of the child sex slave owner.

Sen-shi told him we would toss a coin to see who went first. I lost.

He cut the cards and cut the seven of diamonds. I cut the nine of clubs. One for me. He looked at the gold again and I responded by running my fingers through it. We cut the second time. Aces were high. He cut an ace and I cut a three. A big smile stole over his face as he looked at the gold.

One more. He cut the third time and cut a queen. I felt the pit of my stomach fall open. He leered at the gold and then at Mi-Ling. "Dear God," I whispered. "I could use some help." I lifted the card—the king of spades. Two out of three. "Thank You, Lord Jesus, for showing up!" I breathed.

Sen-shi emphasized the point that a gambling debt was a debt of honor and that the master of the House of the Little Cygnets kept his word. I put the gold back in the bag. Something told me we should get the girl and go quickly.

Mi-ling had a pathetic little bundle thrown out of the house behind her. We high-tailed it for Lucy's house. I promised myself I would never gamble again. I also knew that, in my time, shamefully, child prostitution continued. Victoria had been right. With just a veneer of respectability, we had learned nothing from time. The vulnerable were still exploited.

I tried not to think of the children left behind in the House of the Little Cygnets. Sometimes, it is all we can do to change one life. The real crime is in not doing anything.

When we arrived at their house, Lucy and Caroline took Mi-Ling. Lucy could speak some Mandarin. I got down to Mi-Ling's eye level. "What you have been forced to do will never happen again," I told her, hoping she understood. I had to keep the anger against the owner of the House of the Little Cygnets out of my voice to keep from alarming her. I didn't want her to think the anger was directed against her. "You are welcome in our lives."

Mi-Ling's eyes looked at me impassively. Why should she trust an adult when all she had received from adults was abuse? How do you teach someone to trust or love? It was probably easier to solve the problems of western civilization than teach an eleven-year-old victim to trust.

Lucy put her hand on my arm. "Drew, we will do our best."

I had to believe that their best would be good enough.

CHAPTER 18

I returned the money to the bank. Whereas the gambling debt would be honored, I didn't fancy being relieved of several thousand guineas by a gang of thugs. I had left the bank and was hungry. I needed some of Mrs. Jamieson's packing.

I was on the way back to the room when two Sikh policemen stopped me and saluted. "Sorry to trouble Sahib, but Vice Consul, the Mr. Willoughby, would like to see you PDQ," one of them informed me, saluting again.

He handed me an invitation that required an immediate response. "Of course, gentlemen. I will follow you."

One went on in front, the other fell in behind. When I arrived at the embassy, a couple of officials and Mr. Willoughby met me. "Captain Faulkner, Lady Gray would like to see you."

I replied that I was entirely at her disposal and was ushered into a room in what I thought was the private part of the embassy. Lady Gray, dressed in mourning, rose to meet me.

I said to her, "Lady Gray, if I had one wish it would be to see you dressed in any color other than that which you are wearing."

She smiled a gracious smile and inclined her head. "Drew, I have a service to ask of you."

"But of course, Lady Gray. You have only but to ask."

"Charles' funeral is the day after tomorrow. Sir James Hiram, the ambassador in Beijing, was to deliver the funeral oration, but he has been struck down with a sickness and cannot make the journey. I can give you details about his life and accomplishments, but would you do it in his place?"

I was staggered. No, I was floored. "But Lady Gray, I wouldn't know what to say…I…I…"

"Charles thought very highly of you. Indeed, he had the highest respect for you."

A man like that respecting someone like me? I remembered my English teacher at school. "Faulkner," he had delighted in telling me. "You are a useless moron. You will never amount to anything. You are totally useless. You know what you will be doing when you leave school?" He had come out from behind his desk and done an imitation of a street sweeper. "That's what you will be doing."

Lady Gray was waiting for my answer. "Of course, I will…Father would want that. But you must help me with a resume."

Lady Gray extracted some folded paper from a writing desk. "I took the liberty of presupposing your answer," she said with a fragile smile. "These are his honors and achievements—but these are on paper. Please, Drew. Bring out the man, what he was in his heart. My daughter Christabel approves of the choice of speaker. She is Melissa's mother."

"Is Melissa well?"

"Yes, all thanks be to God. She has recovered and keeps mentioning the 'winsome young man' who rescued her." I blushed.

There was a knock at the door and a voice inquired, "Mother, may I come in?"

"Christabel, darling, do come in!" She did. "We were just talking about you. Captain, this is my daughter, Christabel."

Christabel smiled at me and extended her hand. I put it gently to my lips.

"I wanted to thank you in person for what you did for Melissa," she said.

"Melissa really rescued herself," I told her mother. "She showed remarkable courage."

Christabel Gray, or Hunter as I later found out her married name was, had lovely grey eyes and straight blonde hair that she wore not in the usual ringlet style of the time. When I looked into her eyes, I fancied that I could almost see her soul. She lacked deceit. She was her father's daughter.

We sat and talked and when I asked her about her father, she spoke not of his degrees or honors, but of his kindness. "He would take Melissa out and tell her of the animals and of God's creation and about plants and trees. He painted the most beautiful flower pictures—not botanically exact, but drawn to please a little girl. Sometimes there were animals hidden in them and Melissa had to find them and try and identify them. She loved their game."

I had much of the picture I needed now, but I had to make sense of it—pull it all together.

I was feeling ravenously hungry by the time the interview was over. Mr. Willoughby stopped me on the way out and told me that my tea was being bought and stored, ready for loading. The job was nearly complete and Sen-shi would bill me. So all that was required of me for the moment was preparing for the funeral. I decided to send a report to Adrian in case they wondered what had happened to me.

* * *

The next day, Sen-shi called on me with the bill for the tea negotiations. He had sought to do much of it by numbers. The buyer was given a number and that way he could not be influenced by any rival. We set out for Parsons and Sons and a draught was given to Sen-shi on which he could draw to pay the individual agents and growers. The conversation got round to Sir Charles.

"He helped me get a start in tea buying," Sen-shi said. "Taking me away from hopelessness to a future. It is good when you give someone a future. Word like a wind-backed fire spread of how you risked many thousand pounds to set free a young girl whose parents had sold her. It took great courage. Now, she too, has a future. When it comes to loading your clipper, it will be done well."

It amazed me that anyone else knew about Mi-Ling. "Thank you," I said, too surprised to think of anything better or more original to say.

Curiously, he asked, "Are you going to adopt the little girl?"

"Yes, I would like to—hopefully along with the young lady whom I plan to marry if she will have me."

He thought and said, "It takes courage to be different. To think differently. To look beyond what you see—to look into the heart and not at the color of the skin."

"Sir Charles was like that," I supplied.

"Yes," Sen-shi agreed. "Just like his master."

"His master? But he was the one in charge."

Sen-shi raised his hands. "Yes, on paper. But he, too, was a man under authority."

"Yes, under the authority of Queen Victoria in London."

Sen-shi touched my arm. "Mr. Faulkner, Sir Charles' Master did not live in London—but in his heart and life. He called Him Jesus."

I was ashamed that I hadn't realized what Sen-shi meant without an explanation. It made me feel more inadequate than ever to deliver Sir Charles' funeral oration. We shook hands and parted.

I decided to go and see Lucy and Mi-Ling. Lucy and Caroline had told me that Mi-Ling had started eating, but she could not sleep at night. The girls had moved her bed into their room. Mi-Ling kept expecting the hurtful, dreaded visits from sick, twisted, evil men. She got up frequently during the night to use the toilet.

When I came to the house and she saw me, she ran to the bed and lay on her back. I was shocked. Lucy and I went to her and Lucy tried to explain to her that those days were past. Lucy knew some Mandarin, but the vocabulary of a child brothel had rightly not figured into her learning.

After it seemed that Mi-Ling understood—at least somewhat—I told Lucy about the funeral and asked her to accompany me. She pointed out that decorum dictated that if she went with me, Caroline would have to come, too, and that would not leave anyone trustworthy with Mi-Ling.

I went to see Lady Gray, but she was occupied. Christabel came to see me and I asked how they were. "Truthfully," she said, "it still has not sunk in. Yet, despite the sadness, I know where he has gone. So why should I be sad or afraid? We will meet again."

I admired her confidence, but I couldn't share it. Loss and sadness dogged me with every memory of the gallant Sir Charles Gray.

"I don't know how to ask this, but tomorrow, may I bring Lucy? It would give me moral support and courage."

She smiled. "Of course. She may sit in our party. It would be a pleasure. My father approved of the work she conducted through her school—to give the children an opportunity. We can send the two Sikh policemen to escort her."

A few minutes later, I took my leave, for the funeral was scheduled for eleven a.m. in the church. I had seen such funerals on television— but in those, someone else was doing the speaking. I found Lucy and told her about Christabel's invitation. Lucy was relieved and touched my arm. "I am glad I can be there for you. Thank you for asking me, Drew. Although in saying that, I don't know which one of us will be the most nervous! She added, "Caroline is willing to look after Mi-Ling." She smiled impishly at me. "In fact, if Mi-Ling is to be our daughter, we may have to fight for her. Caroline, I think, loves her as much as I do. It is wonderful to have the benefit of her wisdom and teaching."

CHAPTER 19

Mrs. Jamieson was waiting for me when I got back. "Drew, the *Allegheny* has been seen just outside the harbor limits."

Oh, heavens! It doesn't rain but that it pours. "Have any of them been seen in town, do you know?" I asked.

She replied, "My sources say that the second in command has been going round town with a guard of about six sailors."

Oh, boy. That was all I needed. I was the only witness to Lancaster's murder of Sir Charles and with my goose cooked, he would be free to move about. I was also the corroborative witness to Melissa's kidnapping. It would be easy for Lancaster to avoid the American Delegation—they didn't know what he looked like. I decided to move around during the day and only go out at night if necessary. I needed to tell Luke that the chance to impound his ship might still be there.

My first question to him was, "Luke, any word of your fiancée?" He smiled—which I expected to portend good news. "She was recaptured shortly after the Indians took her. The Comanche had also found whisky and decided to celebrate early. All it took was a couple of guys to get her out. Well, they were used to cutting out Yankee horses, so to get someone out when the guards were seeing double already was no sweat. Once she was out, the other guys attacked and that was it."

I didn't ask for more details. It was a hard, cruel time on the American frontier.

Luke added, "I'm getting to go home on the next ship out. I'm taking a command at San Antonio. That's in Texas. A big state. Lots of room. Lots of opportunity."

I smiled. "Congratulations! Will that include a promotion?"

He sighed. "That would be sure mighty fine. I'm thinking about leaving the army for the marines. I got a taste here for getting my feet wet. San Antonio's a fast-growing town, but getting your feet wet is not one of the main occupations there.

"Besides, the Marines seem to bring the best out in guys and I've had just about enough of hot and dry where your throat gets so parched the vultures even bring you water."

He stared at me. "Now, what's up with you, Drew? You have that 'I'm in trouble look and I need the U.S. Army to get me out of it.'"

I explained to him about my part in Sir Charles' funeral and about Lancaster and his coterie being seen about the town. He realized immediately that my life was in danger.

"Come on. We gotta go see the Major."

Major Piper listened. "Captain, your life is in danger. That's obvious."

Luke asked how far it was from the church to the grave yard.

"I think about two miles," I replied.

"You will be in an open Landau," Piper noted. "In that, you could not be more exposed on a two-mile drive." The clinical way the major explained things brought two words out of a tragic history that had not yet happened—Dealey Plaza in Dallas, Texas, where President Kennedy was assassinated some ninety-six years into the future. I was worried because in the cortege, and maybe next to me, could be Lucy. I was also concerned about the Gray family who had had enough of death to last a lifetime. If Bryant did cause Lady Gray's death, or any of the other diplomats, every ship in the British Navy would be looking for him. If one person were shot—me—and the perpetrator was not caught, then there would be no big investigation.

It was a daft idea. There was no way to obtain body armor quickly enough, but how thick or how thin would metal need to be to stop a bullet in 1867? We were not talking about a high-power sniper rifle, but rather a Springfield or Remington. I asked Major Piper, "Sir, could your blacksmith make me two plates of body armor, one front and one back that I could wear under a shirt? When he is finished, we could try firing a Sharps at close range and if it stops that, it will stop a Springfield Musket or anything else."

Major Piper nodded his approval. "It could work. We used it during the war."

I was picturing the Australian armor-plated bush ranger Ned Kelly, who nearly got away with his robberies until someone realized that his legs did not have any armor over them and brought him down. Time to go see the blacksmith.

The blacksmith was big and powerful, Mick Collins Finnigan, known as MC. Luke told him what was wanted and that it was top priority.

"Stoppin' a rifle bullet is it? Well, now there is a thing. I t'ink we can oblige you, Captain, but wearing this, sir, you won't be able to duck as quick as you normally might." He took some measurements and began hammering metal plate. Then he stopped. "Sir, if the armor fails to do its job, I promise ye yer money back. Me word on it."

We had a laugh, as he said it with a straight face. I thanked them and left, but first I had a pleasant job to do.

I visited Anton and gave him the medal that would gain Czar Alexander's pardon and get him home. His face was a picture—no, it was a masterpiece. "I—we can go home! Away from here! Out of this humidity back to where the wind sets the blood coursing round your veins—black bread, cabbage soup, good vodka and venison. The scent of the pine and birch tree. Clean cold water. Home…wait until I tell Julie! Thank you, my friend. Thank you so much. I can not repay you. Not ever."

I smiled at him and said. "Good! You can buy me coffee at *Starbucks*."
"Starbucks?"

I dismissed his question with a wave of my hand. "Long story— dosvedania."

I rested well. Mrs. Jamieson had Irishized some hot milk with some whisky, in portions of what I reckoned to be thirty percent milk and seventy percent 'purely medicinal' whisky. That was one of the things I had learned from several sources in China. With the use of whisky strictly for medicinal purposes, folks seemed to feel unwell more often, but to enjoy it more.

Anyway, I slept like a log and after ablutions and breakfast, I read back over my diary notes, which I had penned the night before. It was starting to turn into a good read!

CHAPTER 20

A carriage had called for Lucy earlier and she was waiting for me as I came into the service. Lady Gray entered on the arm of her son-in-law. She was dressed in white. That caused several gasps and the fact that she had come at all surprised many. She explained to me afterwards, "I was by his side for more than fifty years and I certainly was not going to leave him when I had one last chance to give him honor and respect." Understanding her husband's love for China and its people, Lady Gray wore white——the Chinese color of mourning. (I found out later that they stayed on in China and she wore white for a year and then returned to normal clothing.)

I sat next to Lucy and her party. I had been told that after the hymn *Who is on the Lord's side, Who will serve the King,* I would go to the lectern on which the Bible rested and deliver the oration. I thought everybody could hear my heart beating.

Sir Charles' name, decorations and honors were read out by the bishop. During the last verse of the hymn, Lucy had taken my hand and whispered, "Drew, just let your heart speak."

I squeezed her hand and got up, walking to the lectern. It seemed a long way away. I began, "Sir Charles was a man of vision, of determination and of faith. He never tired of seeking to make life better for those with whom he came into contact. He served his queen with courage and determination, often putting his life in danger. He tackled each task facing him with determination, wisdom and prayer. When he was knocked down, he got back up again and got on with the task facing him with renewed vigor. Yet, in that determination, he took people with him, seeking how he could bless even the lives of the most humble and noticing the smallest service—not with a patronizing nod, but with genuine heartfelt warmth. One minute he would be absorbed in the most complex diplomatic consultation, and the next moment would find him on his knees of the nursery floor drawing pictures for his granddaughter.

"You all know the stories about him and very probably the half has not been told. Yet in his faith he was like a child. He quoted to me Jesus' words in the Gospel of St Mark, 10:13, *Verily I say unto you, Whoever shall not receive the Kingdom of God as a little child shall not enter therein.*

"Sir Charles was a servant of his queen and a child of his King. He was a devoted husband, father, and grandfather. He was also devoted to providing love and care for his wider family in this nation of China..."

The rest of what I said, I quickly forgot. I stopped in front of Lady Gray and bowed in respect. I took the back of her hand, for in the front of her hand was a small card with four words written on it, "Thank you. Constance Gray." I carry it with me always.

I collected the body armor and put it on. I had to move very slowly and, in the heat, the straps that joined the two plates began to rub my shoulders painfully.

We moved out and Lucy and I were seated in a four-seater coach with two family members as we headed off to the escort of some marshal music. Lucy and I sat with our backs to the sun, which meant the other two had their eyes closed to block the glare. Lucy slipped her hand into mine. I thought the best chance for any marksman was after the carriage passed his vantage point, when he would not hit the driver but hit me. The driver was highest up, so to get me, the assassin had to look down over the people sitting opposite.

Luke's men were along the route, and as the carriages moved, the men moved up ahead of them checking empty houses quietly. The only sound was the creak of wheels turning.

We passed two oak trees. Suddenly, out of a bunch of foliage, I saw movement when there was no wind to account for it. A rifle protruded with just the site exposed. It was aimed right at me. MC had tested the armor and I remembered his joke about money back if it didn't work. Only now, I didn't feel like laughing.

I tensed, waiting for the gun to explode. I inched away from Lucy. I couldn't risk her being injured. Then there was a scream of terror. The rifle dropped and Luke's men were there at once. We traveled on to the internment and I was torn between wanting to pay my respects to Sir Charles and family, and wanting to see who it was who tried to kill me and what had caused him to scream.

After the internment, when the family started to move away, I stopped Christabel Hunter and her husband, explaining that I had to get back to see what had happened. Christabel's husband gave me his horse, offering to ride back in the carriage instead.

I got to where Luke's men had been and met Hank from the cave expedition. "They took him to the fort, sir. He's hurt bad."

"What caused the would-be-assassin to scream?" I asked.

Hank laughed. "I guess his boss forgot to tell him snakes climb trees. Funny thing is, he's from Scotland. When I got to the fort, the guy who's—dying said—'I am a ghillie from the Invercauld estate, trained for years in deer shooting."

That explained why he had been so well hidden.

"Then he said," Hank reported, "I found shooting people was more profitable. So I'm only getting what I deserve."

I hurried on to the fort and found Luke and asked, "Luke, do you have a chaplain here?"

"Yeah, Father Parish. Do you want to see him?"

"No, but he might," I said, indicating the dying ghillie.

The ghillie told his story, implicating Lancaster and Bryant, but he was a dying witness and would not be able to testify against the nasties. Meanwhile, word would get back to them that I was still alive. Then they would try again.

When I got home, there was word that the ship would be ready to sail in a couple of days. I hurried out to tell Lucy and Caroline and Mi-Ling. Someone had crocheted a toy animal for Mi-Ling and she held it close to herself, with gentleness and quiet joy. I thought of how many children who had been hurt or lonely would be helped by the silent ministrations of a Teddy Bear, drier of tears, hearer of fears and bringer of cheers.

"We must get packed," Lucy said immediately, displaying her practicality. "We will try to be as economical as possible since space is limited."

Bryant and Lancaster had escaped again, leaving behind some poor sucker to take the blame. What would happen when we set out on the sea? I doubted we had seen the last of them. What I didn't know then was that one of them would meet his end by entirely innocent hands.

After lunch, Mrs. Jamieson confessed, "Tis heartfelt broken that I am that you are leaving. But right glad that Miss Oxford (She said Mrs. Lucy Faulkner several times as if to gift fate with a helping hand.) is going with you as well as Ting-a-ling (her name for Mi-Ling)."

Without Mrs. Jamieson's help and encouragement, I would have been lost in troubled waters, struggling against the currents but still being swept further and further away from shore. I tried to explain that to her and thank her, but she brushed my appreciation away as if it had been spilled flour on the kneading board. "Tis nothing more that I have done above what me heart told me to."

Anton and Julie had passage out on the next Finnish ship and Anton had been given a house in Turku while a place was found for him, perhaps in Petersburg. It seemed that quite a few folks had missed him. What made me suspect that the greater number of hearts missing him would be female?

"If you get tired of a child," Julie told me more than once, "there is a real woman waiting for you here."

We exchanged addresses and I pointedly promised Anton, in front of his sister, that I would invite him to the wedding when I got Lucy safely back to Bellefield.

When I took Lucy to meet Luke, she seemed impressed by him. As for Luke, rescued sweetheart or not—he could scarcely take his eyes off Lucy. "Say," he told us several times as if the more we heard it the more likely we would be to consider it, "there are great opportunities in San

Antonio. Texas is a great place to start a new life. And much warmer and brighter than Scotland. Keep in touch. Write. Send telegrams."

Lucy and I looked at each other speculatively. A new life in a new land. That seemed inexorably to be our direction of travel. Now all we had to do was get home—wherever home proved to be.

PART 3

The Journey Home

CHAPTER 21

The *Night Arrow* looked tall and imposing as we came aboard. Our luggage bar, a couple of cases, had gone on before us. Now this was to be home for as many days short of one-hundred as could be managed.

It didn't seem like much time when you said it quickly, but Napoleon Bonaparte had left Elba in 1815, and had been defeated at Waterloo in just that length of time. I fervently prayed that we would not meet our Waterloo.

Much would depend on Captain Simon Searcher and the crew and the sailing master, Myles Connaught. It was Mr. Connaught who was to show us to our cabins. He was a friendly, open man, who took particular care to see that Caroline had all she needed. "If I can assist you Miss Harper, you need only ask." She smiled her thanks and her eyes lingered a little longer than normal, rather like a child with its first puppy.

Mi-Ling needed company. It would not have been wise to leave her alone. As bad as her life had been before, she now had to learn to interact with people just because they liked her, not because what they could get from her.

Captain Searcher met us. "I want underway as quickly as you please," he informed me. "We should be able to catch the tide and the wind would be in our favor."

A bit later I saw the Captain alone and said, "It looks like Bryant may be out here. The question is where he may attack, or if he has a cargo. He may have entered the race and even if he did not win, he would take great delight in trying to stop us winning, or just in stopping us."

Searcher nodded. "Understood. We will just have to wait and see."

Lucy joined us just in time to hear the last part of the conversation. "Will he never leave us alone? Give us peace?"

"Men like Bryant, Miss Oxford," Searcher responded, "live by pride, not peace. They do what is right in their own eyes and everyone else pays the price. But not this time if I can help it."

Searcher turned away and began to shout orders. We cast off and the tugs began to take us out into the flow of the river. The ship groaned and creaked like one who had been sitting too long and now found movement bringing life back into the joints. Once the wind began to kiss her sails she would fly. When the tugs turned away, the cry came to make sail and in a short time every inch of space had been taken up by the billowing, eager green sails, as we headed for the open sea.

This was the weak point in the whole plan. There was now no time tunnel until we made port. We were dependent on our own ability to deal with any crisis, from a rudder breaking to a pirate attack. There would be no way to call in backup.

Lucy said, "I'm going back to the cabin to rest. Mr. Connaught has been explaining the dos and don'ts of shipboard life to us." Then she looked thoughtful. "I've known Caroline a long time. I never realized that she was so interested in sailing."

I held back a laugh as I looked at her. "Yes. I wonder why? Or maybe, who?"

She sighed. "China has been good to me. I will miss it. Especially teaching. I was so fond of my students and teaching was so fulfilling. I suppose it didn't take a hundred days to get to China in your time?"

"This is my time now," I reminded her. "But it took twenty-four hours by flight."

She looked aghast. "Flying? In something that moved through the air? But, surely that's impossible! Especially to move so quickly."

I smiled at her. "Lucy we have a long way to go. I will answer as many questions as I can during the journey. For now, let's get underway."

I noticed a couple of the crew looking at her and I hoped they did not hold to the old superstition that women on board brought bad luck. I found out later, to my relief, that Searcher had checked with the men before they signed on and told them women would be on board as passengers. When the crew members saw me looking back at them, they returned to their duties, and there was plenty to do.

I went back to my cabin. What did you do for three months? It made waiting at the airport seem easy. This time there was no *Starbuck's* to fill in the time. I had some books, including *War and Peace*, and I was attempting to put everything that had happened into my journal and keeping it up to date. If it fell into German hands, I might have some explaining to do. I was also in close proximity to Lucy and that might be hard to keep cool over.

If Bryant showed up, boredom would be the least of our worries. I checked my arsenal, hoping that I had enough firepower to stop—or at least slow down—Bryant's ship. I remembered the grenade launcher. I also had to remember that damaging Bryant was one thing, but his crew might contain ancestors of future famous people. Who, for example, you ask? Well, gee, you got me there.

It would not be possible for Bryant to load the cargo from one ship to another in mid-ocean, certainly not the way the dockers in Foochow had carefully packed her. If Bryant managed to win the trust and support of the crew, then the rest of us might know nothing about it. "Remember, Captain," Lancaster had threatened, "there's more than one way to skin a cat."

We were well underway and a new chapter had begun. China had changed my life forever and after this journey, my life would change again. Although at this stage, I did not realize how much. I would miss Mrs. Jamieson and her cooking. I had put on some weight, so it would be down to the gym when I got back…except this was 1867 and there were no gyms.

Anton and the "Snow Leopard" were going home, but somehow I did not think I had seen the last of Anton, Julie, or even Luke Carter for that matter. Had Luke already left for San Antonio? I wondered. Had he joined the Marines?

I was heading back to Bellefield to marry Lucy, but I didn't think I could settle in Scotland in 1867. Was that the reason there had been no last name on Lucy's portrait or date of death? And there had been no picture of me. Where were we? Were we on a wall in Texas somewhere? "This is my great, great-grandfather and mother. They were from Scotland."

What about Meryl? I could get back to her via the tunnel, but could I? Surely I must cut my ties with one time or another. We were one hundred days from "make your mind up" time. Lucy was beautiful and gentle and she had real faith in God, something I had not even considered before. That gave her an enviable real-time strength. And there was Mi-Ling to consider.

How would Scottish society accept Mi-Ling? Lucy and Caroline would take turns taking care of her during the trip, but would she have a better chance in America than Scotland, if we did go there?

The events of the last weeks had made me tired. I needed sleep. We all did. But the question that came back again and again like a hungry stray cat was, could we outrun Bryant, pirates, and storms? Through my actions, Lucy, Caroline and Mi-Ling had been thrust into a long, uncomfortable trip, fraught with danger.

Captain Searcher found me to say that another ship had been sighted off the port bow, the *Sir Galahad*. That was a challenge to outrun, but at least as long as she was in sight, Bryant would not attack us. Witnesses might prove inconvenient from his perspective.

Now I had to devote time to getting my sea legs. They were something apparently that nobody could get for you.

The *Night Arrow* gradually found her pace. The crack of canvas, the strain of ropes pulling and easing, the groaning of wood and planking, and the shouting of orders joined the shipboard symphony to form what might have been a film sound track—except this was not a film, but real life. I lay on my bunk and the temperature began to drop away from the high humidity. I fell asleep.

I awoke to a knock on the cabin door. It was Caroline.

"Lucy is watching Mi-Ling," she told me. "The wee lass still hasn't

163

said anything yet." Caroline looked worried. "Drew, how is she going to manage in Scotland if she won't even try to speak?"

"You are both good with children," I said. "Have patience. Give her time. Just think of the pain she has come through—stripped of her childhood and being sold to that awful place."

Caroline went over to the cabin porthole and looked out at the endless, rolling water. "She has never known love. Never known the joy and comfort of getting a hug from a father who wanted nothing from her, only to love and encourage her. She said in a too-realistic voice 'aye quean yer ma ain flesh and blood ...'"

When I looked at her in dismay, she retorted, "Don't ask."

As the days passed, we ate together and played dominoes and 'chase the ace.' I read to them from *Pride and Prejudice*. It was not gripping excitement, but it helped the time pass.

"I wish Anton was here," I told them. "He could tell us tales of old Mother Russia, along with entertaining proverbs."

Lucy said, "What I keep wondering is what will happen when we find Bryant or he finds us."

"I don't know about sea-fighting. I leave that to the movie stars."

"Movie stars?" Caroline asked.

I nodded. "Yes. In the future, people will go to specially built houses to see moving pictures flashed up on a screen. Moving pictures that can tell the story of what happens in a book."

A twinkle came into Lucy's eye, "Why can't they just read the book?"

I laughed, "Oh, darling, the wonderful advances of science could not make much out of you. How can you live without a *Firecrest 200 station TV*?"

"Darling," she repeated as if in a dream. Lucy looked at me. Her smile had gone. The scientific interest and questions vanished. Then I realized what I had said. Out of the mouth, the heart speaks.

"Drew," she asked quietly with wonderment in her voice. "Did you mean what you said?"

We all have a need to be loved, and a beautiful girl like Lucy was no exception. My next words to her, I knew, could decide my destiny for the rest of my life. *Think*, I told myself. *Think and be very sure.*

Just at that point a loud cry sounded, "Ship off the port quarter, it's the *Allegheny.*

"Stay here," I warned the girls. Then I shot out of the cabin.

I joined Searcher on the quarter deck. He had his telescope to his eye.

"She is high in the water. I will wager she doesn't have a cargo."

"But she must have some weight on board," I reasoned. "Doesn't every ship need ballast?"

Connaught joined us. "She would have to trim her mainsail before she could beat up with us."

"Aye," Searcher agreed. "But this is cat and mouse! He is playing a game. Bryant likes to work on fear—to try to make you imagine all the things he could do."

Bryant shadowed us for five days, then he was gone. Perhaps because we were near Shanghai and there was a British Naval presence there and he did not want to be seen.

We made good time, if that was the right expression, and fell into the routine of the ship. I kept busy. Lucy, I was sure, would not bring up the terminology I had so heedlessly used—"darling"—unless I mentioned it again. I didn't.

I tried to talk to and befriend the hands, until Connaught came to me one day. "Mr. Faulkner, may I have a word?"

"Certainly," I replied. I was pleased to see his growing interest in Caroline, and she in him.

"It does not pay to get too close to the men, sir."

I looked at him in surprise. "I was only trying to encourage them."

He attempted the same measure of patience he would have afforded a small child. "Yes, sir, I understand. But it doesn't pay to get too close to the men. You will have heard the saying, 'familiarity breeds contempt.' They understand leadership and leadership, they respect. You are the owner, as they know. It is Captain Searcher who motivates them."

I nodded and changed the subject. "What do you think they will do if we find Bryant again?"

He considered and replied, "That's one question I'm unable to answer." He directed his attention upward. "Mr. Fairbanks, get that foresail loosed." Then to me, "Excuse me, sir."

I had no idea how soon I was to learn what the crew would do. For three days later, the lookout gave a shout that there was a man in a rowboat.

I ran to the port side and what had been a tiny dot gradually filled my vision. "We need to pick him up," I shouted to Captain Searcher.

"Mr. Faulkner, that will cost us time."

I insisted and the man in the boat was picked up.

It was a decision that I was to regret making and it cost us dearly. They got him up by a rope to which he had to cling. When the head came over the gunnels, I was looking into the face of James Lancaster— murderer and sailing master to Caleb Bryant. He stood upright on the deck.

"What are you doing here?" I demanded, fighting to control my anger.

Before I could do anything physical, like attack, he pleaded, "Shipmates, tis' right glad I am to see you. You saved my life. That poxy..." there followed a description of Bryant that covered every invective in the book and sounded entirely convincing.

"Where is Bryant?" Searcher asked.

"How should I know or care?" Lancaster replied. "He done this to me with no water, no food. Mates, I should have died if you had not come along." Lancaster was a good actor and a good-cat skinner.

My thought, which I did not voice, was that Lancaster was now a prisoner on our ship, so to speak, and could be delivered back to the authorities to stand trial once we won the tea race.

A couple of the others took Lancaster below. For now, my hands were tied and Lancaster knew it. He had made Bryant out to be the baddy and with that, all of Bryant's captains and officers.

Captain Searcher asked me to join him in his cabin. After we got there, he closed the door, clearly angry. "Mr. Faulkner, you may be the owner of this vessel, but I am the captain. I must ask you not to countermand my orders in front of the crew again. A ship has but one captain."

I apologized and extended my hand. "I'm sorry. I was out of order."

He accepted my apology. "Think no more of it." Then he scratched his head. "What could Lancaster have done to make Bryant react in such an extreme fashion?"

"Och," I replied," the man is on a hair trigger, but who would take over?"

"The second officer if he has one."

I considered this and said, "We may need to keep an eye on Mr. Lancaster. Yon laddie has a silver tongue."

"Yes, and don't you go into too many dark places in the ship. I don't want you making an involuntary trip overboard during the middle watch."

I agreed and went back to my cabin, checking to make sure the Webley was loaded. Then went along to the girls' cabin. Mi-Ling was asleep, thankfully.

"We've got James Lancaster on board," I informed them, to the accompaniment of startled gasps. "He's already started to convince the crew that he is a poor, hard-done-to Jack Tar, instead of the murderer that he is."

I handed Lucy the revolver. "Take this and guard Mi-Ling with it. If he forces his way in, use it!"

Lucy sat on the bed, still looking stunned. "Do you think Bryant is in the vicinity?"

"I shouldn't be surprised. I think this is a set-up, but I can't prove anything. He is a bit like a one-man nautical Wooden Horse of Troy, waiting the right moment." I looked round the cabin. "Where is Caroline?"

Lucy's nose crinkled and she smiled. "She has gone on deck with Mr. Connaught." She hoisted the revolver to the shelf above Mi-Ling's berth, covering it with a scarf. "I'll take care of it, I promise." She rubbed my arm in reassurance as I left.

I decided to carry the Bowie knife everywhere I went and to avoid dark corners.

CHAPTER 22

Ship board life continued in its usual routine and Captain Searcher seemed happy with our heading and speed. "We are making about two-hundred-fifty miles a day. Wonderful!" The captain was happy and the ship was happy—except for me. I felt like the specter at the feast. Lancaster went round doing his work but talking to huddles of men, two or three at a time. If I passed by them, they fell silent. Towards dusk one day Caroline came to find me. "Drew, Mi-Ling is gone!"

"Gone? She can't be gone. Did nobody see her leave?"

She shook her head, desperation tautening every line of her body.

Oh, God, where has she gone? I asked myself. I don't know what put it into my head, but I noticed the rope locker where ropes of all shapes and sizes were stored. I told the captain that Mi-Ling was missing and he and Connaught began an immediate search, with Caroline fast on their heels.

I headed for the rope locker, and then my blood ran cold. I heard Lancaster's voice and felt sick to my stomach. "Come on, my litt'l whore. Let's get them trousers off. You won't need them after I'm finished."

I ran as fast as the cramped conditions would allow. There was Lancaster and a half-naked Mi-Ling. Lancaster's trousers were down at his ankles and it was obvious he was about to begin his filthy practice. Livid with anger, I saw red—and nearly every other color.

"You filthy animal! You mongrel!" I shouted, pulling him off her.

Mi-Ling lay placid with the dead face of all abused children.

I hit Lancaster as hard as I could, bringing both hands over his ears, but I only caught one of them. While he was momentarily stunned, I grabbed Mi-Ling's trousers and tossed them to her. "Run!" I directed her, hoping she understood.

Then I focused my full fury on Lancaster. This time I kicked his back and I poured out every ounce of hate I had, every drop of venom, into the attack. I broke McTurk's rule of, "in a fight, never lose your temper."

Lancaster pushed past me, hitching up his trousers with hate in his eyes. He aimed a kick at me, which I dodged, and he was gone. "Coward!" I lashed after him, "You dirty, filthy, murdering coward! May you rot in hell!"

A groan from the tangled bed of ropes brought me back to my senses. Mi-Ling had either not understood my directions, or else had been too frightened to respond. I gently replaced her clothes and carried her to Lucy's cabin where I disclosed what had happened. Through gritted teeth, I added, "I have unfinished business."

"Drew, be careful, darling! If anything happens to you, we're all lost."

I made a quick mental review of McTurk's training. It seemed so long ago now. "I have to stop him. Now, after this, there is no other option. Lucy…God help me…pray for me."

I took her hands in mine. "Lucy, I love you. Marry me. Please?" I looked into her eyes and suddenly all my doubts vanished.

She, being wiser, still maintained doubts. "Drew, are you sure that you would not regret giving up your own time for me? Your own time and your own life and all you know? Even those moving picture screen things you talked about and that fast moving through the sky?"

I smiled at her. "Yes, my darling. I'm sure. Very sure." And inside, for the first time in my life, I felt a flood of peace as if my head heart and spirit had connected and signed a mutual agreement to hang together. "Oh, yes," I repeated. "Sure. So very sure."

She came close to me and her eyes looked into mine. She did not move nor try to avoid me when I kissed her. Then we fell into each other's arms.

"Took you long enough! Congratulations." Caroline, who had abandoned the search for Mi-Ling after hearing that she had been found, had slipped quietly back into the cabin. She hurried directly to Mi-Ling, enfolding her in a loving hug. She dropped a kiss on Mi-Ling's dark head, then released her and hugged Lucy, and then me.

Lucy's hair smelled like a spring garden. Just inhaling her fragrance made me feel slightly dizzy. Then as if her tongue had finally caught up with her mind, Lucy said, "Yes, my darling, Drew! A hundred times, yes!"

I still had to deal with Lancaster, but this time, I was not going into the fight angry. When I reached the deck, I heard part of what he was saying to the crew members gathered around him. Searcher and Connaught were being held prisoner, their arms twisted behind their backs by Lancaster's minions.

Standing on a bollard, Landcaster addressed them. "Mates, the ship can be ours. There's just six of them. Have your fun with the women and the little whore. This time you don't have to pay. Then over the side. The men you kill straight away. Don't forget how they work you to death. The women's yours for fun and games. I know a good captain, a real seaman, who'll take you anywhere and hand out fair shares of loot. Why, you play your cards right—you might end up with your own ship."

Lancaster had not seen me. I shouted, "Men is this the best you can do, this piece of filth that was going to rape a child as your leader? He's using you. How much of this do you think you will get to keep when Bryant and his cut-throats suddenly appear?"

"Lancaster promised us," one voice intoned.

"Have you sunk so low that you would follow an animal like that who would rape an eleven-year-old girl? Some of you have daughters that age. Would you like him to be banging away at them? When his keeper turns up, you will be dumped and you will have to face charges of mutiny and murder—hanging offences."

"Don't listen to him," Lancaster spat. "We can take them now! Who's with me?"

I pulled out my Bowie knife. "I have a knife that says he is a liar." To Lancaster, "Fight me. Square go. Kill me and the ship is yours."

The men drew back and Lancaster pulled out a long clasp knife. "That little whore," he taunted. "Bet you bin havin' fun with her. Worth it, was she?"

Anger ignited inside me as hot and fierce as a raging fire. Then I remembered McTurk's words, "Don't ever go into a fight angry, laddie."

Lancaster lunged at me. I ducked and spun around. He tried again. His knife caught me, dealing a glancing cut. Blood spurted out and some of the crew cheered. Spray flung itself over the side of the ship, wetting my shirt and the deck. That's when I broke *McTurk's Rule 4*: Check the floor, check your footing. When I lunged at Lancaster, he countered. I didn't see the grease on the deck. I slipped and fell back. My knife spun out of my hand and flew across the deck, out of reach.

Lancaster jumped me, pinning my arms to the deck. Just then, Lucy and Caroline were dragged out onto the deck.

Lucy saw the danger I was in and yelled, "Drew! No! Please, no!"

Lancaster spit in my face. "Ah, yer woman is calling for me and after I have finished with you, I will oblige her. You will be no good to her. She will need a real man with all his parts intact. Then she will have to find a new boyfriend as she gets passed round the crew, one by one."

Some of the men chortled. Lancaster's eyes looked glazed. He hooted in what could best be described as a satanic laugh. "Why don't we make him watch, mates?"

Two men forced Lucy down onto the deck. Just as they began to pulling up her skirt, there was an almighty explosion. A red hole appeared in the center of Lancaster's head. Briefly, a look of surprise stole over his evil face. He fell forward, halfway on top of me.

All eyes focused behind me. I turned to look.

Mi-Ling stood next to the Webley, which she had jammed into the rigging and fired.

Connaught twisted away from his captors and jumped up on a bollard. "Men tis' just and fair, but mutiny is mutiny."

Following Connaught's example, I jumped up as quickly as I could to a capstan and faced the men. "Men, get me to London first. Let me sell the tea and I will make the ship over to you. To the captain and crew. This incident never took place. Give me the tea and the ship is yours. Who is with me?"

One of the men shouted, "Aye, lads you heard him. We are not going to get an offer like that again." They perked up as if they wanted to cover their shame. Lucy stood next to Captain Searcher. She was shaking, but she was also praying out loud. I heard the words, "Thank You, Jesus."

McTurk had somehow managed to integrate himself as part of the crew. I looked at him with joy and disbelief as he approached me, "Aye laddie. You have got a bit brain in that head of yours. You owe that wee lass your life." Then he smiled at Mi-Ling and added, "Ach, but that is a girl after my own heart."

Mi-Ling remained silent and fixed beside the revolver. I went over to her and dropped to my knees, putting myself at eye level. She stared at me unblinkingly.

"Thank you Mi-Ling. You saved my life."

The big brown eyes filled with tears. She spoke for the first time. One word, a word that tore at my heart, "Papa." She threw her arms round my neck. Her body convulsed with sobs. Pain and hurt flooded out with the tears. "Papa! Papa! Papa !"

I picked her up in my arms. "Yes, sweetheart. Papa, Papa, Papa."

Lucy drew close and put her hand on my shoulder, wearing the teasing portrait smile. "See. I told you you'd make a good papa."

I turned to her in desperation and said, "But I don't know what to do!"

Mi-Ling's head rested on my chest. Her face held the most beautifully peaceful smile I had ever seen.

Tenderness replaced the teasing in Lucy's smile. "It seems that you are a quick learner."

Mi-Ling stirred. She reached out and caught Lucy's hand, then slipped out of my arms onto the deck. She took my hand and put Lucy's into it. Holding the two hands together, she closed her eyes, as if in supplication.

I smiled at Lucy. "Mama?" I asked.

We took Mi-Ling down to the cabin and tucked her into her berth. She was asleep in an instant. I kissed Lucy, then Lucy pointed to Mi-Ling's forehead. I kissed Mi-ling. "Good night my brave, courageous Mi-Ling."

That night, I was filled with the most wonderful joy. It spilled over into the pages of the diary. I slept like a log. But before my eyes closed, I had time to reflect that perhaps God was real. He certainly seemed to be greater than any "what if?" that life could slam us with.

* * *

It was some two mornings later that Lucy and I were on the quarterdeck. Two of the seamen approached us. I didn't recognize them, but Lucy did and drew back.

Embarrassed, they twisted their caps in hands held behind their backs. "Miss," one of them addressed Lucy. "Daniel and me don't know how to begin. Sorry seems a little word for what big thing what we put you through. The terrible way we treated you. We feel so ashamed."

"What are your names?" Lucy asked gently.

"Daniel Cavendish and Joshua Hemphill," they replied.

I was about to say something when I felt the warning pressure of Lucy's hand on my arm.

Joshua added, "Miss, we are terrible sorry and it's hard when you know you've done something real wrong. It eats away at you."

These were big guys. Lucy seemed small beside them. She gazed at them with compassion—not fear, hate or condemnation.

Daniel agreed. "An' my missus and my babies...I would be so ashamed if they knew." Tears fell from the big man's eyes.

Lucy released my arm, placed her small hands on their thick, muscular arms and said gently, "Joshua, Daniel, I willingly, with all my heart forgive you. We all need God's love and forgiveness."

"Miss, you will be perfectly safe on this ship—all of you," Daniel

173

hastily added. "We guarantee that."

Joshua nodded in the affirmative.

Lucy asked, "Will you make a ship in a bottle for me? I've always wanted one. And Mi-Ling would love it."

The two men brightened. "Sure thing, Miss. That we can do." They saluted and returned to their stations.

"You let them off lightly," I accused in my ignorance, almost angry with her.

"No, darling. Forgiveness is wonderfully liberating. It frees heart, soul, spirit and mind and allows one to see clearly and deeply."

I felt that she was likely right—perhaps with one exception—Caleb Bryant.

CHAPTER 23

That afternoon I went to the girls' cabin and knocked. Caroline opened the door with a smile and Lucy pointed to Mi-Ling.

Mi-Ling had been practicing. "Good morning, Papa."

I smiled. (Actually, my heart jumped for joy.) "Good morning, my dear Mi-Ling. How are you?"

She considered for a moment and said, "Happy. Happy to see you, Papa."

I looked at her with a mingling of love and joy, realizing I had been given the wonderful gifts of Mi-Ling's trust and love. I was determined to do the best I could for her.

Connaught came to the cabin door, seeking me. "The Captain would like to see you in his cabin."

Lucy accompanied us and Caroline and stayed behind with Mi-Ling.

Captain Searcher was pouring over his Mauray Charts. He pointed to two islands as we entered the cabin. "Between these two islands, Java and Sumatra, which are both owned by the Dutch, is the Sunda or Sundar straits, as some maps have it. There is an island there called Krakatau. That area has pirates. If I were intent on some kind of attack, that's where I would undertake it. If a ship got lost there, the pirates would be blamed whether or not they were guilty."

When I heard the name, I thought, *Who has not heard of the massive explosion of the volcano at Krakatau in August 1883? It's estimated that the tsunami from that explosion killed 30,000 people worldwide.* Then I remembered that this was 1867, not 1883, but rather some sixteen years before.

I wish I had a camera, I thought. *What a picture that would be at the local camera club!* Then I remembered that photography was in its infancy.

Searcher continued, "Pray for the wind aft of us. For once through there, it gets us to the Indian Ocean and from there it's 1,300 miles to North Madagascar and next landfall." He looked at me and added, "What we don't want is to become becalmed."

"Is that the Doldrums?" I asked, "Or am I thinking of somewhere else?"

He nodded. "Good. Near enough."

"Is that the only way?" Lucy queried.

"Yes, if you want to get home first. A lot depends on the pirates, but above all the wind direction. To the pirates, Bryant is a target as well."

"Yes," I admitted, "but he doesn't have 765 tons of tea aboard."

Searcher nodded. "All we can do is our best. The rest is in God's hands."

"God's hands," I repeated, rather surprised to hear him state that.

"Aye. God's hands. When you've been in the middle of a typhoon in the South China Sea, getting tossed about like a cork on the ocean, you get to be glad He's there."

"What Bryant doesn't know," I mused, "is the willingness of the men to fight. For now they will be fighting for what's theirs and yours."

"I only want half the captain's share," Searcher replied. "My ultimate satisfaction will be beating Bryant. Lord above! The look on his face when he realizes he can't stop us and he can't win. Aye, that will be payment enough." The pipe came out and he smoked quickly.

"You hate him that much?"

"Aye, that much and more. Besides, from what you've told me, it's clear that while Lancaster may have pulled the trigger to murder Sir Charles, Bryant loaded the rifle. Lancaster is paying for what he did already. Now I want Bryant to pay his share."

I noted that Lucy was silent, not urging the captain to forgive Bryant.

Searcher's eyes refocused on the past, as if a path had opened in his mind. Tears came to his eyes as he remembered the woman who still held his heart. The tears touched the cord of kindness in Lucy and I squeezed her hand gently to let her know that I would relate the captain's story to her later.

"Was Martha very beautiful?" I risked asking.

"She was the breeze that filled the sails of my heart. Martha was spring in winter. I only had to look at her and my heart sang. And when she was in my arms, I knew that dreams can come true." His face darkened. "Bryant ruined her and her name. If I had been there, I would have killed him. No, Mr. Faulkner, you are not the only one with a stake in this. Bryant and I have unfinished business."

He seemed to have forgotten Lucy and me, retreating into memories where only his foot could find purchase. But his face registered his determination to settle an old score and the resolve to carry it through.

Callous and nefarious as he was, Bryant had likely already forgotten Martha.

Lucy and I returned to tell Caroline what Searcher had said.

"We are all in danger," Caroline realized. She turned to Lucy. "But the consequences could be worse for you. If we are boarded and there is no escape, use the revolver."

"To kill ourselves?" Lucy asked aghast.

"No, Lucy, not unless absolutely necessary. To take out as many of them as possible."

"Darling, Caroline is right," I told Lucy. "You would likely be safe temporarily because Bryant is determined to have you for himself. But the others…"

The color drained from Lucy's cheeks. "Surely, it won't come to that!"

Caroline noted, "There are six bullets. That would take out three of them and still leave three for us. How does this thing work?"

I showed her the double-handed grip. "Pull the trigger and don't jerk it."

Meanwhile, we made good progress towards the straits. I was with the Captain on the quarterdeck. "One thing, Bryant doesn't know is who has control of the ship," Searcher said. "He doesn't know whether his pernicious plan worked, or not."

McTurk joined us. "Captain, may I make a few suggestions?"

Searcher was surprised and I intervened, "Captain, it would be worth listening to what Sgt. Major McTurk says. He is an expert military tactician.

McTurk asked me, "Laddie, do you have that Blooper Grenade Launcher to hand? If you do, now would be a good time to get it."

I went to the cabin and pulled up a couple of incendiary cartridges and loaded up, then returned to the bridge. McTurk continued, "Captain with your permission, if we see Bryant, clear the quarter deck except for two or three of the men and Miss Oxford. You and Mr. Connaught stay out of sight. And you, too, laddie," he added, indicating me.

"We must make Bryant think that his plan has succeeded and get him close to the ship." McTurk took the loaded launcher from me. "When Bryant's ship gets close and I fire this, the sails should burn. Slow them down enough. That should get us away out into the Indian Ocean, where it will be more difficult for Bryant to surprise us—at least during the day."

Searcher nodded. He and I were impressed. We got three of the crew on the quarter deck and let Lucy in on the plan. She had nerve, my Lucy-to-be. We tied her hands. She stood in the open waiting. We didn't need to wait long.

We had briefed the crew and told them to be sloppy in ship handling.

Bryant was on the deck of his ship, confident and cocky. Seeing no officers, he called over, "I'll rig up a buoy chair and you put the girl in it. She's the one I want. No doubt you're having fun with the other two. Where's the officers and where's Faulkner?"

McTurk replied in his best New England accent, "The captain's new command is a hang sight wetter than this command is, and Faulkner is feeding the fish."

"Where's Lancaster?" Bryant demanded.

"We took aboard some bad grub and he's got a belly ache. He's in the captain's cabin. The woman's with him. He said he was going first. The rest can have her after he's finished."

I watched from concealment. "Faulkner left something for you," McTurk added as the ships drew closer.

"What?" Bryant asked.

"This," McTurk said. He raised the Blooper and fired. The shell hit the sail and mast and it started to burn. McTurk threw the gun to me. I reloaded and came out of cover.

"This is for Sir Charles Gray," I yelled at Bryant. "You slimy, yellowbelly, bat-fowled coward!" I fired, hitting the foremast. It began to burn.

It was then we heard the watch in the crow's nest. "Three sails leeward."

We started to pull away. Bryant fired a revolver at us and we were followed briefly by sporadic rifle fire.

"Save your ammunition, Bryant," I warned him. "You're going to need it." Searcher had identified the Lateen-sailed ships as Malay Pirates.

We needed to make ourselves scarce. We opened up a good distance. Two of the pirate ships went for Bryant—his was the misfortune to be on a wounded ship. One pirate ship came after us.

The lighter ship would catch us. Our escape depended on whether the Malay had any cannon. The pirate Captain wanted the *Night Arrow* as a prize. The tumult of the fighting between Bryant and the two other pirate ships receded as we attempted to outrun the third ship.

McTurk said to the captain. "Sir, if a ruse works once, why not try it again? If we let him get closer, we can aim for his mast. He only has two."

Searcher looked at him. "Sir, I don't know who you are, nor what kind of weapon that is, but I am heartily glad you're not on the other ship."

McTurk leaned toward me. "I hope you didn't send back that Heckler & Koch yet. Best get it, but keep it covered. It may be that

179

Captain Searcher has had enough surprises for one day."

The Malays began to fire. They had more guns than we did and two of our crew were hit.

"Blast," McTurk said. "We can't afford to lose anyone." He pointed to the two at the wheel of the pirate ship and I fired, hitting both. With no hands on it, the wheel of their ship started to spin. It was at that point that McTurk fired the Blooper, hitting the Lateen mainsail. It started to burn even brighter and hotter than had the *Allegheny.*

The pirate ship was burning and was dead in the water. In the distance, one of the two pirate ships at the *Allegheny* peeled off, then followed by the other left the *Allegheny* burning, but not sunk. Pirates, Searcher explained, worked in families, protecting each other.

A thick mist crept up the strait, hugging the water and covering the *Allegheny*, leaving only flames visible. The pirate ships were coming together to support each other, especially the crippled one.

The wind picked up and Searcher took advantage of that to use every scrap of canvas *Night Arrow* possessed. We were into the Indian Ocean. The unspoken thought in all our minds was what serious damage had been done to Bryant's ship. We hoped against hope that we had seen the last of him—but like an injured rattlesnake crawling into the woodpile, there was always the possibility that he might turn up again and inflict venom without warning.

When I went to the girls' cabin and knocked, laughter met me. Mi-Ling and Lucy were playing a game, *Rock, Scissors, Paper.* You put your hand behind your back and on the count of three you bring out your hand either flat for paper, in a fist for rock, or with two fingers cutting for scissors. Paper wrapped up the rock, scissors cut paper and a rock blunted the scissors. Sometimes Lucy won and sometimes Mi-Ling won. One thing that caught my ear was Mi-Ling seemed not to be able to say "Mama" and instead said "Amma." Lucy tried to correct her. I intervened. "Leave it," I told her. "In India, Amma is a term of deep affection."

Lucy thought and said, "Yes, Amma. I like that. Amma," she repeated and Mi-Ling beamed with pleasure. They continued their game. The winner would play Caroline for the championship.

I left them to it and went to see Captain Searcher in his cabin. He poured over his charts and I remarked, "You're deep in thought, Captain."

He looked up at me. "Hmmm…Well, I'm trying not to be pessimistic and I hope that pirate ship and that bomb contraption of yours stopped Bryant, but sails can be replaced and re-rigged. He would need to make repairs not just to the sails and cables and rigging, but to the superstructure, as well, if it had been damaged. We don't know what crew he lost in the fighting, but what was left Bryant would push till they dropped. If he saw us first, he could wear up on us, then lay back 'till night time."

How could I tell the girls? I decided there was no point in telling them unless Bryant reappeared.

There was plenty of time to record everything in the diary I maintained so carefully, and even for poetry and other writing. True to their word, Daniel Cavendish and Joshua Hemphill presented ships in bottles to Mi-Ling and Lucy, both of whom were delighted. With her active imagination, the bottle entertained Mi-Ling for hours at a time. We kept an eye open for Malay pirates and for any other kind of pirate. We saw the clipper *Sir Lancelot* off the port bow, but got separated in a mist. We still had India to pass. After that, an attempt to sail around Cape Horn. We had come a long way, but still a long way to go. When we reached Arabia, we would have to be careful of pirates and slavers, but every day brought us closer to our goal. When Lucy and I married and Mi-Ling joined us, then what would we do? That question circled around my mind in quiet times like a pup chasing its tail and never quite catching it. Could I settle with becoming a Victorian country gentleman?

Sometimes danger pulls people together. But what would happen when the danger was gone and we were safely alone together? *Oh, Lord, I* found myself half-praying, *I wish someone would send me a postcard of what to do, even if we are still the middle of the Indian Ocean.*

The wind continued behind us and every sail that my layman's eye could see was filled.

CHAPTER 24

You can't know ahead of time what a day will bring. You can get too much thinking time. Life away from Edinburgh had been exciting. How many things that I had gone through in 1867 would have happened to me in 2000-plus? None. Not without forms, applications, risk assessments—a sepsis that had taken the challenge and risk out of life.

Would Lucy leave Scotland? Luke had painted such a glowing picture of the challenges of life in Texas that it made pioneering there tempting. It would be rough, but not any rougher than China had been.

The more the days passed, the more I began to realize that to go back to a safe 1867, to the life of a country gentleman, was not for me. I suspected that Lucy, too, would die of boredom. After we were married, I wondered how long it would be before Lucy got pregnant. I had to help Mi-Ling, but how would she fit into Scottish society? I wanted to adopt her, but I got the impression, somehow, that adoption might be easier in Texas. Texas was a new frontier with more freedoms and fewer conventions than Scotland.

I knew I must talk to Lucy about all these doubts. If we went to Texas, what would happen to Bellefield? Was that why there was no date in Lucy's picture there? Had Lucy become a rancher's wife? No, I guessed not, but she was a teacher and teachers on any frontier were as valuable as gold. Moreover, she loved teaching.

It was a hot day, somewhat alleviated by the sea breeze. So far we had been blessed—always with a good wind behind us. I had become well acquainted with the captain, and now I took the step of asking permission to come on the quarterdeck. He was the captain and it was his bridge. He was the inspiration behind the hard-working crew.

"The boys have done well," he said with satisfaction. "By my reckoning, we should be about two days in the lead."

This was good news, but sometimes problems could remain hidden. My granny used to say, "Don't worry about today what you can put off worrying about until tomorrow." Unfortunately, tomorrow had a habit of arriving right on schedule.

It was about fourteen days after we had sailed through the Sunda Strait when Connaught came to the Captain. "We seem to have a problem, sir."

"What is the nature of it?" Searcher asked. It struck me that Connaught could handle most things that cropped up and the fact that he was bringing a problem to the captain gave me a sinking feeling. I stood back and shut up and let the captain be just that.

"One of the water butts has been holed, Captain. It must have been during the fight."

"Bad?" Searcher asked.

"Aye, sir. The butt is near empty and that leaves one butt. To complete the journey in this heat I think we would need two and even that would get us home with a fair thirst in hand."

Connaught and Searcher trusted each other and each other's judgment implicitly. Even I knew enough to realize that water was the one thing we couldn't do without and expect the ship to run well. Working sails and rigging was a thirsty business in this humidity.

Searcher sighed and looked at me. "It looks like we need water."

"Yes," I replied. "But where can we get it?"

"We are going near Trincomalee, Ceylon. We can put in there."

"We should get water from a reliable source," Connaught warned.

"Right," Searcher agreed. "Let us make haste—fast as you like, Mr. Connaught. Note, too, anything else we need. Can the butt be repaired?"

Connaught affirmed that it could and we made haste. "Three-quarter ration of water, I think, till we get there—and pray to God we don't hit a storm."

Searcher was concerned about the effect of dusky Celonese maidens on the crew. But we needed the water, and there was always the continued incentive of finance for the crew if we won the race.

We managed to sail and to dock with the help of a couple of small boats. The place was thronging with loading and unloading. The British presence was near the harbor and I used Sir Charles' name which opened a few doors. We met Darjit Singh, a huge man. "If I can help you, Sahib, I will be pleased to do so," he assented. I asked him about water and clinked some gold coins.

"I personally will attend to your needs," Singh assured. "I will myself supply the much clean water. It will be at once taken to your ship." I paid him and asked for fresh bread as well and fresh flour without weevils.

"The flour is so fresh, Sahib, that it does not know that it has been ground yet."

Connaught, who was with me, wanted to stretch his legs. "It's good to get the legs going again and to get some exercise and feel firm ground under your feet," he told me.

"Yes, I still feel the movement of the ship when there is no movement."

He looked thoughtful, "Caroline is a bonny girl. My word, what a handsome woman!"

I smiled at him. "Yes, it has been noticeable that you two have been seeing a lot of each other. May I ask if there are any plans?"

"Do you think she would…"

"Marry you? I am not her keeper. The young lady very much has a mind of her own."

We continued walking. "I would need to get a post where she could join me on board," he mused. "I can't leave the sea and I won't leave her."

We climbed one of the hills overlooking the two harbors and a dock. The view was good until…"Oh, dear God no…" Connaught pointed.

It was the *Allegheny*. It had a small amount of scaffolding around it, but nothing that couldn't be cast off.

"C'mon," he directed, grabbing my arm, "back to the ship."

We came down the hill much more quickly than we had gone up. *Oh, dear God,* I thought. *Let Darjit Singh have at least finished getting the water aboard.* If Bryant were to spot us, we would be in deep trouble.

The jolly boat was waiting for us and it was a relief that financial constraints had in this instance overcome the desire for dusky pulchritude. "Quick boys, back to the ship and look lively," Connaught commanded.

We must have approached the *Night Arrow* at torpedo speed. The lighter had already delivered the water and was just leaving. Darjit Singh had kept his word.

We told Searcher what had happened.

"Did he see you?" He asked

"Not to our knowledge," Connaught replied, "but he could have had someone on the hills watching."

Searcher swung into action and began shouting orders. When he seemed satisfied at the immediate progress he said, "Well gentlemen, we will soon know!"

"We could have gone anywhere," I said. "Could it be more than just a happenstance that he turned up there?"

"Bryant may be a foul character," Connaught negated. "But he is a first class seaman and navigator. He knows the best route as any good seaman would—but Searcher also knows the best routes."

Lucy, Mi-Ling and Caroline were on deck trying to get some exercise. It was important to walk but also not to get in the way on an active ship. We strolled out to the Fo'c'sle, which was a short raised deck above the bow of the ship. The bow cut through the waves and dolphins raced along side, effortlessly matching the speed of the ship. Caroline, who had an amazing ability to think about three stages ahead of what I was going to say, sought to distract Mi-Ling. Lucy looked at me and asked, "Bryant?"

"Yes. He was in the harbor at Trincomalee. We need to get away as fast as we can. We need to make the assumption that he has seen us and

185

does know we are in the vicinity."

Mi-Ling and Caroline went down to the cabin. I walked Lucy back.

When we got there, Caroline was playing patience and Mi-Ling was following a passage from the Bible. She tapped the top of the Bible and said to Lucy, "Doesn't Father God say no fear, do not be afraid? He is big. He will take care of us."

Her faith caused Caroline to respond, "Yes, Mi-Ling you are quite right. God will take care of us."

It was not Mi-Ling's words that touched us. It was the absolute conviction behind them. I wondered if I had been missing something.

CHAPTER 25

I had to tell McTurk. I found him playing poker with two others. With the new orders, the game came to a quick end. It looked as if McTurk had been winning. "There are few things in this life more aggravating than to get a royal flush in clubs and have your opponent produce a royal flush in hearts," he reminisced.

"I remember one game back in Abilene in 1887, when I produced a royal flush in hearts and another at the table produced a royal flush in hearts. Such eventualities are amazingly sharpening to the mind." He grew serious. I was left with the impression that the poker player in 1887 might have come off worse than McTurk, who was still breathing.

"I don't suppose," I said to him, "that you have any tricks up that sleeve of yours should Bryant show up?"

He looked up his sleeve. "Well, laddie, let's say sequentially that first he has to see us, then he has to try to catch us, then he has to try and stop us. He's going to be cautious. He doesn't know what we can do and the next time someone drops a match in his wee boatie, the ensuing fire might not be so easily put out. Will caution outweigh revenge—or will revenge outweigh caution? The faster we get wind to canvas, the better. Oh, I went ashore while you were sightseeing with Mr. Connaught and got these."

He pulled out a box of what could only be described as primitive hand grenades. The fuse had to be lit, but as McTurk pointed out, "When they go off, it's not just a big bang."

Waiting. Waiting. If this were a computer game, you could speed it up—but it was real life.

Suddenly a vision of Texas played across the screen of my mind. It seemed a safe haven compared to where we were and what we were doing. A safe haven with land under your feet—even with the possibility of justifiably irate Comanche Indians as neighbors. I thought of the old Finlander Bar in Edinburgh and I seemed to have been away for months. When you have been on an adventure of a lifetime, it seemes impossible to go back to the status quo. I had done things in 1867, that I would not have been allowed to do in my own time. How could I go back to the quiet life and the mind-numbing boredom of "modern" day life?

If Bryant caught us, it could be an end to life—and certainly not quiet! Once we got back to dry land in one piece everything else would fall into place.

We still had to round the Cape of Good Hope, which seemed to me to be one of the world's most misnamed places, judging by the number of sailing ships that came to grief there. Searcher thought we had managed to make up time, but whether it was enough to give us the lead he was not sure.

Those were good days and we had done well to be without sea sickness, but one day the smell of cooking food from the galley reached us and it seemed as if we had been eating fish since time began. That coupled with syrup pudding, fried fish and syrup pudding twenty-four hours, seven days a week, suddenly hit Caroline and me. Lucy and Mi-Ling did not seem to be bothered.

There's an old sea shanty, "What shall we do with the drunken sailor?" Then the line, "Hooray and up she rises." In the song it referred to the ship. In real life it was the food, any food. Greasy food lay in my stomach like a U-Boat stalking a convoy and suddenly attacking. The heads were occupied and often Caroline and I supported each other in our joint misery, with what could be termed for 1867, "a distinct lack of decorum," although Connaught came to the aid of his beloved when he could.

Our state brought some amusement to the sailors. Harbinger, the sail maker who had an amazing ability to keep his glasses perched on the end of his nose, ran me up a hammock. "If things get bad, sling it up and sleep in it," he said kindly. "That way you move as the ship moves and you won't feel so bad. Try and give yourself plenty of fresh air, sir."

I would have tried anything.

One time Lucy and Mi-Ling came up on deck after lunch to see how the invalids were and Lucy decided to enjoy herself at our expense. "You missed yourself, Drew," the minx said cheerfully. "Lamb stew and bread and butter pudding. What's that word you use when you like something? Yummy. Mmmm. Definitely yummy."

Caroline looked at her friend with a distinct lack of endearment and headed for the side with an "awwwwgh," that might have been Mandarin, but probably translated into, "for pity's sake, change the subject."

We passed the clipper *Charles W. Morgan,* as we bit through the foam. Two days passed. Then came a call from the watch, "Deck, there's a ship off the port quarter."

"Can you identify her?" Searcher shouted back.

"It's the *Allegheny*," I said.

"It's the *Allegheny*," came the cry from a long way above us.

Suddenly my sea sickness vanished and even Caroline started to get color back into her face again.

Then resounded another call from the watch, "Deck there. Sail off the starboard quarter."

Searcher shouted up; "Can you identify her?"

There was a brief silence. "The American clipper, *Martha Washington*, from Baltimore" came the reply.

"She's got a cargo," Searcher said.

McTurk noted, "Perhaps our help has just come. The *Allegheny* flies the American Flag even though it's a travesty. We fly the British Flag. If Bryant attacks us, he will not want a witness. Once he gets Miss Oxford off the ship, as far as he is concerned, what you can't carry away you destroy.

"Captain, can we keep pace with that ship?" I asked. "It may be our opponent, but it is also our shield. Are we not the faster of the two ships?"

"Yes," Searcher avowed. "If we trim sail, we should be able to at least be level with them."

So there we were, two rivals traveling together, the *Martha Washington* to starboard with her surprised master Captain Kildonan. Searcher knew him and said he was a good master. Kildonan had seen the *Allegheny* and when she kept pace with us, he must have wondered what was going on. He must also have noticed that the *Allegheny* sat high in the water and had no cargo. If you are sailing with an empty ship, you have either been somewhere or are on your way to get a cargo. Either way, time is money and you want to get to where your next pick-up point is as fast as you can—unless you are up to no good.

I could see Bryant and he was not looking happy. I have to admit the thought that we might be keeping him off his sleep didn't upset me, especially when the picture of Lady Gray at the funeral sprang to mind.

Captain Searcher asked McTurk and me to join him in his cabin on the third day after Bryant seemed to have gone. He offered us a glass of port, which we declined. Captain Searcher didn't take any either. "Gentlemen," he said. "We have Madagascar and the Cape coming up." He looked at me and said, "You must remember the journey round the Cape on the way out. Well, it's probably worse on the way back. We have to beat up the coast of Africa and pray the wind keeps up. We have to remember the conditions that affect us will affect every other ship as well."

McTurk and I walked back along the deck. "I don't suppose you have any gizmo for finding out if we are being shadowed or not?" I asked him dispiritedly.

He thought for a bit, then replied, "Sometimes, laddie, such a thing as old-fashioned greed may be useful. When you were in Trincomalee, I went poking about. I visited a couple of the bars and passed on the information to any listening ears that if a ship called the *Allegheny* came in, it was carrying Chinese silver and silks. They were not to tell anyone because it was a secret. And then I brought some people a drink to ensure their silence.

"'Shipmates,' says I, 'I would get into terrible trouble if it was

190

found out that I had said anything. They said they would all be rich men when they got to America."

I looked at him with heightened respect. "So the hunter becomes the hunted?"

"Hopefully, yes. It just takes time to filter through to the right people. He beamed at me, assured of success. "So all we must to do is wait and let human nature take its course." He disappeared below decks as an increasingly confident Mi -Ling joined me.

She put her arm through mine, scanned the horizon and then asked, "Papa, can Mi-Ling stay with you and Amma always?"

"Dear One," I told her. "We will be here for as long as you need us. One day in the future you may be a wife and mother. I and Amma Lucy will be proud grandparents and I shall be very old and have a long white beard and very wobbly legs and you will have to catch me in case I fall."

"Papa, I know what you do for Mi-Ling. Mi-Ling will always be here for you. Heavenly Father is always here for you, too. He is good. Not bad like in the bad place."

"I am very proud of you, Mi-Ling," I told her. "After we get to Scotland, we may be moving to another land called America."

She thought with her heart. "Then you and Amma Lucy and Mi-Ling and Carol Lady will be strangers together in a new land." She took in a deep breath and said, "I can scent it. The scent of home. Home," she repeated with confidence, "home."

Gradually the sky began to darken and the wind grew in intensity. Connaught came to us, "Better batten down the hatches," he advised. "Not to be indelicate, but I would keep the lids on the chamber pots in your quarters."

I never realized that there were so many shades of gray. The sky was the color of my old school house roof. Much of our time was spent in attempting to keep our balance as the wild tossing on white-crested waves was different from the side-to-side swaying that brought on sea sickness. That being said, the smell of food began to be less appealing and less prevalent as galley fires had to be reduced. The number one fear on any sailing ship was fire. A fire fanned by a breeze could be the end.

All these technical points I knew, but was caring about less and less. Thunder roared and lightning flashed. How sails were lengthened or shortened in these conditions was a miracle, but somehow, they were. Waves came over the gunnels and out through the limber holes interspersed along the length of the ship. In the calm and smooth days, limber holes seemed unimportant. Now they proved their weight in gold.

My stomach shared with Caroline's a feeling of being in three separate parts of the ship.

The cook who went by the name of Nehemiah Famine (Honestly— he said his father had a sense of humor and had always wanted to cook.) and looked as though he was careful to sample his own creations before passing them onto the crew, was upset at the change in routine. It was also obvious from his bulk that he did not have the same physical activity in the rigging to carry out, but he took his job of supplying food on schedule seriously. "There is too much water getting into the galley," Famine complained. "The galley keeps shrinking." Still, even hampered by storms and rough seas, he did provide some good warm tucker for a hungry crew whose physical exertions burned off every calorie with which he supplied them.

I was in my hammock and at least the swinging motion helped to stop the inside of my head from feeling as though it was getting thrown about. Connaught came to my side. "Drew," he said, and his voice seemed to come from miles away. I think I replied in best BBC English, "Awwwwwwish," which translated into, "Apart from the fact I am dying, I'm fine. What do you want?"

"There is a sail to starboard a long way out. It's the *Allegheny*. He may not have seen us," Connaught said encouragingly.

"Ohhhh," I said discouragingly. The way I was going on you would have thought that I was the only person in the world to have ever been sea sick. The trouble is that when you are sea sick, you feel as if you *are* the only person in the world feeling that way. Well, I was. All the rest were malingerers!

I got up. At least, what there was left of me that was alive got up.

McTurk kept his balance well and was scanning the horizon through a telescope. "Laddie, you have to learn to be patient. There is a possibility she is being shadowed and remember, it only takes six or seven big jewels to make piracy worthwhile. Once you get aboard, you never know what else you may find."

When the lookout announced three sails, one was the *Allegheny* and the other two were dhows, Arab gun boats that were taking one big chance. If the British Navy caught them, they would be shown no mercy.

Searcher cried out, "Reef top sails."

I worried that we might slow down too much, but from the extreme distance between us, they might not have seen us as a clipper. Then a mist arose and we were sheltered.

The weather was still foul. "Safe until the next time," I remarked.

"Aye," voiced Connaught, "But when will that be?"

Then we hit the Doldrums.

CHAPTER 26

McTurk had had that look on his face—the best way of describing it was grim resolution. "I don't know about you," he said, "but I am getting tired of this cat and mouse game."

Searcher, Connaught and I looked at him. "What do you mean?"

"We need to take the fight to him. If you were him, what would you least expect us to do?"

"I hope you don't mean surrender," Searcher said dryly.

"No, of course not. I mean, he wouldn't expect us to attack him. At least, carry out a commando raid on him."

"A what raid?" Searcher and Connaught said almost simultaneously.

McTurk explained. "Commandos are special soldiers who specialize in attacking behind enemy lines. The secret of their success is anonymity and nobody knows where and when they are going to strike. You see where they have been—or at least, the enemy does."

We looked at one another and my mind went back to the raid in the caves and the damage it caused the Germans.

McTurk continued. "I think that if the wind decreases, Bryant will pull into an anchorage and wait until the wind rises. Then he can easily catch up with us. You can have an anchorage, lift crew morale, and you never know what interesting diversions you may find.

"One night, when there is not much of a moon, two of us slip up with muffled oars, attach a bomb (He looked at me in such a way that I knew he meant what I had left of the Semtex.), and blow up his rudder. And if we can get on board, blow up one of the masts. Two or three of these hand grenades, if they were tied together, could do damage—split the mast if not bring it down. If we can get it to fall to damage the rigging on the main mast and get away, then we beat it out of there and head for home. It would take a while to repair the mast and a while to jury-rig a rudder. Would you be wanting to take any chances when you don't know if the rudder will stay attached?"

"How do we find him?" I asked.

"That's the problem," McTurk admitted. "Captain, where would you go in the midst of Doldrums if you wanted good food, entertainment, and a chance to strengthen your crew for one last push against us—yet you wanted to keep an eye on everyone so you can get them together at a moment's notice?"

Searcher put his hands behind his back and paced the deck. Stopping suddenly, he replied, "Saldanha Bay. About one-hundred-eighty miles north of Cape Town. It has the largest and deepest anchorage and he will know it. When the wind picks up to a point that he feels he can maneuver the ship as quickly as he likes, he will be out. It's still a race and he still wants to stop us from winning. We can locate him. Then the rest is up to you."

When Lucy found out about the commando raid, she was not the happiest of bunnies as they say.

"Drew, you were nearly killed before and they caught you. Bryant will kill you if he catches you."

"If we don't stop him, then he'll keep coming back. We have to hope that Captain Searcher knows his enemy, and that we get away and get you—get all of us—to your house in Bellefield."

The wind died down, but we had reached Saldanha Bay. There was just enough wind to move the ship in the calm.

We were there a couple of hours when the *Allegheny* sailed in and gradually reduced sail until they anchored. We were hidden back out of sight and watched them from the top of a hill.

We called a council of war in Searcher's cabin. "We must strike tonight," McTurk said. "We can't afford any more time."

"That's true," Searcher agreed. "We are going to need every good going wind we can get to get home first, and Divine Providence, as well."

"One boat," McTurk directed. "Muffled oars. We time our arrival for the middle watch, probably between 2:00 and 3:00 a.m. At that time, the watch is commanded by John Branson."

"Who is he?" Searcher, Connaught and I asked, nearly in unison.

McTurk answered, "One of the good guys. The folk I work for got him on Bryant's ship about a week before Sir Charles' murder. To them, he is a British Navy deserter who has a rope waiting for him if he is caught.

"Sir Charles was aware of a big drugs' trade—much more going out than was thought. Bryant is trying to build up a drug circle in the American cities. Increase the opium dens and add more sinister and easily hidden forms of the drug. That's why Sir Charles was murdered. But we need to get John off the ship.

"We have the grenades and we have a version of dynamite called Semtex. We attach that to the rudder and use the grenades to try to damage the mast. We can't sink him or else we become pirates. There is nothing more self-righteous than a crook and murderer who knows how to use the law."

"Then...?" I asked.

"Then," said Searcher with a sigh, "we move and stop for nothing."

That night we planned to set off. McTurk estimated twenty minutes to row to the *Allegheny*. We were counting on the men having drunk a good bit and that John Branson was still undercover. The Semtex could be detonated from a distance or with the aid of time clock. The grenades we had to deploy the old-fashioned way with a lit fuse and hope that no one saw it. It should go off first and divert attention away from the rudder before it blew up.

As it headed towards evening and dark, someone turned butterflies loose in my stomach to torment me. "Suppose...suppose...suppose..."

I grabbed McTurk and demanded, "How do you know all this?"

"Micro-transmitter, laddie. Great wee gadget. Johnny is going to try and lower a rope near the stern, so I hope you are fit for some rope climbing—or have you been too free with Mr. Famine's puddings?

"Remember: the idea is to get on and off as quickly as possible and try not to get into a fire fight. He would not credit us with such action, but if he sees us—we're in trouble." He paused, "We are technically pirates."

"Right, let's do it," I decided. "Anything within reason for peace. I promise never to complain of inactivity again." I tried not to let my imagination run away with me. Maybe some sleep would be a good idea. On the other hand, my brain had to cooperate as well—which at this moment it refused to do.

Covert operations in 1867 still needed the elements of silence, speed and success. With McTurk, that was almost guaranteed. With me, my track record was not exactly alpha-plus. We rowed, not in a rowing boat which would have been white, but in a rubber inflatable dinghy that McTurk had in his kit. It was dark green, low on the water and was easy to propel despite our weight. It was also big enough to hold three, giving us room to pick up John Branson.

McTurk warned me not to splash. "Smooth strokes as silently as possible," he ordered. I realized the reason behind his order when halfway there, just visible by the light of the moon, a triangular fin cut the surface of the water. McTurk reassured me. "Don't worry, laddie. He is just curious. Just checking. Let's give him a few minutes to get bored and move on."

Remember, reader, this was not imagination or a film set and 1867 sharks had real teeth. What slid past me in the water was real—and seriously big.

It sounds stupid, I know, but the thought that passed through my mind as he slid past was, *I wonder if he has already eaten today?* Funny what you think of when you are scared.

I heard McTurk's soft voice calling time with the paddles. The *Allegheny* swung into view and we kept in the shadows. The ship was quiet with just a voice or two singing, rather like drunken clockwork toys that needed wound up again. A rope hung down at the starboard side of the stern of the ship. We paddled to the rudder, being able to reach one of the locks into which the rudder was slotted. The timer,

McTurk whispered to me, was set for forty minutes. He then pulled my sleeve and pointed up the way with a sense of urgency. We could not afford to lose track of time. McTurk went up first and when I came up, a second head had joined him. I could not see the figure clearly and when I got to the top, both McTurk and Branson had headed for the rear mast and started packing the bombs round it with the fuses rolled into one. A light showed from the open door in one of the cabins and a figure emerged.

"Everything okay, Johnny?"

"Yeah. Fine. Nothing that some rum wouldn't cure. Still, if I can get off the ship tomorrow, I can find me a woman on shore."

The speaker finished his cigarette, then headed for the door, tossing the cigarette stub on deck. It rolled, and as he went back through the door, the fizzing started.

"Come on," McTurk said. "Move!"

Branson grabbed a bag and we headed down the rope. I jumped in the water, praying for real this time, "Please, God—keep the sharks away!" We pushed off and the dinghy caught up with me.

"Come on, paddle, laddie," McTurk whispered. I counted twenty-five strokes, then the mast blew up.

"Don't stop," McTurk said. "Keep going. Your life depends on it."

We pushed further out into the dark. The *Allegheny* was a hive of activity. We decided to wait in the dark for fifteen minutes. Then, bang! The rudder erupted in orange flame as the time pencil went off.

We made it safely back to the *Night Arrow*. I was the last one leaving the dinghy. Suddenly, the surface of the water churned and the shark came out of the water and right across the dinghy.

Man! I went up that rope faster than you could believe!

The sails erupted on the *Night Arrow* and our deck became a hive of activity. The wind had picked up slightly and we did not want to be around when dawn came. We saw the *Allegheny,* not sunk, but partially on fire.

Suddenly, orders stopped flowing. When I turned around, John Branson was standing by Captain Searcher with a gun to Searcher's head.

"That's fine, gentlemen," he said in a cold voice. "Let's just stay nice and steady or you won't have a captain. Now, Angus, drop that blade you carry up your sleeve onto the deck and kick it over here—gently now."

McTurk obeyed. His eyes never left Branson.

"Now, gentlemen, here is what we are going to do. Miss Oxford and I are going for a little paddle over to the *Allegheny*. Bryant has promised me ample recompense for getting him the love of his life. Some jewels, when taken back to 2012, will sell for a great deal of money. I will disappear out of your lives. Your Captain will come with us just in case we need his help in sailing the ship."

"Ah, Johnny," McTurk said. "So they got to you?"

Branson shrugged his shoulders. "Business is business."

Lucy had waited up to assure herself of our safety. Unfortunately, she chose that moment to wander out on the deck to see if we had returned. When he saw her, John Branson smiled broadly. "Now, Miss Oxford, if you will join me? Oh, yes. I have one other task to do. I have been told to shoot the little whore, justice for Lancaster's death—such a nice man.

"So, Mr. Faulkner, if you will go and get her?"

I didn't move.

"Go on," Branson said, "She will never know what hit her."

Still, I didn't move. My feet felt like they were tied to the deck.

"Let me make this clear, Faulkner," Branson snarled. "No dead girl, a dead captain. I'll count to three."

"You murdering..." but before I could spit out the profanity that had risen up in my mouth like bile, I felt the gentle pressure of Lucy's hand on my arm.

"The girl now...one..."

Oh, dear God, what do I do? How do you combat a murdering thug with a flawed sense of injustice?

Mi-Ling was asleep. Caroline, who was reading by candlelight, looked amazed when I entered the cabin without knocking, even more amazed when I went over to the bed and gently shook my daughter awake. "Mi-Ling, I have to take you up on deck."

"Drew! What's wrong?"

"Everything," I told her. "There is grave danger. There are hostages and he wants Lucy and Mi-ling or the captain dies."

"Dear God, help us!" Caroline exclaimed, clasping her hands across her chest.

Mi-Ling said in a sleepy voice, innocently trusting, "Mi-Ling come with you, Papa."

"Take her, Drew," Caroline said, laying a hand on my arm and kissing the top of Mi-Ling's head. "But walk slowly—no! Don't ask. Just do as I say."

May you never be put into the situation I faced. I had no degree in psychology. If I could have died in Mi-Ling's place, I would have done it in less than a heartbeat. But I was leading my loving, trusting daughter to her death. To be murdered by a calm nut case.

When we came out, Branson, Searcher and Lucy were visible from the cabin door. The gun was at Searcher's throat. Branson quickly switched his knife to the captain's throat and pointed the gun at Mi-Ling. "You are a little whore," he told her in a scathing voice. "You're no good and you murdered my friend."

McTurk's eyes had never left Branson. He was waiting for his chance. But, oh, Lord Jesus, would he get that chance in time?

Branson's calm voice droned on as if he enjoyed the sound of his own voice. "So, little whore, here's the deal. I am going to execute you for…"

At that moment, Caroline walked out on the deck as naked as the day she was born. "Come on, boys," she invited in a saucy voice. "Who's next?"

Her diversion was just enough. Branson looked and McTurk moved.

Lucy fled from Branson. McTurk grabbed his blade from the deck and freed the captain. Branson and McTurk fought, a karate battle back to the bulwark on the port side of the ship. Branson side-stepped McTurk's lunge. McTurk just caught his grip as he went over the top of the bulwark.

"Angus, laddie, never loose your temper," Branson mocked. He hammered at McTurk's fingers in an attempt to loosen his grip and force him to fall into the waves below.

Then a lash of rope from the rigging came over the top and hit Branson across the face. McTurk's arm came up and Branson flew over the side of the ship. He hit the water and began to swim. As quick as he was, the white shark was faster. We heard a garbled scream, then silence.

Connaught took off his jacket and covered Caroline. I heard him telling her that she was a real-life hero.

We all gathered around Mi-Ling and hugged her and told her how good and brave she was. It was the only antiseptic we had to fight infection from the wound that Branson's heartless-soulless words had caused. Then Lucy and Caroline, taking turns hugging her, took Mi-Ling back to the cabin.

The *Night Arrow* began to flow with life. McTurk stood on the deck. "Is it cold or is it just me?" he asked. "Everywhere that Bryant goes he causes death and misery. He would have had Branson shoot that little girl. That is unforgivable—and all for his own ego."

"Hopefully we've done enough—at least to stop him," I said, realizing that I was still quaking from Mi-Ling's close call. "We owe you again, Angus McTurk. Thanks." Then through the dim light I saw his swollen fingers. "Are your hands okay?"

"Still got five fingers," he answered nonchalantly. "I'll see if Mr. Famine has got any ice. If Caroline had lacked courage, Branson might have killed us all. And that's a plucky wee lass you have, laddie."

"I couldn't have dealt with Branson alone," I acknowledged.

"No, laddie. He was out of your league, but you have come on in leaps and bounds."

"Thanks, Sergeant Major. But as my teacher used to write on my school reports, *Room for Improvement*."

McTurk went off in search of ice.

I went to thank Caroline. Caroline was fully dressed, but clearly in shock. No 1867 female would have presented herself naked in public. A man counted himself fortunate to ever see a glimpse of anything below the knee!

Mi-Ling lay with her head on Caroline's lap. Her face was stained with tears. Caroline was stroking the girl's hair and repeating, "Peace, Mi-Ling, peace. You were a brave girl."

"That goes for you, too, Caroline," I told her. "Thank you. We owe our lives to your courage and quick thinking. McTurk says nothing else would have saved us and I think he's right."

A tear rolled down her cheek. "But what will people think?" she whispered.

"What they already think. That you are a remarkably brave and courageous woman. We all know we owe you our lives. Look at Mi-Ling. She's thanking you in her own way."

"But Myles…"

"Myles will love you more than ever," I assured her. He is telling everyone how brave and courageous you are right now. He's repeating it to everything that stands still long enough to listen."

Mi-Ling sat up. "Papa," she asked, "can I thank Mr. McTurk?"

I lifted her off Caroline's lap and held her in my arms, hugging her tightly and kissing her cheek. "In the morning, Angel. Right now we all need to get some sleep."

Lucy hugged me. "I hope we've seen the last of that evil man."

"I hope so, too. All we can do now is wait."

After I left the girls' cabin, I remembered the shark gliding past my boat and how Branson had not escaped. "Thank you, God!" I exclaimed loudly, unashamed of who might hear me. I was beginning to believe that God was real. That might be a flawed deduction, but why take chances in case He was real?

CHAPTER 27

The journey home. But when we got home, everything would change. We had been through a lot together. Everyone had played a part in getting the ship this far. Some parts had been less or more dramatic than others, but it had taken everybody working together. I thought the worst might be behind us until we hit one more major obstacle, a thing that frightened every sailing ship—fog.

From North Africa, on north, fog could happen at anytime. It could be local or it could cover a wide area. In 1867, there was no global positioning system or helpful shipping forecasts. You could navigate, but you had to be good. What you could not account for was any stray ship passing by. This is where time could be lost or made up.

Fortunately, it was possible to hear in a fog and you hoped and prayed that the lighthouses along the way were functioning. Before lighthouses had become automatic, it had taken a three-man crew to run them. The Fresnel lens had just been invented. It boasted the brightest light. I was not the only one on board hoping for as many of these as possible. I kept reminding myself and Searcher kept reminding all of us that what slowed us down could do the same for others. While that was true, it also meant that any clippers who had not had as good a start as us could catch up. They could be making headway in fog-free waters a good bit south of where we were.

The important thing was to keep going. The greatest danger was at night.

Apart from Lucy and Caroline, we needed as many eyes as possible. Mi-Ling had different ideas about what she could do and hear. She was younger than any of us and her vision was excellent. All she had to do was warn us. In return, we tried to keep her warm. I stood watch with her and it was amazing what she could hear. She would point out into the fog. "Ship, Papa. I hear." Sometimes the rest of us could see nothing. Not all the ships were tea clippers. After nearly every warning Mi-Ling gave us, a ship would glide past or be seen in outline.

McTurk, who was his usual sanguine self, said, "That wee lassie is worth her weight in gold." The two of them got on like a house on fire. After the incident with Branson, Mi Ling had thanked McTurk the following day. She had stood on a capstan and as he went past said, "Thank you for saving my life, grandfather," and put her arms round his neck.

Since then, he and Mi-Ling had become good friends. Love changes people. McTurk used his skill and strength to teach Mi-Ling self-defense, amazed at what she already knew. If I had not wanted to adopt her, I'm sure McTurk would have. Or perhaps even Myles. Mi-Ling had become a favorite of the entire crew.

No matter how much we tried to keep it out of our minds, we were not sure if Bryant would turn up again. He couldn't prove that we had blown up part of his ship, but he knew it. And we had no idea of how much damage had been inflicted on his ship—or on him.

Searcher kept us on the ball. This was his time. He took advantage of every blast of wind, spreading canvas to catch every breeze, and taking risks in the fog. Taking risks was part of the life of a successful captain. Other captains who had lacked courage to take risks, or who had hesitated at the wrong time, were at the bottom of the Bay of Biscay. Connaught described it as "a real mean piece of water."

It makes me feel seasick just remembering. We slowly ploughed our way north. In the distance, and a good bit astern, sailed the clipper *Ariel*. We had seen her fading in and out of sight for several days. Like us, she was on a swings and roundabout sail—gain sea, lose sea.

One of the key positions on ship was the helmsman, or as was sometimes the case, the helmsmen. They kept the ship on course, following any changes in course that the captain ordered, a point here, or two there. We beat up through Biscay in really rough weather and a certain amount of fog.

Suddenly, from out of nowhere, another ship cut across in front of our bow, sails flapping. It wasn't the *Allegheny*, but big enough. It was only the alertness of the helmsmen and some prompt action on their part that the *Eglantine* did not cause considerably more damage to us. The helmsmen turned to starboard, risking the danger of heading for a lee shore, but the spanker sail (the very back one) caught round our bowsprit breaking, but not sheering it. That was bad enough. We had lost what Captain Searcher called the flying jib, the furthest out sail over the bow. It now blew loose and with that, the wind began to drop.

Searcher and Connaught worked like Trojans. The crew was magnificent. The chippy earned his wages ten times over in trying again and again to repair the bowsprit.

Caroline, Lucy and I planned what to do when we landed. The tea would be auctioned, ours first if we got home first. We would get the banker's draft from the sale of the tea and travel to Aberdeen and out to where Lucy could get her estate, Bellefield. It would take nearly a week to get there by coach, or shorter by train for as far as the train went.

All this was academic if we didn't stay ahead of *Ariel*, who was dogging our every movement. Thousands would be lined up to waiting to see who would be first and second and wire the results back to London. If we won, Captain Searcher would have pulled off a wonderful feat of seamanship.

Searcher saw *Ariel* and said to us, "*Ariel* is a fine ship and Captain Keay is a supremely competent master. They won last year's race. We can't let up."

In the cabin, Mi-Ling asked a flood of questions about her new home and her new mum and dad. When Connaught came to the door, he looked nervous, glancing first at us, then at Caroline. He was twisting his hat in his hands.

Appraising the situation quickly, Lucy said, "Drew, Mi-Ling and I would like a turn around the deck. Would you come with us, darling?"

Dumb me. "Won't Caroline want to come?" I objected.

"Not this time, darling," Lucy replied with that quizzical portrait smile that did strange things to my heart.

"Yes, Papa," Mi-Ling said, taking my hand. "Tell me about Scottie Land."

What follows is what I wrote down in my diary through details Caroline recounted.

"Caroline," Myles said. "We will be back in England soon, and I hope, safely."

"Yes, Myles."

He took a quick turn around the cabin and whirled to face her.

"Caroline, everything that I held dear in my heart, everything that is important to me—apart from God—has been turned upside down. I am a seaman who loves the sea, yet I know that my life is empty or it was empty before you came into it.

"Caroline, I love you. I love you because you are beautiful, unique, brave and special. If I spent the rest of my life searching, I could never find another you. Somehow, I have stopped breathing on my own and your name has become the air that I breathe. I go about the ship holding conversations with you in my heart and listening for the sound of your voice and laugh.

"When I am with you—it is only then that I feel complete. Caroline, there is no other way of saying I love you with all my heart except to ask you to marry me. I can get work on board ship where you, as my wife, can come along. So, Caroline, will you marry me?"

After Caroline told me all this so that I could write it down in my diary, I'm afraid to admit that my remark was, "So, what did you say?"

She looked at me with that look that women have for a man who is particularly dimwitted. "Nothing," she said.

"Nothing!" I exclaimed.

"Not a word. I just let my lips and arms give him his reply."

They announced their engagement before we landed.

I turned ownership of the *Night Arrow* over to Searcher and the crew, as I had promised, writing a letter to that effect. We agreed to let a lawyer seal it when we landed.

The bowsprit was repaired but *Ariel* had drawn closer. *Ariel* did not draw much water, but *Night Arrow* drew less, a fact known to the builders. At the time, I had wondered why Captain Searcher had enquired about that. Now I knew.

As we streamed past a cheering throng at the Lizard Lighthouse in Cornwall, we were just ahead. Something had happened to slow the *Ariel* down. As we gradually pulled away from her, we saw *Sir Lancelot*, under Captain Keay's command, sailing in behind.

We were towed into Tilbury. The place was alive with cheers and shouts. Mi-Ling was in her element. She loved the excitement.

Searcher found me and said, "We left Foochow on 29th of May and it is September 5th—exactly one-hundred days."

"Well done, Captain! I owe you much more than a ship! And if it had not been for your skill, we certainly would not have made it."

Connaught joined us and Captain Searcher looked at him and said, "I do believe that you have been the most blest recipient from this trip, Myles. It is my belief that your mind will not be on things of the sea for some little while."

Connaught looked like an embarrassed ten-year-old. "Aye, Caroline is really something grand."

"Caroline Connaught has a lovely ring to it," I noted.

Connaught's hand went to his mouth. "Bless me! A ring! I don't have a ring. Goodness, I have to get ashore…"

We laughed and slapped him on the back. "Relax, Myles," Searcher told him. "The race is over. We won! We can all go to shore."

Lucy, Caroline and Mi-ling joined us. There was a look of awe on Mi-Ling's face. "Ohhh," she kept saying, along with something in Mandarin.

"What's she saying?" I asked Lucy.

"Well, dearest one, it depends if she is talking about you or about London."

"Come on, don't tease."

"She is saying, 'wonderful, wonderful."

The gangway lowered and a gaggle of men came aboard. One in a brown suit came up to us. "Well, well! Which one of you is Mr. Faulkner, the owner of the *Night Arrow* and how do you feel on this wonderful occasion?" A battery of notebooks flipped open, ready for my words.

"We are glad to be home safely and we give thanks to Almighty God for a safe return," I said, surprising even myself with the sincerity of those words. I added, "And, speaking for all of us, we hope there are a lot of thirsty people who are waiting for tea."

That earned laughter and applause.

Mr. Brownlow of *The Times* looked questioningly at Lucy, Mi-Ling and Caroline.

"May we be introduced?" He asked, doffing his hat.

"My fiancée, Miss Lucy Oxford, and her companion and now-fiancée to Myles Connaught, sailing master of this vessel, Miss Caroline Harper."

Mr Brownlow looked at Mi-Ling and then back at me. "And this young lady?"

Mi-Ling looked at me shyly and I was suddenly back on deck, Mi-Ling, standing next to a smoking revolver as Lancaster fell dead, momentarily wearing a surprised expression that he was not immune to death after having inflicted death on so many others without retribution.

I placed my hands on Mi-Ling's shoulders and stated proudly, "This young lady is my daughter, Mi-Ling, and she is a blessing from God. I can safely say that without her I would be dead right now. Now, please excuse us, gentlemen. It's been a long time on ship and we have business to conduct."

I got down eye level with Mi-Ling. She threw her arms around me and said, "I love you, Papa." Her face broke into a big smile.

Angus McTurk came up to me and said, "I'm going to look after the tea and I will get the draft for the money into your hands. Stay at the Palace Garden Inn. It's far enough away for the ladies to be safe. I will make sure the draft gets to you. I think you may be busy in the next few weeks. We will keep an eye on you."

I drew McTurk aside. "One other thing," I asked quietly, "Is Meryl still alive?"

He sighed and shook his head. "Laddie, I tried to help you avoid this heartbreak. Yes, she is alive and fully recovered." I looked at him, my eyes begging him to tell me what I wanted to know but was too afraid to ask. "Yes," he admitted reluctantly. "She still loves you—though by telling you this—I think I have made your life much more difficult."

"When you get back tell Meryl…" But what could I tell her? I had a daughter now and I had promised to marry Lucy. "Tell her that I still have her perfume…it's like *The Scent of Time*. And tell her I …" But I couldn't finish the sentence.

McTurk sighed and shook his head again. "Aye, laddie. Just so. Just so. But was it not Shakespeare who said 'Conscience makes cowards of us all'? I can teach you combat and how to survive a fight or a battle, but the decision you have to make—well, only you can decide. Perhaps we will serve together again. Who knows?"

He slapped me on the back. "We'll make a soldier out of you yet."

That was a scary thought.

Our luggage was sent along ahead of us and I had a last wander round the ship and what seemed a lifetime of memories. I turned back to look at the *Night Arrow* as we headed for the Hansoms that had come for us. The *Night Arrow* had done well. Tribute was equally due to the sailors who sailed her and to the skill of the captain and sailing master.

Building the *Night Arrow* had been more than just a job to men who built her. Pride spoke from every clean line. The craftsmen realized that for many journeys, the lives of brave men would depend on the quality of their work. There she stood, gently rocking from side to side as she was unloaded.

The ground under my feet at Tilbury dock seemed to move from side to side. I could still feel the movement of the ship. I sighed. "Goodbye, old girl. Thanks for everything."

Then I did something that was becoming more a part of my nature. I prayed. "Thank You, Father God, for getting us safely to land and for all of us being alive and in good health. In Jesus Name."

CHAPTER 28

Daniel Cavendish and Joshua Hemphill had taken our luggage to the cabs. I tried to give them something in thanks.

"No," Daniel said, pushing the money back to me. "You gave us a second chance. The Lord bless you."

"Aye," Joshua added. "And a long and happy marriage."

Yet I felt like many who had come back from war into peace and had found it difficult to settle. I felt the scent of home—but it was blowing in two different directions. *No, enough of this,* I told myself. Then I realized that I had spoken aloud and the others in the coach had quit talking and were watching me with questioning eyes.

"Sorry," I improvised. "Daydreaming. I can still see that shark."

Tea prices were good and the draft was put into my hands, along with money for meals, accommodations and train tickets.

We took the train from Euston to Edinburgh. It was a long, cold journey, even though during daylight the September sun warmed the place somewhat. I had been living on adrenalin without realizing it. Now that danger had ended, I felt tired and dispirited. The train stopped in various places, forcing us to disembark for food.

It was obvious that Caroline missed Myles. I was thankful for telegrams and so was she. Contact was so vital, I thought. I decided not to tell them about the ease and swiftness of e-mail.

Was it really over? The most exciting time in my life? Now, willingly, I had a daughter to parent and I had to think of her. Time can make us forget what we owe to people; the fear we were in, the danger. Gradually, memory glamorizes it. Real love sticks with you all the time, like the warm winter fire on a windy winter's night.

In Aberdeen, I had never seen so many fishing boats, all seeking mainly one very exportable fish—herring, also called "the silver darlings." Herring from Aberdeen was shipped around the world.

From Aberdeen Station we were directed to Mealmarket Street off the major King Street thoroughfare and told we could purchase coach tickets there. When we arrived, we found that four tickets had been brought for us and were waiting. The Coach left at 8:00 a.m. and if you think cities in 1867 didn't have rush hours, think again. It was like the chariot race from the *Ben-Hur* film, only worse. I didn't know when the first stop would be, so emphasized with my vestiges of 21st Century "anything goes" to Lucy that they should they "go" before going on the journey. Lucy blushed and said in a gentle voice, "Beloved, don't be indelicate." I forgot that even after everything intimate we had shared together, I was in 1867, and some subjects remained taboo.

Slight regret nipped at my mind and I realized that I was missing something to blow up.

One other thing about a journey in 1867, is that you sit and sit and sit and then you sit again. It was a warm autumn, and when you weren't hitting potholes in the road, you were choking with dust. We were exceedingly glad to arrive at the 1867 inn. I missed *Starbucks*. We all took light ale, even for Mi-Ling. We couldn't risk the water because we didn't know its source. Folks, if you think life is tough and inconvenient now, you should go back to 1867. We negated giving Mi-Ling ginger beer. At that time, sugar was applied in newly discovered fizzy drinks as if it would be a threatened commodity by tomorrow.

Thankfully, the lawyer we had gone to see had been located in King Street. We had passed the money over to Isaac Porthero and he had given us the title deed to the house and the estate.

"May I offer my congratulations as you begin your new life together," he had said. "It is quite a responsibility running an estate and making it pay. I am here at your service. Miss Oxford. You have grown up in China. It is much colder here, and I do not mean only in temperature. He looked at Mi-Ling. "May I suggest a tutor for the young lady rather than the local school? I do not know of any other Chinese persons in the area—but being Jewish, I do know what prejudice is."

He had adjusted his papers on his desk and added, "It is amazing how much money changes people and suddenly how many friends you have. Beware those who rush in to greet you when you arrive. They are rarely there when you leave. If you are given business propositions, I beg you let me see the small print first before you sign anything."

Isaac Porthero had given us sound advice. I was also aware that we were getting closer to Bellefield, where there would be an 1867 time portal.

We clattered into the main Square at Huntly and I hired a buggy. We headed out for Bellefield. Thankfully there was a driver to take us out.

"Ah weel, nae doot ye'll be lookin' farward till taken o'er at Bellefield," he said. I replied on behalf of Lucy, who had clearly not understood a word of what he said, "Aye, aye, fairly, fairly. It's sic a bonny spot."

He visibly lifted, "Aye, ye'ill nae get better in the hale o' Aberdeenshire. You will be Miss Oxford's affianced? Richt pleased I am tae meet you an were fairly glad yer sae trickit wi'the place."

There was no A96 paved roadway yet, just a track road worn by generations of carts and farm carts and all the other agricultural activity of Aberdeenshire.

Then I nudged Lucy, for I recognized the house. It had not changed that much in some hundred and fifty years. Everything looked new. The stone work was clean and bright. I wondered if the front door was the same. Turned out it was and the lock was still stiff. It made me wonder if Adrian had ever fixed the lock.

"I will always love you…" Meryl's voice came back to me like a long forgotten poem released by a mind that realized its tardiness in not having remembered sooner. I could count the steps from the front door to where she had told me she loved me. Clyde, the butler, opened the door. Lucy entered first, followed by Caroline and Mi-Ling.

"Sir," Clyde welcomed. "We have been expecting you."

Then I saw other members of staff lined up in the hall and Lucy doing an amazing impression of royalty as she greeted everyone. No difference was shown to Mi-Ling. She was being treated like the daughter of the house, which she was—or would be once Lucy and I got married.

I unpacked in my room which was small by choice with an open fire. It was the same room I had slept in some one-hundred-fifty years later. I even thought of scratching on the wall, "Kilroy was here."

Lucy was chatty at dinner. "Darling," she said. "Do you want me to wear ivory or white for my bridal gown? You choose, my love. I want you to be proud of me."

I smiled at her and nodded, but in my head and deep inside my heart I knew the choice was about much more than the color of Lucy's wedding dress.

Normally the gentlemen would retire after the meal to drink their port. I was the only man in residence, however, so I took my port outside and walked down the steps. The night before I had left, Meryl had come to me out here. "Just look and listen," she had said. "Look at the stars and the vast expanse of the sky. We seem so small, just you and me. All we have is tonight and nobody can take that away from us. Tomorrow everything changes"...and so it had. Suddenly, I wanted to close my eyes and feel Meryl's arms around me, assuring me that everything would work out and that she loved me. When I went to our tree, it was still light and the last rays of the setting sun shone through. When I looked at the flowers round the tree, they were forget-me-nots.

I went to bed after some difficult conversation in the drawing room. We dismissed it as due to the fact that we were all tired. Maybe this was a dream and we needed rest—peaceful rest without someone or something trying to kill me, or eat me, or blow me up, or shoot me.

Over the next few days, many came to visit Lucy and to a certain extent me. I directed them to Lucy. It was her estate. Maybe my nose was just out of joint.

I was in the library one day and Lucy came to me. "My love, what about a Christmas wedding? By the time everything is arranged and invitations sent out and returned it would need to be about that. And darling, have you seen the minister yet? We should ask him if he is free."

So we made an appointment to see Mr. Thorburn, the Church of Scotland minister, to discuss the wedding. Meanwhile, Lucy spent her time doing a guest list. It was our chance, she said, to make an impression on society. There would be an evening meal or a wedding breakfast. The questions proved endless: would we need champagne? What about Switzerland for a honeymoon, to Berne or Lucerne?

"Just as you wish, my love," became my standard reply. I was even starting to sound like them, the 'toom tabards' (empty coats) of Scottish society.

CHAPTER 29

I went outside for a walk around the estate. It was raining and I did not really care. I started out through the trees and walked and walked. Suddenly, I was joined by a dog, a lively brown-and-white rough collie with a friendly manner. Then a man dressed in tweeds and accompanied, not only by the collie dog, but by a shotgun as well, broke out of the line of trees. He approached me.

"Aye. I'll be askin' ye yer business on this estate—oh it's Mr. Faulkner, the mistress' intended. How do you do, sir? Jock Shepherd, the estate ghillie."

He noticed my puzzlement when he used the word "ghillie."

He explained, "I take care of all things to do with hunting and stopping poachers."

"I see," I said unenthusiastically.

"Well, sir, it'll nae be lang till the big day for you both. Everybody thinks the weddin' is just fine an we all want the two of you to be happy —weel, the three of you to be happy. Thon wee Chinese girl is a bonnie wee lassie. She'll dee ye both proud."

"Aye, we owe her a lot." In fact, I had been forgetting what we did owe to Mi-Ling. We had started taking it for granted that she would always be there. I, with the usual rationalization of the human mind, had forgotten as the empty days had stretched out on top of each other, that were it not for Mi-Ling, I would be dead. Lucy would have been in Bryant's bunk until he got tired of her and passed her on to someone else.

"Mr. Shepherd," I suddenly thought to ask, "What do I do on the estate?"

"Weel, sir, beggin' your pardon, but its no fur the likes of me to be tellin' you. You have so many social things. You get invitations to their house and you invite them to yours. These things are awa above the likes o me. Then you'ill have events in the county—dances and parties as well as raisin' money for folks what's fallen on hard times. An the estate Christmas Dinner. They all look forward to that. Then when ye ging to the kirk on Sunday, ye meet all kinds of people."

"I wish I had your satisfaction."

"Satisfaction? Aye, I have a lovin' wife who cares for me and when work is nearly done we go walking through the forest and heather. We have been side by side for forty years. When we go out walking and talking, no two days are the same. No two walks are the same. She kens as much about beasties as I do and has a great love for them.

"See, sir," he continued, "when ye see an eagle in the sky, lord of all he surveys, hardly moving his wings, it reminds me of God. Like in Isaiah 40:31 when the Bible says, *They that wait upon the Lord shall renew their strength; they shall mount up with wings as eagles; they shall run and not be weary; and they shall walk and not faint."* He looked me straight in the eye. "Maybe, sir, if you were to wait on the Maister in yer walks and ask Him what to do on the estate, it might be a surprising answer you would get."

"But I am still not sure about God," I admitted to the stranger. "I thought I was on the trip getting here. He seemed to deliver us from so much danger. But now that we're safely here…God suddenly seems far away. Almost as if we don't need Him anymore."

"Weel, sir, that I canna say. But ae things for certain. He has enough sureity for baith o you."

"Thank you," I said. "You could be right."

He had struck a chord and I decided to get back to the house.

When I got there, Mi-Ling was skipping around a tree with one of the girls from the estate. When you looked at Connie on one side, she was lovely. But when she turned her head, a fiery birth mark marred the other cheek. Mi-Ling saw me and ran up to me. "Papa, this is Connie,

Mi-Ling's friend. Nobody else plays with Connie because her face has the mark. Papa, she has no friends. Her face is different. They laugh. My face is different. I know. So I tell her to come to Mi-Ling and we play together. Is that okay, Papa?"

Tears of pride for my daughter stung my eyes. "Of course, Mi-Ling. Connie, you are always welcome here."

Connie's face broke into a lovely smile. She curtsied. "Thank you, sir. That's kind of you. And then she began to sing. As her voice rose, I swear the birds stopped singing. She sang in Gaelic and tears began to run down my cheeks. I was down at their level and Mi-Ling put her arm around me. "Thank you, Papa. You look at her heart. Not outside where the face has the mark."

"What are you singing?" I asked Connie, "Because I do not speak Gaelic."

She thought for a moment and then translated, *I stand on the shore, is my longing in vain, will he come to me, my love again? Will we be in each other's heart, beating as one and never apart? Oh, when, oh when will I be home?*

"That's beautiful, Connie. Where did you learn it?"

"My mother, sir. She was a teacher but stopped to marry my father. But now he has died and we work some of the land."

I knew I had found Mi-Ling's teacher. Connie told me where they lived and I told Connie that I would be along tomorrow to speak to mother and ask her if she would like to tutor Mi-Ling.

Feeling much better than I had when I left, I went looking for Lucy.

"Where have you been dearest?" she asked, not at all sweetly, when I found her. "I have been worried sick about you."

Wow! Where did that come from? I wondered. "I went for a walk on the estate."

She walked up and down in front of the fire. "You should tell me where you are going." Then she must have realized the fractious tone of voice, for she attempted to ameliorate it. "Dearest, you could have fallen and be lying on a hill somewhere injured—laying out there all night and chilled to the bone."

"Darling, this is Bellefield estate, not the Himalayas. Someone

217

would have found me. And speaking of finding, I found a tutor on the estate for Mi-Ling, a lady who used to be a school teacher. She can speak several languages, and her daughter, Connie, who is ages with Mi-Ling, has the most incredible singing voice."

Mi-Ling, who had followed me in, attempted to add her explanation. "Amma," she told Lucy excitedly, "Connie is Mi-Ling's friend. She plays with Mi-Ling. Connie's mother is nice to Mi-Ling when we play at Connie's house."

Lucy frowned at Mi-Ling. "You never told me you went to an estate worker's house to play."

Caroline, whose breathing had grown heavier and heavier, said in a quiet voice, "She told me. I gave her permission."

"In the future," Lucy ordered, "Let me know where she goes. You never know what will happen in some of these rough estate houses."

I looked at her in total astonishment. I was speechless.

Lucy added, "This my estate. I am the mistress of it and I would ask you to take cognizance of my wishes."

"Of course," Caroline said, then turned to Mi-Ling. "Sweetheart, will you please go to your room for me? Don't worry. You have done nothing wrong. I will be in later with some warm milk and biscuits for you."

Looking puzzled, and slightly apprehensive as if she feared she had committed some unintentional wrong, Mi-Ling came to hug me. "Goodnight, Papa."

I tried to reassure her with a long hug and kisses all over her face. She giggled and went to Lucy. "Goodnight, Amma."

Lucy snapped. "It's not Amma. It's MAMA. Good night, Mi-Ling."

Mi-Ling fled. The pain on her face made me feel as if an unseen enemy had thrust a hot poker into my gut and twisted it.

Caroline, red-faced and stiff, looked like an ignited firecracker right before it exploded.

CHAPTER 30

After Mi-Ling fled the room, Caroline turned like a tigress on Lucy. "Lucy! How dare you talk to Mi-Ling like that?"

"What do you mean? I was just trying to help her with her English. This is my estate and I have a right to…"

Caroline was fizzing. I had never seen her so angry before. "Damn you and damn this estate! Look what it has done to you—changed you beyond all recognition."

I opened my mouth to intervene.

Caroline whirled to face me. "And you! You have died inside. You won't stand up to her and put her in her place. You bleat 'yes, darling,' as mindlessly as a sheep. And then you have the nerve to stand there as silent as a rock and let her talk to Mi-Ling like that! What kind of a father does that make you? Mi-Ling would be better off if Myles and I adopted her and took her away from here with us. Perhaps we will. What has that wonderful, priceless, precious little girl done to you that both of you cause her so much hurt and pain?

"Dear God in heaven as my witness, has she not had enough hurt and pain? What has that blessing of a child ever done to have deserved all this hurt?" She stopped to draw breath.

Lucy attempted to speak.

"Shut up, Lucy. I'm not finished. Do you know what I wish? I wish that Bryant was here. When he was around threatening our lives, we worked together. We encouraged each other. We would have died for Mi-Ling and for each other. If Bryant could see you now, he would be rubbing his hands with joy because of the bickering and suffering. He's won, Lucy. You've let him win without him ever firing a shot or killing anyone."

"Bryant's dead," I reminded her.

"Oh, Mr. Knowall, you know that for a fact? You have seen his body, have you?"

I took a breath because I knew she was right. "We are in a small corner of the world," I said, trying to convince myself first of all. "He will never find us here."

Caroline snorted. "Myles says Bryant is ninety-nine percent bad, but he has one strong point. He is an exceptional navigator. He specializes in finding little islands, bays, and pieces of land. What he can do on the sea with a map and compass, he can do on land."

"Get away," I objected. "We left him, hopefully, at the bottom of Saldanha Bay."

Caroline tossed her head. "Drew, think! If he is still alive, what is to stop a man like him from getting another ship? Another lucky card game and—presto—he is the owner of the *White Hind* and off on his travels again."

She sighed and shook her head. "But that's not the point. You both owe Mi-Ling an apology and if you don't give her one, I am out of here. I only have to wire Myles and he will meet me. And I will ask him if he would like to begin our marriage with a daughter. He loves and admires that little girl. I expect he would be delighted."

Lucy was astonished," But, Caroline, dear. I don't understand why you're acting like this. Why you are treating me like this. We've been friends all our lives."

Caroline looked at her, her newly grown scorn evident. "I don't care if we have been friends since Noah's Ark. You are wrong and you know it."

Lucy began to cry.

"It's not nice being hurt, Lucy is it?" Caroline asked with steel in her voice. "That little girl has been hurt all her life and she thought that she had found happiness with you and Drew. And what does she get?" Caroline mimicked, 'It is Mama, not Amma.'

"Well, Lucy, you are not fit to answer to the title of either the way you've changed since coming here. My word for you is used in the animal kingdom with reference to dogs that have puppies."

I jumped to Lucy's defense, albeit only half-heartedly. "Steady on, Caroline…"

"You shut up, too, you gutless windbag. If you let her run all over you now, you had better start practicing saying, 'woof-woof.' For unless you take a firm hand with her at once, all you will ever be is a lap dog.

"Now, if you excuse me, I'm going to get that broken hearted-kid —whom I would be proud of to claim as my daughter—some milk and biscuits. And you two have something to say to each other. At least, if you don't, you're thicker than I thought you were." She stormed out of the room leaving Lucy and I broken to bits.

Lucy was still crying. I felt like crying myself. The door opened and Mi-Ling, with the immediate sense of feeling that children have, came in and saw Lucy sobbing. She went over to Lucy and put her arms around her shoulder, running her fingers gently through Lucy's red hair.

"Mama," she said clearly. "Mama, don't cry. Mi-Ling loves you." Hearing Mi-Ling say "mama" instead of "amma" made Lucy cry harder. Mi-Ling took out a hanky from her pocket in her nightdress and started drying Lucy's tears.

"Ammas don't cry. They make tears better," Mi-Ling said. Neither Lucy nor I could speak.

Still hugging Lucy, Mi-Ling said, "When Mi-Ling was in bad place before she get set free, Mi-Ling be Amma to the little ones when they cry, or afraid, or hurt. They come to Mi-Ling and Amma would make gone the tears till the next time bad came."

I looked into the eyes of this incredible young woman that God had given me as a daughter. "What happened when you hurt, Mi-Ling?" I whispered, afraid and not really wanting to know.

"God put arms around me. He tell me one day Mi-Ling be free. Then you come. I know Father God keep His promise to Mi-Ling."

Lucy quit crying. "Mi-Ling, I am so sorry for the way I spoke to you and for hurting your feelings." She hugged Mi-Ling tightly to her. "I love you, sweetheart. Please forgive me."

"I forgive," Mi-Ling said with puzzlement drawn across her dark brows. "But why forgive? When Mi-Ling little, Mi-Ling go see my friend in big house. Friend had puppy. Puppy was fun. He would lick Mi-Ling's hand. One day Mi-Ling go see him and he not happy. He growl and hide in dark place. My friend think he was sick, but Mi-Ling see a thorn in his foot. Puppy let Mi-Ling take it out. Then he be happy again. It's okay, Mama. You had thorn."

"Yes, Mi-Ling, I had a thorn and you just removed it. But it is not right that I let my thorn hurt you."

"Mi-Ling, I'm sorry, too," I told her. "Lucy I have not been spending enough time with you. Please forgive me."

She nodded her dark head. "Mi-Ling loves you and Amma loves you. You in most happy circumstances—two people love you and still you are free—not in bad place."

She yawned. "Mi-Ling is tired and go to bed now."

Lucy and I kissed our daughter and sent her off to bed. Then Lucy looked at me. "Drew, what can I say except that I am sorry? I have behaved like a real horror. The worst kind of person and one that I thought I could never become." She reached for my hand. "There is something else. Drew, I hate this place. I see what it has done, or nearly done, to us. What it would have done had it not been for Caroline and Mi-Ling. I hate it here. This is no life for someone with a mind. When we were teaching in China, at least we were making a difference. We changed people's lives for the better. I miss teaching. I miss having a purpose. I'm just play acting here, pretending to be someone grand—and that isn't me."

She paused. "I was only doing this because I thought it was what you wanted. You risked your life to help me get here safely. I feel like an ungrateful fool to admit that I'm not happy here."

"Lucy," I said in amazement, "I was only doing this because I thought this is what you wanted. I hate it, too. I am losing my soul here. I need to be with you where we face challenges together. Where we can build our own life together and not feel like we are just stepping into someone else's. Lucy, can we sell this?"

"There is one other thing," she said. "I will cancel it if you don't want me to do it. I'm getting my portrait painted. The artist was trained by…"

"John Everett Millais," I finished. "No, darling. You must get the portrait done. It will catch my eye in some hundred and fifty years and get me back to China where we meet. Hang it in the alcove on its own where the wall bends in. We need to go and see Isaac Prothero again, which means going back to Aberdeen." I paused, then asked, "Do we get married before we leave?"

"Yes. If it's possible to arrange it so quickly—but, darling, it may not be. But if we were married first, we could travel alone together and spend time together learning to be just us. But just a quiet wedding. Not the grand affair I was planning."

We talked for most of the evening, sitting in front of the fire. The door opened behind us once and then again about ten minutes later. We ignored it.

The next morning, the sun shone and the sky was a bluer blue and the grass a greener green. Lucy looked even more beautiful than usual. The artist turned up, so we had to delay our visit to Aberdeen. Mi-Ling was getting on fine with Connie's mum and Caroline returned to being her old self, the tumultuous storm of the previous night spent.

When the artist "sat Madamoiselle" for preliminary sketches, Lucy fiddled when I was absent.

"If monsieur could remain? Mademoiselle is less agitated and thus we shall the quicker progress make."

Earnestly desiring that the quicker progress be made, I stayed. I also suggested the gown that she was wearing in the completed painting. When Lucy came down the following day with it on, the artist went into raptures. *"Charmante, tres charmante, si belle,"* he effused.

In my mind I was saying, *"Come on, pal, get the paint on the canvas."*

When it was left to doing the "fiddly bits," I was not needed, and I left artist and model to achieve the perfection that I knew would be in the final portrait. I got a lamp and explored the basement. I had not previously attempted to locate the time tunnel. There was everything in the basement; rusty iron work, flags, regimental colors, a couple of old muskets, some empty champagne bottles and a modest wine cellar. I poked and prodded, wishing I had McTurk's Kairon detector. Finally, I found something made of stainless steel, a box the size of a cell-phone. I stood outside the room and pointed the box toward the far wall. There was a colorless light and when I moved the switch up, a green light flashed on. I got outside the door. Then the place began to shake, but only in the room I had left. The far wall opened and there was a carriage just like the one I had left in to go to China.

The door opened after I pressed the button on the outside. It hummed. At least now I knew where it was and how to get it. I had written an update outlining everything about our trip from my diary entries. I placed it on one of the seats and thought, *Do I? Why send just the note when I could be with Meryl in an instant?* Then I remembered Mi-Ling. I left the note inside, threw the switch and got out before the door locked. I went outside just as the thing vanished again. I checked, but there was no sign of the small tunnel that had been beside the large one that I had left in. Maybe it had been an afterthought.

I went back upstairs and decided to keep this to myself. I kept the switch box, but did not know its effective range.

I went back upstairs and the artist was saying, "Two hundred guineas is a modest fee, Madamoiselle, but these are hard times. I hope it will bring you great joy and *votre mari aussi.*" Lucy said something to him which I could not hear. When I saw the completed painting, it looked some one-hundred-fifty years younger and when Lucy came into the room I said, "Mmmm, you improve with age."

We went to see Mr Prothero and told him of our decision to sell the estate.

"No doubt you want to go to the United States," he mused, "though I cannot see many going to some of the far northern states. It is so cold there that your words come out as blocks of ice and you have to thaw them before you hear them."

He chuckled at his own humor. Then he said, "It may take a little time to sell Bellefield, or then again, there may be someone waiting in the wings as they say in the theatre."

"Any ideas for overnight accommodation?" I asked. "It will be tomorrow before we can take the coach back."

"Douglas Hotel in Market Street. Tell them I sent you. You can take your choice of dining places round about," he replied.

We went to the hotel. Outside the front door I said to Lucy, "This place is still standing in my time even though it was built in 1856. It looks a little newer now than it will some hundred and fifty years from now."

The next day we arrived at the coach terminal and got our tickets. The horses must have eaten well, for they were eager to work.

I happened to glance across at a coach that had just arrived. One of the figures alighting was tall, with a black cloak wrapped around him and what looked like a seaman's cap like the one Searcher had worn. His face was hidden in the shadows but when he walked, he limped badly. I could not be sure. I didn't think he had noticed us. We got in the coach and sat back into the seat as far as possible, Lucy following my example instead of asking questions. Thankfully, her hair was hidden beneath a large, ornate hat. I decided not to say anything. If I was wrong, there was no sense in creating panic. But what if I was right? *No*, I thought. *It's coincidence. You've got Bryant on the brain and that's stupid because you left him behind in Sandalha Bay.* I wished I had McTurk to converse with, though, and to reassure me.

We got back to Huntly and then out to the estate. There was a certain sense of safety in that. I went to find Jock, the ghillie, and came across him setting traps.

"Good afternoon, sir. Fit can we dee for ye on a bonnie day like this?"

"Mr Shepherd, I have a favor to ask of you."

"We'll, sir, if it's in ma power to help, I will be glad till."

"Jock, would you know what an American sounds like?"

"Aye, sir. They used to come shooting in the auld Colonel's time. Good shots and Purdy guns."

"Jock, if you see a party of Americans on your travels, will you come and tell me? One of them will have a pronounced limp, though he does not need a stick. The others I don't know about. Please don't approach them. They could be dangerous. And please don't tell the mistress. She fears and distrusts them as well, but if I've made a mistake in identification I don't want to worry her."

"Sir, there are twa under keepers. May I give them the same warning so that they may be vigilant?"

"Yes, of course. Six eyes watching are better than two. These men may be armed with handguns and they may have explosives," I warned.

I went back to the house, trying to stay calm.

Lucy was radiant and her face was flushed from the heat of the fire. Mi-Ling and Connie had eaten and they played together happily in the room. *The ideal family portrait*, I thought. But if I had seen Bryant, how long would it last? "Let's stick together," I suggested, attempting to sound casual.

Caroline's eyes opened wide. She motioned me over to the far side of the room and waved at the high bookcase. "Drew, can you get me volume two of *Caesar's Gallic Wars*? I can't reach it."

"Of course," I said, stretching up.

"What's wrong?" she whispered. "And don't say 'nothing.'" Then in a louder voice, "No, silly, that's volume one."

"You were right, Caroline. He got off a coach. He was wrapped up against the wind and was a seaman and he had the pronounced limp I gave him after the sword fight. But I don't want to say anything to Lucy in case I've imagined the whole thing. Caroline, can you load an Adams revolver? There's one in the gun room. You could put it where you keep your clothes. Lucy is not liable to look in your things."

Caroline retired early. I made sure I still had the Webley and the other equipment from China. Then everyone retired to their rooms for bed.

Thankfully, nothing happened and I decided I must have been mistaken. A batch of wedding invitations arrived, brought by carrier. Lucy had decided on a simple dress and we had postponed the wedding long enough to enable us to send off invitations and receive replies. We had gone to pre-marriage classes as the minister requested. He had intoned, "You are asking God to be witness to your vows. Though you, Mr. Faulkner, probably know very little about God or the Lord Jesus."

"Mr Thorburn," I asked, "have you ever been to China?"

"No, I have not."

"Have you ever been shot at, or had a fifteen-foot shark swim up so close to you that you can touch his skin? Have you ever fought pirates and prayed that you would come through, then given thanks to God when you did? Have you ever set yourself up as bait for an assassin's bullet and then breathed a sigh of relief to God when he was caught?"

"No, Mr. Faulkner. No, to all of those things."

"Then, Mr Thorburn, you have not really lived close to God."

He cleared his throat in embarrassment. "Perhaps you are right. What date did we say for the wedding, December 26th?"

"Aye, that 'ill dee jist fine," I told him.

We sent the invitations and replies arrived quickly. Most were acceptances. We decided against a honeymoon. We had to be ready if a buyer appeared.

Meanwhile, I wired Luke Carter and told him what was happening. I knew that if we made it to San Antonio, he would help us.

We also wired Anton in Finland. He wired back that he would come to our wedding. "Freezing cold here. Hope you have heat there. I missed the cold in China, but this is much cold. You will get heat on the honeymoon—old Russian saying."

It was about two days after the telegrams arrived that Sandy Gordon and Duncan came up from the village, bringing some things we had ordered. "Fine news about the big day. We were awe delighted," Sandy assured us.

He started to leave, then turned back. "Aye, an' there were twa Americans lookin' for you. He scratched his head, trying to remember. "It was some kind o' a Biblical name he gave."

"Luke," I asked hopefully. "Was it Luke Carter?"

"Naw twas nae that name…Caleb. Aye, Caleb Bryant. An' he asked me to give you this." He handed me a note, doffed his cap, and left.

"The color drained from Lucy's and Caroline's faces as I opened the note. It was short and to the point. *"ACCOUNT OVERDUE. COMING FOR PAYMENT. SEE YOU AT THE WEDDING. BRYANT."*